A DUKE OF [illegible]S OWN

EMMA ORCHARD

B

Boldwood

First published in Great Britain in 2024 by Boldwood Books Ltd.

Cover Artwork and Design by Rachel Lawston

A CIP catalogue record for this book is available from the British Library.

Paperback ISBN 978-1-83561-055-8

Large Print ISBN 978-1-83561-051-0

Hardback ISBN 978-1-83561-050-3

Ebook ISBN 978-1-83561-048-0

Kindle ISBN 978-1-83561-049-7

Audio CD ISBN 978-1-83561-056-5

MP3 CD ISBN 978-1-83561-053-4

Digital audio download ISBN 978-1-83561-047-3

Boldwood Books Ltd
23 Bowerdean Street
London SW6 3TN
www.boldwoodbooks.com

To my mum: I miss you every day.

PROLOGUE

LONDON, SUMMER 1816

Lady Georgiana was beginning to be certain that she'd made a terrible, terrible mistake in coming to this party. She'd made a lot of mistakes in the past – last summer had been one huge blunder, she'd done one stupid and irresponsible thing after another for months – but this was something altogether different. A spectacular disaster, even by her standards.

And it wasn't really a party, was it? To call it that implied that it was just like all the other parties she had attended in her past two London seasons, or while travelling abroad with her brother Hal after Bonaparte's final defeat last year. There were elegant, expensive rooms here, to be sure, filled with elegant, expensive people. There was fine wine – oceans of wine, she had just seized a glass herself and gulped it down – and beautifully presented food. There was the hum of conversation, laughter, a little music, liveried servants, and candlelight reflecting in lovely Venetian mirrors. She might easily have been in Venice, in fact. How she wished she were. Everyone here was masked – that didn't signify anything by itself; she had attended many masquerades before. But all those similarities didn't make it a party. The differences between this... this gathering and every other she had ever been to were some of them subtle and some of them all too obvious.

Georgie had often, especially last summer, complained of the restrictions imposed upon young ladies by chaperons, and spent a great deal of time trying to evade them. Now it seemed she had her wish: there were no chaperons here. They would be distinctly de trop in such a setting. And she found she desperately missed them now they were gone; one of her aunts, her sister-in-law Cassandra – anybody, really, who could rescue her from the consequences of her own folly, even at the cost of a severe dressing-down.

But no. She'd thought herself too worldly-wise, too clever to need a chaperon, she'd been restless, discontented, a little bored, and so she had sought out a faster, more fashionable set this season, and had swiftly become firm friends with the dashing Mrs Aubrey, a widow a few years older than herself, a lady understood to be of respectable birth and slightly spicy reputation, but one who was received everywhere in the haut ton. They had found each other entertaining company over the past few weeks, had swiftly become firm friends in a superficial sort of a way, and there had been nothing at all before tonight to raise the slightest doubts on Georgie's part about the lady's intentions towards her. And Mrs Aubrey had brought her here, telling her that she would enjoy herself excessively; that she was sure Georgiana had had enough of Almack's, and vacuous debutantes, and dull, dull respectability. She would show her, Mrs Aubrey said, something *much* more interesting. Georgiana had agreed fervently, secretly thrilled that Caro, who was so clever and sophisticated, could see she was not just another silly girl.

And now here she was. At an orgy.

She should, she thought, have made her escape when she noticed that the servants and musicians were masked, as well as the guests. That had been the first warning sign, which she would have been wise to heed. But this was an elegant townhouse in Mayfair, much like her own family home, thronged with fashionable people, not some den of iniquity in Covent Garden, and Mrs Aubrey's hand at her back had urged her on, the older lady laughing a little at her sudden hesitation, mocking her. She had told herself that it was foolish to be apprehensive; Caroline Aubrey's friends might indeed be interesting, free-thinking people of whom prudes would disapprove, but nothing more extreme than that. She had been wrong.

Mrs Aubrey, having brought her here, had abandoned her almost immediately. The house, it seemed, was a labyrinth of small rooms, and Caro had disappeared into one of them with another lady and a gentleman, clearly intimate acquaintances of hers, shooting an enigmatic glance at Georgie from her glittering, suddenly malicious black eyes as she did so.

They had attended another, perfectly ordinary masquerade first, a respectable private ball, shrugging off Georgie's conveniently casual chaperon, a schoolfriend's mother, along the way, as it was easy enough to do when everyone was masked and disguised. Mrs Aubrey was dressed in a daring low-cut scarlet gown in the extreme of fashion, covered by an anonymous black domino. Her face was largely hidden by her black loo mask, but her new companions here at the orgy had gone some way beyond conventional dress; the lady who had kissed Caro full on the mouth in greeting then grasped her hands tightly and drawn her away had remembered her stays but forgotten her gown, and the gentleman... Georgie did not want to think about the gentleman. Suffice it to say that he was not sporting conventional eveningwear. Or daywear. Or... any wear. Various questions of a precise anatomical nature that she had wondered about for years suddenly became clearer to her, and in the light of them it seemed unlikely that the trio were going apart to discuss the news from overseas or the latest Paris modes. She was not completely naïve, and was growing less naïve by the second.

At least they had sought privacy. Many of the party guests had felt no such need for discretion. It seemed, instead, that conspicuous public display added to their pleasure. In the largest room, on, around and in several cases under the elegant velvet chairs and sofas, couples, groups of people, were...

Huddled in a corner in her mask, trying to make herself small and inconspicuous, Georgie was dressed as a boy. Tiring of her long curls and suddenly finding them childish, heavy and restrictive, she had recently had them cropped, and perhaps that had put the idea into her head. It was not entirely unknown that ladies should attend masquerades disguised in masculine attire, and she had found that her brother Fred's best suit, outgrown by him and put aside until it should be required by one of the twins, fitted her perfectly. It was surprisingly comfortable, and unlike a young lady's thin muslin gown had any number of useful pockets. The cloth was a very deep red, a crimson, and as she had admired herself in the mirror, swaggering a little and striking amusing masculine attitudes, she had thought that it presented a pleasantly dashing appearance, and set off her short dark hair and bright blue eyes, not to mention her long legs, extremely well.

Clearly, others were of the same opinion, and Georgie found herself paralysed. Her swagger had deserted her entirely. She knew beyond a shadow of a doubt that she should leave. Immediately. Her safe, respectable home was only a street or two away. It might be highly improper for a young lady, even one dressed as she was, to walk unescorted through London at night, but there was no question that it was far more improper to stay here and witness... this. All this. And that was setting aside any question of participation.

She might have imagined that the nature of her masquerade dress would protect her from any unwelcome invitations, since at a casual glance she would pass for a boy, but the truth was far otherwise; in the few moments she had been here, both ladies and gentlemen had approached her, had made suggestions, some of them shockingly explicit, which she had refused with a forced smile and a brief, emphatic shake of her glossy dark head. These ladies and gentlemen all seemed to share a positive mania for acquainting themselves with the contents of her breeches, though it was not entirely clear to her whether they were all fully aware of what she kept concealed there. Perhaps they didn't care either way. Perhaps they liked surprises. She felt eyes on her now, assessing her, undressing her.

And still, despite all this, she could not force herself to go. Her mind was a blank – she could not muster sufficient coherence of thought to force her legs, her body, to turn, to make an exit. She was reasonably confident that no one would try to stop her if she moved with sufficient assurance, and she hardly owed Mrs Aubrey any consideration. She would have a great deal of explaining to do, of course, when she gained the safety of her family home, but that could scarcely be her chief concern now. And yet she stayed, watching almost in a daze as a voluptuous blonde lady, masked and dripping with many-coloured jewels but otherwise essentially unclothed, encouraged a gentleman armed with a short riding whip to... Good God.

A voice in her ear, rich, deep and honeyed. 'You find their activities... interesting?'

Another one. She sighed, and, making her voice gruff – not that it had helped before – said, 'No, sir. I thank you for your kind offer, but I was about to go.'

'Were you, I wonder? But in point of fact, fair Rosalind, I made no offer, kind or otherwise.' This man, at least, realised she was a girl, and thought to make a Shakespearian joke of the fact, though she wasn't in the humour to be amused. But there was no denying that it was an extraordinary voice, more expressive, she thought, than any she had ever heard before, and containing, especially in such a setting, a wealth of highly dangerous possibilities.

She turned involuntarily to look at him. Up at him, for he had bent his head to address her. He was very tall and well-built, dressed in immaculate evening black cut by the hand of a master, and his mask was plain black too. Behind it, unusual silvery-grey eyes glittered, and his glossy black hair too was streaked with silver-grey, and longer than the current mode for gentlemen, though his face, what she could see of it, was unmarked by age.

His expression seemed to change as he looked down at her. His mouth was resolute, sensual, beautifully sculpted, and as he regarded her searchingly it thinned into a grim line. 'Oh, you really don't belong here, do you? I thought as much. Come with me!'

He took her firmly by the arm and drew her, without unseemly haste, from the overheated room into the marble hallway. She went, unresisting. A door opened across the passage, providentially discharging a dishevelled, laughing group of people in scanty Grecian costume into the atrium, and one of the female members of the party seemed inclined to engage her in drunken conversation, but her – what, her rescuer? Her abductor? – made a small sound of satisfaction and pulled her swiftly into the room they had just vacated. He closed the door behind them, locked it in the woman's flushed face, and turned to survey her.

Georgiana had had previous experience of gentlemen, or so-called gentlemen, locking her in rooms and advancing upon her with dishonourable intentions. Last year Captain Hart, who had most improperly met and wooed her in secret for months while she was still at school and had wished to marry her – or, more accurately and humiliatingly, to marry her substantial fortune – had attempted as much, had tried to force himself on her, and she had fought him off, taking no hurt and leaving him much the worse for the encounter. She was on the alert, ready to defend herself by the use of violence if necessary. She had done so before and could do so again. If all else failed, she could always scream. Loudly.

But the masked stranger did not attempt to pocket the key, nor did he approach her more nearly now. Instead, he said abruptly, 'You are obviously an innocent, and a full ten years younger than anyone else in this *maison d'intrigue*. How in God's name did you come to be here? Were you brought here against your will, or are you, as I conjecture, a complete fool with a reckless appetite for danger and far more hair than wit?'

This was the point at which Lady Georgiana Pendlebury should have told the truth, confessed that indeed she had been brought here under false pretences by someone she had mistakenly thought a friend, and begged the formidable stranger's help in making her escape. Undoubtedly he would have conveyed her home in safety, at the cost perhaps of a stinging dressing-down for her folly. This evening would then have become merely an embarrassing incident, but one which had, after all, done her virtue and her reputation no lasting harm. Nobody had laid a hand on her with amorous intent, nobody here could have the least idea who she was. Caroline Aubrey, who was plainly not the friend she had foolishly believed her to be, she would deal with later. She could have made a naughty story of it, and later have related it to friends in strict secrecy, to scandalised giggles. One day, when she was married, she might perhaps tell her husband of it, supposing he turned out to be the right kind of husband.

But she did not.

1

NORTH YORKSHIRE, A FEW WEEKS LATER

Georgiana sighed and leaned back in her corner of the luxurious Pendlebury travelling coach. Even this, the most modern of vehicles, sometimes struggled to cope with roads that were axle-deep in mud in many places. The lurching and jolting motion was wearisome.

The season was over – God knows she was glad of it – and in normal times she would by now be settling in to her brother Lord Irlam's house in Brighton, looking forward to all the fashionable amusements the summer there could offer. But these were not normal times; no al fresco entertainments or riding parties on the Downs could be expected when the weather continued so very inclement, and icy showers greeted every attempt to venture outside. The harvest was set to fail, or had already failed, and there was hunger in the towns and unrest in the air. It was not the time, serious-minded persons felt, for idle pleasures. Or at least, not public idle pleasures.

Though she knew it was selfish to think so when it was causing so much suffering, the disturbed, disturbing weather suited her mood. The events of a few weeks earlier, her visit to that house and its aftermath, had been a salutary shock to Lady Georgiana; she had looked at herself coldly in the light of them, and she had not liked any part of what she saw.

Last summer, when for pure love of excitement and attention she had entangled herself with the fortune-hunter Captain Hart and thought herself so clever, so adult, she had been in reality foolish, reckless, immature. She had hurt others who by no means deserved it – not least her brother Hal – and had been very lucky, she knew, to escape the imbroglio that she had created with her reputation and even her person intact. Hal had talked to her very seriously about her irresponsible, careless behaviour, as had her aunt, but she had not really been punished for her folly; she had instead been taken on a luxurious tour of Europe, and seen beautiful cities, ancient ruins and natural wonders few girls of her age were privileged to see. They'd spent months abroad, in Italy and elsewhere, and Hal had even trusted her to visit Venice with a friend's family, away from his supervision. She'd spent Christmas there, and had behaved well, self-consciously properly, still chastened by her brother's gentle reproaches – but look how she repaid his trust now.

She knew she was spoiled and over-indulged, as the only girl among her numerous orphaned siblings; last year she had apologised for her follies a dozen times, and cried, and promised to do better, and had thought she meant it, but once again she had allowed her impulsiveness, her thoughtlessness, that wild streak that she did not yet know how to control and sometimes feared she never would, to lead her into dangerous behaviour.

Much more dangerous behaviour. She had gone to that cursed house – perhaps that could be excused, as Mrs Aubrey was greatly to be censured for her mischievous and apparently pointlessly cruel deception – but when she, Georgie, had realised what manner of place it was, she had not instantly fled. She had stayed.

She had watched, seen things it was not safe for her to see, and when escape had offered itself to her, she had not taken it. Instead...

Georgiana was resolved not to follow that thought to its conclusion. Her experiences in that house, in that room, which she was determined not to think about now, absolutely refused to think about now as they brought a fiery blush to her cheeks, had at last caused her to reflect seriously upon herself, as, she now recognised with pain, she had not truly done last summer. Her apologies, her tears last year, had been worthless, since they had not in truth caused her to alter her behaviour one jot.

It was all very well to scoff at stuffy, outmoded social restrictions, as she had done when she chose to make Mrs Aubrey her friend; to use all her ingenuity to evade chaperonage; to say airily that the restrictions placed upon young women – never young men – were monstrously unjust and should be overturned. No doubt all these things were true, but she was obliged to live in the world as she found it. She was the daughter and sister of earls, she would be wealthy in her own right as far as a woman could be, but that did not give her some special magic that would enable her to defy society and its rules with impunity. She knew that a young gentleman in her position of great privilege would be free to behave more or less as he chose, to toy with women, to sample any and all debaucheries that caught his wayward fancy. But she, struggling with the same impulses and desires, was not similarly free. She had only to examine the career of Georgiana, Duchess of Devonshire, her mother's friend, for whom she had been named, to see the truth of that. The Duchess's husband had been constantly unfaithful, unfaithful even with her dearest friend, and his wife had been obliged to accept and even to raise the results of those irregular unions, but when she in her turn had strayed, had sought a little happiness and caused scandal because of it, her husband had been merciless and she had been forced to give up her dearly loved natural child.

The problem was not just society, Georgie had some while since admitted with a dull sort of a pain; no, she was torn over what she wanted. That was at the root of it all. The Duchess of Devonshire was not the only example set before her eyes. There were many other noble ladies who, after presenting their husbands with an heir or two, took lovers as they pleased, and left their complaisant husbands free to do the same. If these ladies were reasonably discreet, their social position did not seem to suffer. *Their* wild and reckless impulses could, it seemed, be indulged. She might, she supposed, marry suitably and then, a few years later, claim this very special, limited sort of freedom, though she would have to choose her husband carefully if this was the path she followed. If she wanted passion, if she courted danger – as it seemed she did – then a suitable marriage need not entirely close these possibilities to her. The idea simultaneously fascinated and appalled her, as if she stood on a cliff edge and toyed with jumping to her ruin.

She was coming to believe that it would be ruin for her. It must be so, because she must face the fact that this dangerous existence was simply not what she had been raised to expect her life to be. Those other ladies who gave their affections and their persons so casually and so frequently had perhaps grown up with parents who lived in this manner, who thought it entirely normal, when surely it was not. But her own parents, despite their milieu and some of their friends, had loved each other on sight, till death and beyond it, and, she believed, never thought to stray. Her brother Hal had married his Cassandra for love, and after initial misunderstandings was now blissfully happy. Had her mama been living still, and not lost to the grave these eight years, Georgie thought she would have been horrified to think that her daughter was so much as contemplating such an arrangement, even hypothetically. She would have counselled her, surely, to curb her impatient, passionate nature, to wait, to trust to time, to believe that one day she would meet and fall passionately in love with a man who loved her as deeply in return and could fulfil all her needs.

I must do so, Georgie resolved again now with a slightly watery sniff that she hastily suppressed. I must restrain my wild impulses – while recognising that they exist, for I have to be honest with myself from now on, or I will be lost – and be patient. Though it is very hard.

Because she had been so very lucky that night a few weeks ago. The man – she still did not know his name – had offered his carriage to take her home, eventually, and she had alighted from it just outside the elegant square in which she resided, so that his servants could not see her destination and thus learn her identity. She had to her astonishment entered her brother's house entirely undetected, climbing in through a first-floor window, assisted in her exertions by her male attire. Nobody seemed to have wondered where she was, as her brother and sister-in-law had not attended the masquerade she had gone to, but had spent the evening at home alone together and presumably gone to bed hours since. She was excessively glad that she was not obliged to face them in her state of dishevelment and confusion. Her maid, who must have perceived her absence, she had bribed, as she had done on many occasions the summer before.

The next day she had written to Mrs Aubrey, telling her that she had left the house to which she had been brought as soon as she had realised its disreputable nature, and terminating their acquaintance. She could not know, for she dared not ask, why Caro Aubrey had effectively set out to ruin her. But it scarcely mattered now. Should Mrs Aubrey feel inclined to spread malicious rumours, she had told her in her letter, she ought to know that, if Lady Georgiana's reputation suffered the least hurt, the fact that she had been so shockingly tricked into visiting such a place and then abandoned there would be spread abroad. As would exactly what Georgie had observed of Mrs Aubrey's subsequent behaviour – she described it in great detail – and the fact that she was plainly a regular visitor. Lady Georgiana Pendlebury required no further communication from Mrs Aubrey, other than a credible assurance that her letter had been destroyed – and it was returned to her without delay, in fact, torn into dozens of tiny pieces but still, to its author, recognisable.

Other consequences had perforce been left to time, and there had been none. No gossip, not a whisper of scandal, no glances bright with malice, no laughter stifled behind gloved hands. Nothing save the memories that tormented her.

Georgie shook her head in unconscious denial and returned, with an effort, to the present. She had been excessively glad to leave London, glad to escape the risk of seeing *him* again. She had been run ragged, looking for him wherever she went, and her family had noticed the dark circles under her eyes, and pronounced her fagged to death by the demands of the season; she had perforce assented with what she was aware was a slightly wan smile.

Fresh air was what she needed, it was agreed by everyone. The family had always intended to visit Lady Irlam's childhood home in Yorkshire at some point this year, and had carried out the plan as dismal June ended, even persuading Hal and Georgie's aunt, Lady Louisa, normally the most indolent of women, to accompany them north, since her companion Miss Spry was keen to come and see more of the north country. Cassandra was plainly delighted to visit her old haunts, and to show them to her husband; Georgie was happy enough to wrap up in voluminous layers and accompany the pair on bracing walks across the moors when the weather allowed. She felt better now, she told herself, now that she knew she was safe – she could hardly imagine that he, that the man, would appear from behind a drystone wall or wind-blasted tree, striding across the wild moors towards her, though in truth he still haunted her dreams, some of which were nightmares and some of which were decidedly more pleasant, though still disturbing in their own way.

But the company of two such besotted lovers as Hal and Cassandra, not yet a year married, was bound to pall in the end, and so Lady Georgiana, Lady Louisa and Miss Spry had with alacrity accepted an invitation to visit Louisa's old friend, Lady Blanche FitzHenry, at her brother's home on the Yorkshire coast. They had spent a couple of nights in Harrogate to break the journey into easy stages – Lady Louisa was not a woman who could ever be hurried – and were now on its final leg, approaching Northriding Castle.

'Have you ever been here before, Louisa?' Georgie asked idly now, as she gazed out of the carriage window, shaking off her lingering thoughts and looking about her. There was a change in the quality of light, even on such a grey day; it was plain that the sea was nearby, even though it was still unseen behind a low rise of wooded hills. They must be close, she thought.

'I have not,' her aunt replied. She was a handsome, statuesque woman of a little more than forty, with a drily humorous, languid manner and a decided air of fashion. She was unmarried, but nobody had ever had the temerity to call her a spinster. 'Blanche and I first became acquainted at school in London, and endured our first season together – well, I endured it; Blanche liked it, I think. She is a fearfully energetic creature; you will see soon enough. And then she married FitzHenry directly and went off to live in Ireland, and I have not set eyes on her for twenty years or more. But now, of course, she is a widow, and has brought her children to stay with her brother for a while.'

'Her brother, the notorious Duke,' said Miss Spry wryly. 'I confess I am all agog to meet him, and picture him very much as the villain in a Gothic tale. Montoni, perhaps. Is he as bad as he is painted, Louisa? Has he really seduced and left heart-broken quite half the ladies of Italy?' Miss Jane Spry did not in any sense conform to the picture held by most people of a lady companion; she was not a small, timid, retiring woman, dressed in drab, self-effacing garments, but was tall, blonde, cheerful and outspoken, dressing with careless flair and addressing Lady Louisa, her intimate friend, with no marked degree of deference. She came from a notable literary family, and herself wrote poems and learned articles that had been published in journals to some acclaim, but despite this Georgie liked her.

'I have not the least idea how bad he truly is,' said Louisa. 'He is eight or nine years younger than Blanche, and I was not at all acquainted him when he was a child. Odd to think of a famous rake once being a child, is it not, Jane? I know him by sight, of course; he is quite unnecessarily handsome, albeit in a sinister sort of a way that would quite fit your Gothic picture of him. You will not have set eyes on him, I suppose, Georgie, for you do not frequent the kind of parties he is rumoured to attend of late years, I am happy to say. But apart from gossip, I know as much or as little of him as you do.'

'How disappointing.' The older ladies shared a smile.

Then Louisa said, with a brief burst of uncharacteristic animation, leaning forward urgently and tapping her niece on the knee with her lorgnette for emphasis, 'I do not need to tell you, Georgiana, that you must never be alone with him. I know you have a long history of evading chaperonage, which it would be far too fatiguing to pick over again today, but whatever the truth behind it, his reputation is, as Jane says, atrocious. I should never have agreed to come here with you if I had not been given to understand that it will be quite a large party, containing several young ladies and their hopeful mamas, along, I trust, with more interesting people. But this time all the proprieties will be observed by you, do you understand me? Your good name would not survive an entanglement with *him*. And no, I do not propose to give you any more details of his exploits, so you need not think to ask me for them.'

Georgiana shuddered a little; thank God her aunt had no notion about her own latest and worst escapade. Long might it remain so! 'I promise you, Louisa, I have learned my lesson long since and will not do anything to put you to the blush. No, truly, I mean it!' she said, when the response was an incredulous snort. She was grateful when Miss Spry turned the subject.

'"Hopeful mamas"?' asked that lady thoughtfully. 'Do I understand you to be implying that the Duke is contemplating matrimony at last? That young ladies have been gathered here expressly for that purpose? If so, this is the first I have heard of it!'

'It may be so, I cannot say,' replied Lady Louisa airily. Then, 'Do not look at me in that odiously quizzing way! I will not be accused of matchmaking! You both know I would never contemplate such a thing, least of all with a man whose reputation is as bad as his. I am here to see my old friend, my dears, and nothing more. I promise you, I have no sinister intention. Jane, Georgiana, come: you wrong me!'

'Good!' said her companions in unison.

'But,' pursued Lady Louisa with a twinkle in her fine blue eyes, 'it might be amusing, might it not, to observe as disinterested outsiders the lengths that others go to in order to trap such a great prize?'

'To see young women offered up as sacrificial lambs can hardly be considered amusing,' said Miss Spry with a little heat; it was an old debate between them, for she was known to harbour radical views on the condition of women.

Her companion was of a more cynical turn of mind, and said merely, 'Well, we shall see, shall we not, dearest Jane, whether the innocent lambs are sacrificed, or run eagerly to the slaughter, jostling each other as they go? Presumably even a man as infamous as the Silver Duke cannot marry more than one of them at a time.'

'The...?' Georgie began to ask, prey to a sudden ridiculous fear. But there was no time to question her aunt further.

'We shall know soon enough,' said Louisa, 'for I perceive that we have arrived.'

2

The carriage passed over a bridge that seemed to span a deep moat, rattled over wet cobblestones under a mossy stone arch, then crossed a courtyard and pulled up smartly at the foot of a flight of weathered stone steps. The ladies were handed ceremoniously down from the carriage by a pair of impressive footmen in black and silver livery, and looked about them curiously at the ancient ivy-covered buildings that surrounded them. As she set one elegantly shod foot on the cobbles, Lady Louisa staggered slightly, finding herself enveloped in a warm embrace by a whirlwind in human form: Lady Blanche, tall, plump and flushed, dark hair touched with grey, come out in flattering haste to greet her. 'My dear Lou!' her hostess cried. 'I am so happy to see you at long last! You have not altered one jot!'

Lou? mouthed her companions to each other, but then it was their turn to be welcomed. Their hostess drew them inside to take off their bonnets and pelisses, and pressed them to sit and take tea by the huge and welcome fire in the Castle's cavernous great hall. A regiment of servants bore away their outer clothing, and they were left alone with Lady Blanche. 'I am sorry my brother and the rest of the family are not here to greet you,' she said, 'but we could not be entirely sure of the hour of your arrival, and they have taken advantage of a break in the incessant rain to go out riding. My children are still quite new to the estate, and Gabriel is showing them around. He is ridiculously proud of the place, though I am sure one would not think it of him when he affects to care for nothing and nobody.'

While her aunt and her old schoolfriend exchanged reminiscences of people and events that meant little to her, Georgie looked about her in quick interest. She had grown up in a castle with medieval origins, and this was another such. But her home had been tamed, she thought now, by centuries of peace, and was set, besides, in the gentle countryside of Hampshire. Surrounding its towers and battlements were rolling landscaped acres, a man-made lake created by Capability Brown, a Grecian temple; not, as here, jagged cliffs, lonely beaches, and the wild North Sea. And the Pendleburys, her own people, were an old family by most people's standards, but the Mauleverers, the feudal lords and now Dukes of Northriding, were, she understood, older still, and had ruled this starkly beautiful country with a mailed fist since the Norman Conquest.

The difference was reflected inside the ancient building. This great room contained little that told an observer she was in the nineteenth century; massive oak furniture, faded hanging tapestries, burnished armour and weapons, smoke-blackened beams, all were perfectly and deliciously medieval. Even the pair of enormous grey wolfhounds slumbering by the mighty fireplace were in keeping, and might have stepped out of a poem by Mr Scott. It was undeniably impressive, even a little intimidating. The room's current inhabitants, thought Georgie, idly weaving a fantasy as the three older ladies chatted, were the interlopers here – not just her party, southerners as they were, but Lady Blanche too. Their modern dress was at odds with their surroundings – they should have been wearing fur-trimmed velvet gowns with long sweeping sleeves, and elaborate pointed hennin headdresses over shaved brows. But then, she mused, it would be foolish to forget that such times were harsh as well as romantic, and at the advanced age of nineteen she would presumably already have been a mother several times over. Or dead in childbirth.

She took herself mentally to task for wool-gathering, and returned her attention to the conversation around her. Lady Blanche was describing the other guests, who were, she explained, most of them currently taking tea in one of the sitting rooms in the more modern part of the Castle. 'I am sure they are all excellent people in their way, and full of every accomplishment, but I do not find them uniformly sympathetic, Louisa, and I am excessively glad that you are all here to bear me company in my time of trial. For you must know,' she said, leaning forward a little and including Miss Spry and Georgiana in her confidences, 'that my exasperating brother has at last been brought to see that he must marry, and I have therefore assembled the cream of feminine society – or so they plainly consider themselves to be, and I have no particular reason to disbelieve them – so that he may look at them, and they may look at him. Of course, you might with justice wonder why such an awkward exercise was not performed in London, during the season, rather than dragging half the ton up to the wilds of Yorkshire.'

'I believe I can understand why. You had not until recently put off black gloves, had you, Blanche?' said Louisa softly.

Her friend sighed. 'It is true, alas.' She turned to Georgie and said, with a sad little smile, 'I had two brothers, but the younger, Ashby, was killed at Waterloo, and the next in line for the dukedom after him, our cousin John, who grew up here and was like another little brother to us, also took injuries there that he later died of. So after such heavy losses, Gabriel must reconcile himself to marriage, however much he has always said that he dislikes the idea, and I am returned from Ireland to help him. It is an onerous enough task, I do assure you.'

The ladies all murmured their condolences, and their hostess said in a brighter tone, as if deliberately shaking off lowering thoughts, 'It must also be admitted that Northriding Castle and its surroundings will not appeal to everyone, even if *we* think it the finest place in the world. Therefore it is by no means a bad idea that any woman who fancies herself as Duchess should see what sort of bargain she is taking on. For Gabriel, as I have said, is excessively attached to the place, and will wish his children to be reared here, as we were.'

Georgiana found herself more than a little surprised that Lady Blanche should be so frank, and this must have been reflected on her face, for that lady said, 'My dear Lady Georgiana, I would not speak so plainly to everyone, but you must know that I do not include you as one of the marriage party, as I term it. You and Miss Spry, and dear Louisa, are my guests, invited expressly by me, and you may be pleased to consider yourselves above the fray. My son Bram is a little older than you, I think, and my daughter Eleanor a little younger, and I hope you will grow to be fast friends and contrive to amuse each other. Please do not think that I have brought you here as one of the aspirants for my brother's hand; I am sure Louisa would never consent to such a cold-blooded plan, even if I had contemplated it for a second. Apart from any other considerations, I know the Pendleburys generally marry for love, and this can be no love match.'

'Thank you for restoring my character, Blanche,' said Louisa drily. 'I was saying as much in the carriage not half an hour since. I have no taste for matchmaking, but I have not the least objection to watching others' exertions in the field. Tell me, have you made any progress? Is any one of the horses in the race favoured over the others?'

Georgie did not doubt that Lady Blanche was about to answer this question with what appeared to be her habitual devastating frankness, but she was not to have the opportunity to do so. The dogs, which had been snoozing peacefully all the while, so that she had almost forgotten their presence, suddenly twitched, as at a sound only they could hear, and as suddenly were both fully alert, springing to their feet and rushing lithely to the great oak door that led to the courtyard, where they milled impatiently, letting out the odd excited bark. The massive portal opened, and several people in riding dress entered, in a great gust of cold air that made the fire waver and smoke billow into the hall for a moment. The dogs jumped about in ecstatic welcome, but were quelled by a firm word. The newcomers were a young man, pale and fine-featured, with dark auburn hair, a young lady of an appearance so similar that she must surely be his sister, and an older gentleman. He was perhaps in his early thirties, tall, well-built and coldly handsome, his long black locks streaked liberally with silver and his eyes of a similar unusual, striking shade. There could be no possible mistake. It was him. The Silver Duke.

3

It took every atom of Georgiana's self-control to preserve a fragile appearance of composure as Lady Blanche presented her family to her newly arrived guests. She smiled mechanically at the young people, and murmured polite commonplaces, which they returned. The young gentleman was plainly taken with her, and asked her what seemed to be a great many questions, but she had no thought to spare for him, and returned only mechanical answers to his civilities.

The Duke bowed over her aunt's hand, greeting her with cool courtesy, then turned to Georgie. She curtsied, and raised her eyes to his. The hand he took in his much larger one was trembling, she noted with little surprise. She could do nothing to prevent it. Their eyes locked as they had done once before, bright blue to silvery grey, and she was so close that she saw the flare of utter astonishment as he recognised her. There could be not the least doubt that he recognised her. She saw his pupils dilate as memory flooded them. Flooded him. She was sure she must be flushed, her breathing constricted, and hoped distractedly that others, if they saw it, would ascribe it to the heat of the fire. Not him, of course – no, he knew better.

'Lady Georgiana,' that instantly recognisable voice purred. 'What a... pleasure it is to make your acquaintance.' She could only pray that no one else noticed the minute hesitation before the word 'pleasure'. But she heard it, and her whole body tingled at the recollections it evoked, the recollections it was surely meant to evoke. That he should dare to speak of pleasure... He had recovered his composure with astonishing swiftness; indeed, unlike her, he had never truly lost it. He was, she thought, toying with her deliberately. This could hardly be a surprise to her.

And then he had released her, and moved on to greet Miss Spry, and Miss FitzHenry was shyly addressing some cordial remark to her about her journey to which she was obliged to reply. There was a general movement; the Duke and his nephew took their leave with many expressions of regret – Georgie avoiding her host's penetrating gaze all the while – and went off to take tea with their other guests, and Lady Blanche and her daughter summoned the housekeeper. They would take Lady Louisa and her companions up to their rooms, they said, where their luggage (which had arrived in a separate coach with the abigails some time earlier) had already been unpacked, and allow them to rest for an hour or two before it would be necessary to change for dinner and greet the rest of the company.

Georgiana pasted a smile to her face, and said everything that was proper, until at last she was left alone in her chamber, sinking into a chair set beside her bed and putting her cold hands to her face in sheer unbelieving horror. There was a spectacular, dizzying view from the room's casement down to the beach hundreds of feet below, where angry waves roared and lashed across slick black rocks, but she did not see it. She was blind to her surroundings, back in that warm, sensual, depraved house in Mayfair, and that small, locked room. She felt now as though she had never left it. As though she never would leave it.

She could almost have laughed when she reflected on her thoughts during the carriage ride, and all her pitifully sensible resolutions. To wait, to be patient, to curb her wildest impulses. To behave properly, like other young ladies, and to wait for love, and marriage. The trouble was, it had been so very easy to form such a purpose over the past few weeks. Then, she had been secure in the belief that the latest and worst instance of her recklessness had been entirely and most providentially without consequences. Up till this afternoon, she had believed that once again she had shown evidence of bearing a charmed life. She'd heard nothing more from Mrs Aubrey, she'd been touched by no breath of scandal, she'd come hundreds of miles away from home, and she had convinced herself that her ridiculous imaginings about meeting *him* again had been just that – ridiculous.

Of course, Georgie had wondered a thousand times who the man could possibly have been. She'd spent many hours wondering. He was plainly someone of great experience, she could vouch for that. Her whole body tingled at the recollection. His honeyed, seductive voice, his glittering eyes, his long, clever fingers, the smile that just touched his firm lips, his mouth: good God, his beautiful, sensual mouth. His kiss, his... All these things and more had obsessed her, waking and sleeping. But as the weeks went by, she had convinced herself by sheer force of will that it did not matter. That she had put the past behind her, and learned her lesson from it. That they would never meet again, and he would not recognise her if they did. That he was nothing to her, just as surely as she was nothing to him. And most of all that she was safe. She didn't deserve to be safe, but she'd persuaded herself that she was.

But now she was in his home, he had recognised her – this she knew with every fibre of her being – and she was so very far from safe. She was in his hands – an entirely involuntary shudder ran through her at the thought – he was the notorious, scandalous, dangerously attractive Duke of Northriding, and she had not the least idea what he would choose to do with the power he held over her.

4

Georgie dressed for dinner that evening with unusual care. She, Louisa and Miss Spry were housed together in a tower, each with a bedchamber that opened into a comfortably furnished shared sitting room. The walls of all these chambers were curved, wood-panelled, and the small windows offered magnificent, albeit currently rain-drenched, views out over the sea, the wild coast and the inland moors. It was undeniably picturesque, said Miss Spry, but must be extraordinarily inconvenient for the servants. At least they were not obliged to haul all the water for the ladies' ablutions up the steep spiral staircase with its timeworn stone treads; there was an ingenious dumbwaiter, operated by a pulley, set in one of the thick walls. Unconsciously echoing her niece's thoughts upon arrival, Lady Louisa said that she would never previously have imagined that any dwelling-place could make her own venerable childhood home, Castle Irlam, seem almost modern. And yet she admitted that this place did. 'I suppose it is the proximity to the sea and the height of the cliffs that produce much of the powerful effect. It is sinister, even in summer. Can you imagine,' she said with a shiver, 'what it is like here in the depths of winter?'

'You have no appreciation for the sublime,' Jane Spry replied with fond mockery. 'I find it magnificent; do not you, Georgiana? One of the most striking places I have ever visited. Although I shall be sure to take my warmest shawl down to dinner, and I recommend you both do the same or risk dying of pneumonia, so perhaps I am nothing but a sad hypocrite.'

Georgiana agreed that the prospect was indeed magnificent to contemplate, and hoped that it might be possible to descend and walk along the beach one day, if the rain ever abated. 'Though I cannot imagine how the strand may be reached,' she said, peering down. 'I can see no path, and if there is one it must surely be dangerously precipitous.'

She was determined to converse as lightly and naturally as possible, and to ignore the lurking sense of dread that haunted her. She had administered a silent, stern lecture to herself while she was dressing, telling herself that she must remain composed at all costs. Any undue agitation she betrayed would be perilous, and might attract attention that she by no means desired. Attention from the Duke himself, and from her fellow visitors.

Whatever might happen, whatever disaster impended, she would not allow herself to imagine that her host had the least intention of exposing her, of revealing to his distinguished guests where they had met and exactly what had passed between them there. She must remember that he had assembled a company here at his home with the fixed intention of choosing a bride from the young ladies present. His sister had explicitly said as much: that he must marry and set about obtaining an heir – what an innocuous phrase that was, if one did not think about it too deeply – as quickly as possible. Such a purpose would hardly be served by creating a fearful scandal with another guest. Young ladies and their families who had travelled so far in search of a rich and titled husband might overlook much in the way of the gentleman's irrevocably tarnished reputation, but surely they would not overlook such an insult.

If anyone learned her guilty secret, Georgie realised suddenly, they would inevitably think the Duke had brought her here to serve most dishonourably as his mistress of a night while he made his choice of bride at leisure and then courted another by day. Such an affront could not be borne, and no woman of birth and breeding would ever look at him again if what he had done became widely known. So perhaps she was not entirely without weapons of her own, although in order to use them – as had been the case with Mrs Aubrey – her own reputation must first be entirely destroyed. But she could threaten, could she not, if it came to that, even if in truth there was little chance of carrying out her threats? This thought, extreme and Gothic as it was, made her feel a little better, and gave her the courage to straighten her shoulders and regard herself with critical attention in the silvered mirror. She would go down fighting if she must, take full responsibility for her own rash actions, and look her best while she did it. She had her pride to sustain her, even if she was quaking inside at the prospect of seeing him again.

'I do not think I have ever seen you looking so well, my dear girl,' Louisa said behind her. 'That gown is extraordinarily becoming, and quite out of the common way.' Louisa was known for her stylish dress, and a compliment from her was a rare thing, and to be treasured. It gave her niece a little much-needed courage. In Venice last winter, Georgiana had found a changeant silk that exactly matched her eyes and yet was shot through with gold – it was an unusual colour, or colours, for a fabric, and she had purchased a full bolt of it and brought it home. When it had become clear that the summer was to be an extraordinarily cold one, she had had it made up into an evening gown with long sleeves and a demi-train. She wore it now with a bright shawl of

Indian silk and an ancient family jewel on a long gold chain. This was no occasion for tiny puff sleeves, demure pearls and white muslin. She needed armour.

The wisdom of her choice was soon revealed to her, after she and her companions made their way down winding stairs, along galleries, and down yet more stairs to the reception room where the guests were all assembled – some might have said, huddled – by another roaring fire. The older ladies were most of them sensibly dressed, with long sleeves, warm shawls and modish lace caps tied under their chins, but some of the debutantes in the party had foolishly chosen to array themselves in thin, clinging muslin gowns that might be appropriate for a July evening in Brighton in any normal year, but not for North Yorkshire in this year without a summer. These gowns, designed to display and to entice, left their bare arms and the exposed portions of their bosoms slightly blue and shivering now, a sad prey to gooseflesh. Georgie smiled inwardly to herself, and moved forward with Louisa to greet the company with a serenity she had previously thought beyond her grasp. She could do this, she told herself. She must.

She soon realised that her presence was creating a certain amount of dismay among the young ladies and their mamas, which they were concealing with varying degrees of success. Of course, she thought, they consider me one of their number, and a rival; they imagine I have entered myself into the lists as a candidate for Northriding's hand. I suppose there is no way of conveying to them that they are fair and far off in such a supposition. They would simply not believe me, and I cannot really blame them. I am here, after all.

They were most of them ladies with whom she had become acquainted in Town, this season or the one before. Like her, they all remained unmarried, unbetrothed, or of course they would not be here, eyeing each other like cats who were currently contemplating arching their backs and hissing in warning.

Only one of them was a friend: Miss Alice Templeton, who had made her curtsey to Queen Charlotte at her side and whom she had always liked, though they were very different in character. Perhaps that was why she liked her. At least *she* is glad to see me, thought Georgie as they embraced each other, and I am pleased to have her company, though I can hardly think her a fit bride for the Duke. She is so excessively gentle, mild and good, and I am sure has never entertained a wicked thought in her life, while he, as I have reason to know... Alice drew her aside, and said, smiling a little, her soft brown eyes warm with affection, 'I was delighted when Lady Blanche told us you were coming, for I had not looked to encounter you here.'

'We had not expected to be here, Alice,' replied Georgiana. 'We were in Yorkshire already, at my sister-in-law's house, when the letter from Lady Blanche was forwarded on to my aunt. Since we were relatively close by, Louisa thought she might take advantage of the circumstance in order to visit her friend; they were at school together as girls, you know, and have corresponded ever since, but not seen each other for an age.' She thought she might at least try to impress upon some of her fellow guests that she had other reasons than theirs for being here.

'You did not think to remain with Lord Irlam, then, Lady Georgiana?' said another voice from just behind her, one far less friendly in tone.

'I did not,' Georgie replied with a false smile. Of all the debutantes she loathed – and there were regrettably many, for unlike Alice she was not a meek or a patient young woman – she thought that Mary Debenham must be the worst; of course fate would have ensured that she would be here. The woman was a harpy in silk and muslin. 'My brother is, as you will recall, not ten months married, and the company of two people so entirely besotted with each other as he and Lady Irlam can be a little trying after a while, dearly as I love them both. I must admit I was glad for an excuse to come away and leave them be.'

'Oh, yes,' said Mary, something approaching a sneer marring her icy blonde prettiness. 'It was a love match, was it not?' It was plain that she found the whole concept perfectly ridiculous and not in the best of taste. 'I do seem to recall that Lady Irlam was a Miss... Somebody-or-other from Yorkshire, I quite forget the name, for I declare it is not one I ever heard before I met her.'

'Cassandra was a Miss Hazeldon,' said Georgie from between gritted teeth, wishing she could think of some witty, devastating set-down to put the odious creature firmly in her place.

'An old Skipton family, I believe.' A deep, rich voice: the Duke had, unobserved by any of the three ladies, joined them, and stood regarding them sardonically, immaculate as ever. For a tall, well-built man, he moved very swiftly and quietly when he chose. 'Be careful how you criticise a Miss Somebody-or-other from Yorkshire, Miss Debenham; my own mother was nothing more.' A cold, glinting smile accompanied these words, and did nothing at all to mitigate the sting they carried.

Mary was aghast, and could scarcely find the words to express her dismay as she stuttered out an apology. She had not meant to imply; she would be mortified if the Duke should think... She lost herself in a morass of confused words. He merely smiled ironically in response and did nothing at all to aid her in her distress. Fortunately for her, dinner was announced at that moment, sparing her blushes, and she was able to escape.

'I believe I am to take in your aunt to dine,' said her tormentor as he turned to Georgie, his silver eyes enigmatic. 'A pleasure, I am sure, but also a shame, as I would have welcomed the chance to become better acquainted with you, Lady Georgiana. But that will have to wait for a more convenient occasion, and I must possess my soul in patience until then. And here is my nephew, more fortunate than I, come to escort you.'

There was no time to dwell on the implications of his words, or to try to decipher the mocking expression in those arresting eyes, let alone to examine the feelings raging within her; Mr FitzHenry was smiling eagerly at her and offering his arm, and she was obliged to smile in return, and take it, and go in, like the civilised creature she was supposed to be but, she feared, most definitely was not.

5

It had not previously occurred to Georgie that it would be so, but the dinner table at Northriding Castle that evening presented a rather odd appearance. There was nothing amiss with the napery, the silver or the china, and the wood was polished till it shone. The two dozen or so persons seated in the grand green dining room were, for the most part, fashionably dressed and suitably bejewelled. They seemed in no way unfit to take their places under the painted gazes of Van Dyck's huge canvas of Mauleverer ancestors, who looked down on them with those distinctive silver eyes from gilded frames in all their glory of armour, silk and lace. But it was customary in society for hostesses to attempt to balance their guests nicely by sex. Given the circumstances of this house party, that must always have been a challenge for Lady Blanche, but the arrival of the three Pendlebury ladies, unaccompanied by so much as a brother or an elderly uncle, had disordered matters further. Some of the other ladies had brought their papas, one had brought a brother too, but still there was a decided shortage of persons of the male sex at the table. The hostess had done what she could, and brought in the Duke's estate manager and the incumbent of the local church. Yet there were far more ladies than gentlemen none the less, and the table placement must have given Lady Blanche the headache, although nobody present was ill-bred enough to refer to it; or at least, not in earshot of their hosts. They all knew why they were there, after all.

Using the already unconventional circumstances as an excuse, and contrary to all rules of precedence – although perhaps the daughter and sister of a duke did not need an excuse, reflected Georgie, but could afford to defy convention in such matters – Lady Blanche had chosen to place Miss Spry at her own left hand. Perhaps she had done this to compensate herself for having Mary Debenham's father at her right; he appeared to be a gentleman not the least interested in conversing with ladies, and very interested in eating his dinner, which he proceeded to do with intense concentration and in a silence more flattering to the cook than to his hostess. The Duke had Louisa at his right, and Lady Debenham at his left, and Georgie, who was determined not to stare at him and even more determined that he did not observe her staring at him, could not help but notice that he and her aunt were keeping each other very well amused. Lady Debenham's face was a picture; she was plainly of a naturally sour disposition, much like her daughter, and, it seemed, thoroughly disapproved of His Grace, of Lady Louisa, and of the tenor of their somewhat flirtatious conversation, which she must be able to hear with perfect clarity. But Selina Debenham was here because she cherished ambitions to see her daughter as this man's duchess, no matter the reputation or the conduct of her prospective mate, and so she must paste on a smile, and present a complaisant face. The dinner itself was excellent, well-chosen and beautifully cooked, but Georgie did not think that Lady Debenham, unlike her husband, was enjoying it to any marked degree.

She herself was better placed, though it did not seem so at first.

Convention would have set her close to the Duke, as one of the highest-ranking ladies present, but Lady Blanche had instead positioned her not far from her own end of the table, with the rector, Mr Summerson, on one hand, and Mr FitzHenry on the other. Georgie hoped Lady Blanche was not matchmaking for her son. The young gentleman was both handsome and amiable, and showed a continuing disposition to flirt with her if given the least encouragement, which she was not in the mood to indulge just now, but he was little more than a boy, after all. When she did not appear responsive to him, he turned without any appearance of chagrin to the young lady on his other hand and tried his luck there. They were soon laughing together as if they had known each other for years.

Mr Summerson was a surprise, though – he was a middle-aged, cherubic man with grey curls and a benevolent expression, and far more entertaining than any gentleman in holy orders she had ever encountered before. 'Now you are thinking,' he had said with a twinkle and a soft Irish brogue, 'what have I, a young lady of beauty, rank and fashion, done to deserve being placed next to a prosy old clergyman?'

She had choked a little, and then laughed despite herself, and they had found themselves excellently suited from then on and well able to keep each other amused; perhaps, she thought, one needed to be a very special kind of cleric to minister to a patron such as the notorious Duke of Northriding. She thought the gentleman would not mind if she asked if his living was in the gift of the Mauleverers. As they were apparently the largest landowners for miles around, she thought it must be so. 'Indeed it is,' he replied easily. 'I owe my comfortable situation entirely to the Duke. It is a shocking and entirely unjustifiable system of patronage, and aren't I a terrible hypocrite for saying so? Lady Blanche's late husband was a distant cousin and a good friend of mine, and thus I came to His Grace's attention, and he was so good as to give me the place here when it came free ten years ago. It would not,' he said thoughtfully, 'suit a fellow who was any holier and more unworldly than he need be, nor of too timid a disposition. He'd have sleepless nights, so he would.'

Once again, Georgie was unable to conceal her surprise, and he smiled at her as he saw it. 'I'm not saying anything the Duke would not say himself, my dear. He has a certain reputation for all manner of wickedness not fit for your ears, it would be idle to deny it, and I dare say some of it was earned and some of it was not, as is the way of the world. But he's an intelligent man, you know, and fearsomely well-read. Not lacking in deeper feeling, too, though he tries hard to conceal it. He keeps me on my toes, for sure, though the rest of my days are as easy as they could be.' He saw she did not immediately understand him, and added, 'The Mauleverers look after their people; it is something of a proverb in their part of Yorkshire. You'll not find shocking hunger, want and ignorance such as you see elsewhere, not in these lands. Even in difficult times like the present, you will not see Northriding people suffering.'

'I am glad to hear it, sir,' she said fervently. And then on impulse she added, 'What do you, think, then, of this party and the reason for which it was assembled?'

'Now there's an interesting and rather indiscreet question from a young lady,' he said. He did not seem offended in the least, but she noticed he had not, in point of fact, answered her question. 'No, I do not mean to reprove you, Lady Georgiana. Frankness is a rare quality.'

'I do sometimes struggle to control my unruly tongue, and too often say what I should not,' she admitted ruefully. 'But it occurs to me as it did not before, talking to you, that the Duke is not only choosing a bride for himself. My sister-in-law has a great many responsibilities as Countess of Irlam, and the chatelaine's duties must be even more numerous here, I should think. His Grace must strive to choose a lady who can fulfil that role too. Not necessarily an easy task, I should think.'

'Yes, my dear, you are quite right, of course, and the Castle has been without a mistress for too long since his mother died. It is four years since the late Duchess left us, good and gentle lady that she was, and her shoes will not be so easy to fill, as you have divined. Quite setting aside her son's own preferences in the matter, of course.'

'My own mother died eight years ago,' she said softly. 'We still miss her every day. Everyone who was at all acquainted with her does. I know my sister-in-law experienced a degree of trepidation upon taking her place.'

'Any woman of sensibility would feel so,' he said with a sympathetic smile. 'The ones who wouldn't, they're the ones you have to watch.' It might be her imagination, but Georgie thought that he was regarding Miss Debenham as he made this last remark. She supposed she could take that as a sort of answer to her earlier question if she chose. But she could not be so impolite as to ask him to elucidate further, and so she turned the conversation into less dangerous channels.

When the ladies withdrew and left the gentlemen to their port, she found herself at Louisa's side, as the other ladies clustered around the piano in heated discussion. 'I see the Duke kept you well entertained,' she teased her aunt in the moment's privacy. She was not, of course, in the least jealous of the attention, for that would be absurd on several counts.

'He did,' her aunt conceded. 'He made me laugh – set out to do so, I am sure. I have no idea why he should trouble to make up to me; perhaps he cannot help himself. He has a degree of charm that is rarely to be met with, he is as clever as a cartload of monkeys, and I would not trust him an inch. Not half an inch. And I am not a young lady with her reputation to worry about. So you bear my warning in mind, my girl. I wonder if I was wrong in bringing you here?'

Georgie feared she flushed. 'Louisa! Hush!'

'No, I do not mean to insult you, so do not put your back up. It's merely that I have met any number of rakes before, and found them exceedingly tedious creatures – the sort of men who can look at a woman, any woman, in only one way. You must know the type of villain by now: a man who sees the mere existence of a woman upon the earth as an invitation, one who would attempt to kiss a girl he met unprotected in the road, or walking in the countryside, or force himself upon an inn servant.'

'Horrid,' said Georgie with a shiver. She greatly feared, though she had not fully understood it until their last meeting, when she had been forced to fight off his advances, that her former suitor Captain Hart had been of such a stamp.

'Yes,' agreed Louisa. 'Horrid, and highly dangerous in the sense that they will molest any woman they encounter without the least compunction if ever they see an opportunity. They should be put in the pillory and pelted with refuse until they undertake to change their ways. Or as a sex we should take up guns, so that we can simply shoot them all and rid ourselves of them for ever.' She spoke calmly and appeared to be entirely serious, and Georgie smiled appreciatively in response; she could not disagree. 'But as long as you do not find yourself in their power in any way, they are easy enough to resist for a woman of sense, and merely nuisances. I do not believe that the Duke is like that, though. I think him far more of a threat. I think...' She hesitated, as if choosing her words carefully.

Her niece regarded her with misgiving. 'You think...?'

'I think he is the sort of man who could make an impulsive

young lady like you throw her cap over the windmill and never regret it until it was far, far too late. I'd wager he could seduce a woman and make her believe it was all her own idea. And I say this to you, never having so much as looked at a man seriously in my life. So have a care, Georgie!'

6

It had been a strange evening, Georgiana reflected much later, and it was no wonder that it left her unable to sleep, a dozen jumbled impressions whirling in her head as time dragged slowly by and still she was wakeful.

She climbed from her bed and crossed to the window, picking up her shawl as she went and wrapping herself in it. Drawing back the heavy velvet curtains, she looked out pensively on the scene revealed to her. The moon was waxing and stood low in the sky, with dark clouds scudding fast across it and obscuring its silver face, and then tearing away to reveal it once more. When it was exposed, it laid down a shining path across the gunmetal waves that bit at the beach. There were no other dwellings on the tall cliffs close to the Castle, and she could see no other part of the building from here, no lights or manmade structures, so all that she beheld was nature, but a much fiercer nature than she was accustomed to at home in Hampshire. There was nothing manicured or cultivated here. She was reminded of mountain vistas that she had seen while travelling abroad last year, in Italy,

Switzerland and Germany. Not by any means comfortable or reassuring prospects, and many people found them unsettling, alarming, even sinister, as Louisa had said. But she had found that she loved them, and she loved this too – the fierce wildness of it spoke to her, somehow, and certainly echoed the turmoil that she felt inside her tonight.

The young ladies and their mamas had arranged an impromptu concert to show off their musical accomplishments. This was quite a usual way of passing an evening in polite society, of course, but it must take on a deeper significance now. Georgiana had been torn – she did not want to participate, did not at all wish to be included in the list of young ladies vying for the Duke's attention, but if she refused to take her part that also would draw attention to her, and perhaps give the impression that she thought herself above her company and wished to stand apart from it. She was the highest ranking of the young unmarried ladies here, and she could already tell that Mary Debenham and her crony Miss French saw her as serious competition, for that reason if for no other. She did not herself believe, though she could advance no solid reason for such a belief, that the Duke would give a fig for such distinctions. Nor did she think that he was in all honesty likely to choose one lady as his Duchess above another merely because she gave a superior performance upon the pianoforte or sang an Italian song in an affecting manner. This was not an audition for a role upon the stage, it was real life. But she would sing, if she must – she thought herself very cunning in manoeuvring matters so that she did so in a duet with Alice Templeton, rather than alone and exposed. She declined to perform again once their piece was done, and though she was sure that Miss Debenham sneered at her for it and whispered that she was an indifferent singer and knew it, she did not care. She had felt Northriding's eyes on her as she sang, and whether this was in common courtesy – she was singing, he was looking at her singing, just as anyone might – or some more disturbing reason, or even her own fevered imagination, it made her uncomfortable and she wanted no more of it.

They had had no private or public speech after the brief, snatched interlude before dinner, and Georgie was glad. He unsettled her beyond all measure, and her own recollections unsettled her more. She would do her utmost to avoid him for the rest of her stay, and certainly she would take Louisa's words to heart and be very sure never to be alone with him for as much as a second. She had better reason than her aunt could possibly suspect to know that Louisa had been entirely right when she warned of his dangerous charm. He was perfectly capable of mesmerising a young lady into behaving in a scandalous manner and casting all thought of propriety to the four winds. His beautiful voice alone could cause one to...

The silence of the bedroom was broken by a distinct and very curious noise: a sort of sharp creak, which seemed much more distinct than the usual sounds of an ancient building of wood and stone settling as it cooled. Georgie chided herself for falling prey to Gothic terrors in such a cliched setting – she had grown up in a castle and knew better – but all the same she could not prevent herself from turning, and scanning the panelled walls and moonlit four-poster bed with anxious eyes. Perhaps there were mice; she didn't like mice. Could there be rats, even? Surely not.

If there were rodents, they must be unusually clever ones. The moonlight fell full upon a long, straight, perpendicular crack in the linenfold panelling, and as she watched in frozen horror it grew wider, longer, as a gap opened, large enough at last to admit a person. A cloud obscured the moon for a second, or perhaps she blinked, and when the fitful light reappeared she saw that there was a figure standing in the room with her, a tall, familiar figure clad in a sumptuous silk dressing gown. The moonlight drew gleams of silver from his hair and struck sparks from his glinting eyes.

The Duke.

7

He stepped towards her, and she shrank back against the windows, clutching her shawl about her in an action that some part of her knew to be both futile and ridiculous. Being fully clothed – at least at the start – had not helped her before. A light flared, and she saw that he held a closed lantern, and had uncovered it.

He set it down, his lips quirking wryly as he regarded her. 'You are quite safe, Lady Georgiana – or at any rate, as safe as you wish to be. I give you my word I merely came to talk. We have matters to discuss, do we not? Private matters, best examined without any fear of interruption?'

As safe as she wished to be. She forced down the traitorous thoughts his words, his damnably seductive voice set roiling within her. 'How do I know I can trust you?' she said bluntly.

'Have I not given you sufficient proof on our most memorable previous meeting that I will go precisely as far as you desire me to and no further? No matter how strongly my own inclinations might urge me otherwise?'

She flushed hotly from head to toe, and grasped the windowsill for support. It was true, she could not deny it. Neither violence nor coercion nor even any form of persuasion had played the least part in what had happened between them. If he had bewitched her, she must admit that she had been a willing victim. More than willing: eager.

'And besides,' he said, settling into the chair beside her bed and making himself comfortable, just as though they were having some quite ordinary conversation in an ordinary setting, 'you forget that your most excellent aunt and her chère amie are close by. Should you feel compelled to scream, or make any other kind of loud noise, I feel confident they would hear and come running to your rescue. You need not fear scandal, either, since no one else besides your little family party is staying in this tower. Shriek away, the instant you feel threatened, I beg you. There is no denying that it would be a little awkward for us both if you were to choose that course, but I doubt your aunt would spread the matter abroad, for the sake of your reputation – and as for my reputation, of course, it could hardly be any worse than it is already. Sit down,' he added in a less satirical tone. 'I'm not going to pounce on you.'

She came over to the bed, and sat where she could see him, but not too close, her back straight and her hands primly clasped in her lap. Though it was a little late for that. 'Did you have me put in this chamber on purpose?' she asked suddenly.

He laughed softly. 'How could I? I did not know your identity until I set eyes on you this afternoon. I am seldom surprised, but I admit I was then. No: the whole building is honeycombed with secret passages and hidden stairs. My ancestors were both Catholic recusants and shocking libertines, the whole pack of them, and it seems the results in terms of domestic architecture are much the same. In the unlikely event that I should wish to pay a nocturnal visit to Lady Debenham, for example, I may easily do so.'

She felt a wild impulse to laugh, and suppressed it ruthlessly.

'But how did you know I was here, then, and not in one of the other rooms in this tower?'

He waved a languid hand. 'Blanche has a list, which I purloined. She is terrifyingly organised. You might, of course, have for some inscrutable feminine reason swapped chambers with your aunt or Miss Spry, in which case you cannot doubt that I would have vanished as silently as I came. I doubt you would have heard my arrival, you know, had you not been awake and up already. Why were you, I wonder? A guilty conscience?'

She refused to rise to his bait, and would certainly not be discussing her conscience with him. She doubted *he* possessed such a thing. 'I would have heard even so, I think. The panel creaked most shockingly.'

'I thank you for the information,' he said gravely, though somehow she knew his voice and the tiny, fleeting expressions on his face well enough by now to tell that he was mocking her still. 'I will make sure to oil the hinges for the next time.'

'I insist you close up the secret way immediately! Because there will not be a next time!' she shot back, and then moderated her tone for fear Louisa or Miss Spry might hear. 'There will never be another such improper occasion!' she hissed in further emphasis. It was a sentence that lent itself to being hissed, and she was pleased with the sound of it. 'I do not see that we have anything at all to say to each other!'

'Do not be disingenuous,' he said, his eyes glittering in a highly disturbing fashion. 'It does not suit you, my dear. I had thought you fearless.'

God, his voice when he spoke the endearment, even if it was meant ironically! It was like the lightest of caresses across bare flesh, arousing, tempting, promising much more. She could very easily see why so many women had succumbed to him. But she would not be one of them. Not again. She bit her lip, and then realised he had seen her do it, and wished she had not.

'You know we must talk.' He was relentless.

'Why? There is nothing to be said. It was, it is, all a horrible mistake,' she said very low. 'You were in ignorance of my identity, and I of yours – I hope you know that—'

'I do know it,' he said lightly. 'I have good reason to. I do not think anybody – apart of course from a jealous husband on one particularly memorable occasion in my wild youth – has ever been so appalled to see me in all my thirty-one years of existence. My *amour propre* has never been served such a severe blow. Mr Summerson would no doubt tell me it is good for me.'

'I do not know how you can make a joke of such a serious matter!' she hissed.

'Practice?'

'You must be the most provoking creature alive!'

'You are not the first person to say so. But we are dancing around the subject, are we not? I am as guilty as you, for I find an unexpected pleasure in sparring with you. Pray continue. You were saying, most unflatteringly: a horrible mistake. I believe you said something similar last time, too.'

'Yes,' she said very quietly. 'A mistake, a moment of madness on my part. I was tricked there, to that dreadful house – you know I was, I told you so – and then...'

'And then...? There's the rub. You could have chosen to leave when I so nobly offered you the chance. You did not. Moreover, you lied to me, and made me think you something you are not, and I acted on that mistaken belief. If you can put what happened next out of your mind, you have the advantage of me, for I cannot. No matter how I try, and God knows I have tried. As I think I said to you once before, you are not obliged to give me any explanation for your behaviour, and I'm not asking for one. But do you really pretend to be surprised I have come to you tonight?'

She put her hands to her burning face. He was not saying anything she had not said to herself a hundred times, and his words were daggers. 'Why exactly are you here, then? I demand you tell me plainly. Enough with the insinuations. Is it just to talk, as you claimed, or do you have blackmail in mind?'

His beautiful voice was expressionless, but somehow she thought he was angry. 'Blackmail to what end, Lady Georgiana?'

'I would have thought it obvious!'

'I try never to be obvious. I recommend the habit to you, madam.'

'Certainly,' she said bitingly, 'a man who summons a veritable harem of young ladies to his home to choose between them for a bride, and then comes to another in secret and proposes to make dishonourable love to her, while all the others sleep in happy innocence, cannot be said to be obvious. Many choice adjectives could be applied to such a man, but I am sure that "obvious" is not one of them.'

He sighed, and was silent for a moment, looking down at his hands. 'I suppose that that is all too true. Consider me duly chastened. The trouble – one of the troubles – with having a reputation for outrageous behaviour is that sometimes I allow it to run away with me. I am not, after all, as you so pertinently remind me, the Grand Turk.'

She refused to soften at his almost-apology. 'You owe me nothing, sir, but only you can say what duty you owe to your future wife.'

'Yes, yes,' he said with a touch of impatience. 'Consider your point sufficiently well made, Miss Prim. To the victor, the spoils. I will leave you to your virtuous slumbers, and trouble you no more.'

'Good!' she said, standing, flushed with triumph. She had bested him; the new and more prudent Georgiana had won. She had, just this once, defeated her worst self. Perhaps there was hope for her yet.

And then their eyes met, and held, and despite all Georgie's resolutions something flared to instant, insistent, undeniable life between them, as it had done before with such disastrous consequences.

He rose too, and only now did he approach her with lazy confidence, like some big cat sure of its prey. 'Your words are very fine,' he said, his tones silken once more, and lazily amused, 'and I applaud the noble sentiment. Your concern for your sisters, even the ones you don't like one bit, is most affecting. But, my little liar, we both know – do we not? – that if I reached out and touched you now, your body would take fire at my lightest caress. Be damned to sisterhood and virtue, the blood in your veins is saying to you now. Be damned to caution and respectability. Put your hands and your mouth on me, Gabriel, and give me what I crave so desperately!' He was very close, and his voice was little more than a whisper when he said, and now she was unsure if he spoke for her still, or for himself, 'Give me what you gave me when first we met, and give me more than that before I die from wanting it!'

She gasped at the images his words called up in her, and he laughed softly, and then he did reach out one well-formed hand and touched her face. It was the lightest and most innocent of caresses, but the effect was electric, all-consuming. She tried to repulse him, or if she could not repulse him to stay still as a statue under his touch and betray nothing of the effect he had upon her. But it was too late, for he knew already, and in any case she could not dissemble; her physical being simply would not let her. Her face turned instinctively into his palm, her body yearned towards him. And he bent his silvered head and kissed her.

8

He kissed her very briefly and casually, a mere tantalising brush of the lips, as if it meant little to him, and then without another word he left, closing the secret panel with exaggerated care behind him. Georgie collapsed onto her bed with a sob that combined frustration and anger. Frustration that he had not done any more than kiss her; anger that she had so intensely wanted him to. And on top of all that, hot shame that he had known it.

She thought that Louisa was entirely correct: this was a man who could seduce you, and convince you it was all your own idea. It would not surprise her, she mused bitterly, to hear that women by the dozen had been known to beg him to make love to them. Perhaps he thought that she would do so, if not now, then later. Perhaps that was a part of the game for him.

Perhaps she would.

She had before, after all.

When he had turned to her in that room, in that house of sin and temptation, and accused her of naïveté and folly, some species of madness had possessed her. She had no other explanation for all that had followed. In that moment, she simply could not endure that this man of all men thought her an inexperienced little idiot, even if it was all too true. She had summoned a brittle smile and said in a low voice, 'I was tricked into coming here, you are quite correct to guess as much. A friend, or one I thought a friend, brought me here under false pretences. I had no idea... But you need not fear for my virtue. I am not the innocent you think me. I am a widow.'

She heard the words she uttered as if someone else was saying them. She had no idea where they had come from.

'A widow?' He seemed amused rather than sorry. 'I offer you my condolences, madam. You must have been married and then left cruelly alone so *very* young.'

He did not believe her, and no wonder. But she was committed to the deception now. She cleared her throat, and blurted out, 'I was. My husband died at Waterloo. We were only married a few months.'

'Ah.' No trace of humour in his deep voice now. 'Many of us lost dear ones at Waterloo. And many were widowed cruelly soon. You have all my sympathy. But that does not explain why, being brought here by deception, as I can well believe, you stayed. I imagine a young widow might well be lonely, but I assure you – and you must have seen for yourself – that you will find no companionship here. Or at least, not any kind of companionship that will be of use to you. Indeed, quite the reverse. This place is for those who know what they are doing, and despite your long months of experience, my dear, it is all too plain that you do not.'

She did not know why, but sudden tears stung her eyes at his words, even though they were spoken gently enough. He saw – he saw too much – and in a second he had closed the space between them and was standing perilously near to her. He put up her chin with a gentle finger and said, 'Oh, do not cry. Unconscionable! I am sorry.'

'You have nothing to be sorry for. I'm not crying,' she said uselessly, and sniffed.

'Of course you are not; forgive me. I expect you have had a trying time, finding yourself abandoned here. Were you frightened? That can paralyse one, certainly. Outrageous of me to question you.'

Had she been frightened, in all honesty? 'I…'

He shook his head. 'You must be aware that you owe me no explanation.'

'I know I do not. In all honesty… I do not know if I was frightened. Shocked, I suppose. But no, not really frightened. It's not as though I truly thought anyone was going to hurt me.'

'Not unless you wanted them to.'

She choked, aware that she was blushing furiously and grateful for the mask to conceal it, and then said, 'Yes, I could not help but see…'

'Nobody could help but see.'

'It seemed to me that that was the point.'

'I am sure you are quite correct. And I expect it has been an education of sorts for you, but I think it is time for you to leave now. My carriage is at your disposal, madam.'

The formal phrase in such an incongruous setting made her smile involuntarily, her dimples creasing below the mask, and she saw the echo of her reaction in his silver eyes. He was very quick in understanding, she thought. Dangerously so.

'Yes,' she said, 'I should thank you and go.' But still she did not move.

There was a charged silence, which he broke by saying very softly, 'But you don't want to. Do you?'

'No.'

'What do you want, then?' His liquid voice, his intent gaze caressed her, and she shivered a little as the fine short hairs on the back of her neck rose. She wasn't smiling now, and nor was he.

'I don't know what I want.'

'I presume,' he said, his voice liquid honey, 'that, unless I have misjudged you greatly, you do not, unlike the lady with the deplorable taste in jewellery, desire that I, or anyone else for that matter, should lay you naked across the sofa and take a whip to you? If you do, of course, just say the word; I am sure it can be arranged. Most things can, I understand, here.'

'No!' she said, the contrast between his beautiful voice and his scandalous words doing curious things to her breathing. 'No, I don't want that. But...' She was not having this conversation. It was not real. Or if it was, someone else had taken possession of her.

'But...?' The blunt word was a caress. How did he do that?

'You said I must be lonely, and you were right.' As she uttered the lie, she knew that it was true. Hal had Cassandra, Louisa had Miss Spry, her brother Bastian had his Matthew, however complicated their life must always be; whereas she, she had thought Captain Hart loved her, but he only cared for her money. She was a foolish, reckless, lonely girl. That was the truth of it.

'I told you, you will find no companionship here.'

'Not even from you?'

She thought she had shocked him into silence for a moment, and she was fiercely glad of it. It pushed her to be more daring. 'What did you come here looking for, sir? I cannot believe *you* were brought here by deception.'

His laugh was a little reluctant, she thought. Another point scored. 'Hardly. I came here seeking... Well, there is no use in telling you, for I fear very much that you would not believe me. But whatever or whoever I was looking for, I did not find it. I found you instead, fair Rosalind.'

His eyes had darkened as he spoke, and she felt dizzy

suddenly. He went on, 'And you found *me*. And so you are either going to walk out of that door now, while you still can, or you are going to tell me what it is you want from me.'

A whisper, barely audible. 'I said I do not know.'

'Then I suppose I must help you. A kiss, perhaps?'

'Perhaps...' she sighed.

'Then kiss me.' He smiled maliciously as she looked up at him in surprise. 'I will not have you say later that you did not choose this. Kiss me, if you want to, or do not.'

'You don't want to kiss me?'

'Oh, you are spoilt! Do not make me regret the whip. My desires are not at issue here, but yours. Own them.'

He would not make it easy for her, it was plain. She stood on her tiptoes and took his face in her hands. 'It is true that I am spoilt,' she said. 'I know it, and I have been trying to overcome it.' And then she kissed him.

Georgie had been kissed before, but she had not kissed. A lady did not take the lead in such matters. Until she did, it seemed. She was a little unsure for a second, but then sensation and instinct took over. She brushed his sensual lower lip with hers, and then tasted it more fully. She opened her mouth a little wider, and deepened the kiss. His lips were warm and surprisingly soft, and she felt the slightest prickle of evening stubble under her palms as she cupped his face. She feared he would never respond to her – perhaps she did not please him – but just as that thought was about to freeze her into mortified immobility he made a low sound, almost a growl, against her lips, and everything changed. He came alive under her mouth, and an electric current seemed to pass between them.

An instant later they were devouring each other, open-mouthed, and she felt his big hands slide to her buttocks, capturing them, pulling her closer. She should have been shocked by his presumption, by the sudden intimacy of his hands on her, but she was not. She liked it, all of it. She moulded her body eagerly to his and fastened her hands deep in his hair, giving herself up to the embrace and the sensations it aroused in her.

When at last their lips separated, they were both breathing hard. He did not release her, but held her still in a firm grip. His hands had slid up to her back now, under her jacket, warm on her skin through her thin shirt, and their faces were still very close. She could feel his breath on her cheek. He smelled of sandalwood and leather and spiced orange soap. He smelled edible.

'And was that what you wanted?' he whispered, and she thought that despite the ever-present note of mockery his voice was not quite steady. He had a great deal of control over himself, it seemed, but it was not quite perfect.

'Yes.' It certainly seemed as though it was.

'And was that *all* that you wanted?'

It was not enough for him – she could feel the evidence of it, pressing hard against her belly. It did not frighten her; it gave her a dangerous and illusory sense of power. But still he would not take control from her; still he would make her choose and state her choice.

This was the true moment of no return, she thought.

'No.'

He smiled; a new smile, a wolfish one. 'Say it,' he whispered against her mouth, and she shivered at the feather touch of his breath. 'You need to say it.'

'No, it was not all that I wanted. I want more from you than just a kiss.'

'I'm not sure I would call that "just a kiss". Perhaps it was otherwise for you; I found it highly memorable. But very well, madam. I am entirely at your service. What do you require of me?'

As if in a trance, she heard herself saying, 'I cannot do anything that would risk...'

'Of course you cannot; I understand perfectly. But that still leaves a wide enough field of endeavour, after all, as I am sure you know.'

She did know, if only in theory. Georgiana had been cautious with Captain Hart, despite his increasingly insistent entreaties. Caution: it seemed laughable now. They had not gone further than kisses and caresses, which had been pleasurable enough in all honesty. He had told her, of course, what more they might do, in the hope of inflaming her passions so that she lost her senses, and had exerted an insidious sort of pressure besides. If she really loved him, he had said... But Georgie was stubborn, as a girl blessed with five brothers and no sisters must be, and perhaps when all was said and done she had simply not wanted it enough to take the terrible risk, had not wanted him enough.

Yet in this room, with this utter stranger, a man whose name she did not even know, who thank God did not know her name, somehow, it was different. She reached out a finger – she did not have far to reach – and traced the classic lines of his mouth, the sculpted upper, the surprising fullness of his lower lip. He let out a breath, perhaps in surprise, and then his lips parted a little, as if in invitation, under her touch. And then she boldly pushed her finger between them – he did not attempt to resist her – and ran it along the moist tender flesh inside. And his clever tongue came out to meet her exploring finger, and lick it, suck on it, and she shivered as he tasted her. The moment stretched. The most insistent of Captain Hart's caresses, his hands on her, had never made her feel anything like this. She remembered some of the shocking things that people, men and women both, had proposed to her a few minutes ago, before she had come into this room with this man. Oh, they had shocked her then, those whispered suggestions. It seemed a lifetime had passed in a few moments, and she wasn't shocked any more. Forbidden delights suddenly seemed much more tempting as they stood close together, her finger in his mouth, his tongue caressing her skin. She withdrew from him slowly, and said in the lowest of whispers, 'Yes. Your lips, your mouth, I want you to...'

Something flared in his eyes. 'Once again you have surprised me,' he said. 'I congratulate you, for it is not easily done.'

'I am glad. May I have my reward, then?'

'Oh, yes,' he said. 'Oh, yes, I think you may.'

9

His hand went to the buttons at the fall of her breeches. Even then he halted for a moment, as if in question, and she made a low sound of impatience that set him smiling. He undid them deftly, and slid his hand inside. She gasped as she felt his warm fingers slip between her nether lips and gently, very gently cup her sex. She felt dizzy at the intimacy of the action, and was surprised by a sudden fierce urge to press herself against him, to move in the hope that he would move too. He made no further motion, though, but kissed her quick and hard as he held her, and murmured against her mouth, 'Perhaps you will be more comfortable sitting down?' He was right; with his hand on her she felt lightheaded, liquid, flushed with heat and tingling with the promise of fulfilment.

There was a velvet sofa just a step or two away, and he drew her across to it, his fingers still on her. She had no thought to do anything save go with him. He took his hand from her, slowly – reluctantly, it seemed to her – and she had just self-control and wit enough left to her to make no protest at the sudden absence. Then he fell to his knees before her in one graceful movement, drawing her breeches down over her thighs, and as he did so she sank helplessly into the soft cushions. 'Alas,' he said, 'adorable though you are in this garment, I think we will both do better if I relieve you of it.' He undid the buttons at her knees and in a moment she was naked below the waist. Apart from... 'Shall we keep the stockings?' he mused, settling back on his heels to regard her with glittering eyes, eyes that made her shiver with desire and anticipation. 'I think we shall. The black is excessively becoming. They undoubtedly add... a certain something.'

Then his hands were on her legs, spreading her with a gentle but inexorable touch. 'Although you might have noticed that I like to talk,' he said, setting his hands firmly either side of her hips, 'and talking to you has been enormously stimulating, I believe that now the time for talking is done. So I will not make myself tedious by asking you again if you want this. Indeed, you have given me every reason to think that you do. I hope I will find ways to please you, my Rosalind.'

And then he lowered his mouth to the side of her thigh, just above the knee, and began tracing his way slowly upwards. She leaned back against the sofa cushions in a sort of daze and looked down on his silvered head, wondering if she had run stark mad. But the sensations he was evoking soon drove every coherent thought from her head. When he reached the most sensitive and fullest part of her inner thigh, he kissed it lingeringly, and then to her enormous surprise bit it gently. A bolt of pure sensation shot to the hot, wet core of her; she gasped and arched her back. He laughed, a private sound, triumphant. He kissed where he had bitten, then withdrew a little and retreated to her other thigh, and once again he edged his way upwards with great care and deliberation. This time the anticipation heightened the pleasure, for she instinctively knew what he would do next. She was right: when he reached the point once more where her flesh was softest and most tender, there was another long kiss, and then a bite, a little harder this time. She thought she cried aloud.

Then his mouth ventured on further, and she was truly lost. He settled forward on his knees and slid his hands under her naked buttocks, clasping her tightly and positioning her so that she was entirely exposed to him. She raised herself a little in shameless mute appeal, and he buried his face in the curls at the junction of her thighs, and set about devouring her.

His wickedly clever tongue explored her innermost folds and found her nub. When he fastened his lips on it and sucked it into his mouth, once again she cried aloud, and grasped the sofa cushions with each hand and bucked under him, pressing her core against him. Then he released her, but before she could moan in protest his tongue was sweeping along her crease to find her entrance, and laving around and around it, then pushing on inside her in the most intimate action she had ever known in her life. And then it all blurred together and she could no longer distinguish one thing from another; she merely knew that he was carrying her away on a rising tide of pure pleasure such as she had never known or imagined possible. His lips, his tongue, his face buried in her, his hands on her, holding her so tightly... She threw back her head and abandoned herself to it utterly.

When the great waves of sensation broke over her, she closed her eyes and let them take her. He did not stop, his mouth, his tongue still busy worshipping her, still drawing out exquisite sensations from her almost unbearably sensitised flesh, and as she returned slowly to what was left of her wits, she was for a moment unsure if she would die if he did not stop, or die if he did. But at last it was too much, too intense to bear any longer, and she moaned wordlessly in feeble protest. He seemed to understand her, for he drew away instantly, though he did not take his hands from her, but still held her possessively. She was still exposed to him, had no thought of covering herself, and he looked up at her in obvious appreciation, his desire for her obvious, his mouth wet and glistening. He was smiling beneath the mask that he still wore; his black and silver hair was wildly dishevelled and his eyes dark as sin, his pupils dilated. 'I do not think that I would easily grow tired of doing that,' he said, his beautiful voice caressing. 'And nor, I think, would you. And now the question once again must be, was that enough for you? Or do you still want more, as I must confess that I do? And if indeed you feel the same, what next can I do to please us both?'

Something he could read in her face gave him sudden pause, though, and he released her then, sliding his hands from beneath her and reaching up with one long finger to capture a tear where it trembled on her eyelashes. 'I had not known...' she whispered brokenly, hardly aware of what she was saying, all her proud, false defences shattered into a thousand pieces.

'I perceive that you had not,' he said in a low tone, and was silent for a second. 'Tell me,' he went on in a more conversational tone, 'had anyone done this to you before?' She shook her head, any thought of lying to him far beyond her now. 'And are you, in point of fact, a widow, or even – God help me – a wife?'

'No.'

'So what are you then, my delicious little liar?'

'I don't know what I am.'

He laughed rather cruelly. She supposed she had given him reason. 'A virgin?'

'I have no idea,' she said rather dazedly, as the waves of pleasure finally receded, leaving her lost and cold and exposed. 'Am I? Still? You would know best.'

'Good God!' he said with sudden heat. 'Are you completely insane?'

Somehow she found the courage to smile, albeit a little tremulously. 'It seems so.'

He swore again, still kneeling between her naked thighs. 'Perhaps,' he said, 'I should put you over my knee and spank you – since you are undeniably dressed for it – and then send you home.'

Between shame and the lingering dregs of arousal, she scarcely knew what she said. 'Do you think I might like it? Do you think *you* might like it?'

'Oh, no,' he said with some heat. 'Enough of this. Enough of pretending to be something you are not. This is perilous talk, madam. What is to stop me laying you back against this sofa and spending the rest of the night taking my pleasure from you, before I send you on your way greatly enlightened, but no longer any sort of virgin?'

She should be frightened of him, she supposed, but most oddly she was not. Mostly what she felt was regret, and she had no desire to examine the sensation too closely. 'Nothing at all. But you won't.'

'You are very confident.'

'Am I wrong?'

He rose abruptly to his feet, and stood frowning down at her. 'You terrify me,' he said. 'You really do. I don't know if I should flee from you screaming, or carry you off and make you my mistress, and devote the rest of my life to showing you in exquisite detail the true meaning of pleasure. Because you can be sure that was just the beginning.'

His words set little shivers racing all across her body once again, and he saw the effect he had. Of course he saw. 'Yes,' he said softly, 'make no mistake, I could... But no. We both need to leave this place. Dress yourself, while I still have the strength to let you, and my carriage will take you home. I don't suppose it will be a very long journey.'

He was silent for a moment and then said, some repressed emotion in his voice that she could not hope to identify, 'And if by some miracle I were to obtain vouchers for Almack's, I dare say I might see you there any Wednesday I chose, might I not, among the other debutantes? Or at Lady Jersey's rout party, or Princess Esterhazy's Venetian breakfast?'

She was pulling on her breeches with shaking hands, and did not look up at him. Was he trying to discover her identity? The idea was simultaneously thrilling and horrifying. 'Am I likely to encounter you at any of those places, sir?' she asked with a fair attempt at sangfroid.

He laughed. 'You are not. And perhaps it is just as well.' He took her hand and drew her to her feet, but did not release her after he had done so. 'I will let you go now. I do not suppose our paths will cross again, little liar, for I do not belong in the drawing rooms of the haut ton, and *you* do not belong in places like this. I hope that at least is clear to you.'

'Yes,' she replied. 'Very clear. You were right in what you said a moment ago. I know I must stop making these dangerous mistakes. I must do better.'

'Well,' he said with a glinting smile, 'I may be a dangerous mistake – God knows it has been said before, and more than once – but I know one thing.' He raised her hand to his lips and kissed it gently, then turned it over and pressed another kiss into her soft palm. This too was an intimate action, and once more she shivered at the touch of his lips upon her most tender flesh. 'I flatter myself that you will not easily forget me. And I will certainly not forget you. I wonder if I will want to?'

10

It was no wonder that Georgie slept badly for what remained of the night. It had been a mistake to allow herself to remember and relive in exquisite detail what had passed between her and the Duke. Especially as he had made it all too clear that he would be quite prepared to repeat the experience. He knew it would be entirely wrong, entirely unfair to the other young women he had brought here, one of them his future bride; he had accepted as much when she upbraided him, but it seemed to her that if she made the slightest move, gave him the smallest sign, he would come to her again. All the while making it plain to her that this was her choice, and that any moral qualms she might have were her responsibility alone. She certainly could not hope to deceive him into thinking she did not want him. She knew she had revealed herself all too plainly to him once again. Had he not said so? But this was not in the least a helpful train of thought.

As to what he felt – she could not be sure. He had called their... their meeting memorable, had said he could not put it from his mind. It was weak to be glad of it, and foolish too, but she supposed that even rakes – and she knew he was a rake, everyone in England knew it – did not often have such intimate encounters with complete strangers in such circumstances. Or perhaps they did. Perhaps it was a daily occurrence. Twice a day. Entirely commonplace. She felt sick and weak at the thought. At her own weak, foolish, dangerous behaviour. It was not to be repeated.

She breakfasted in the sitting room with Louisa and Miss Spry; she was glad, for she did not think she could face Mary Debenham and her mother over breakfast, feeling as she did. Or the Duke, with his mocking little smile meant only for her. She should flee from this place, to protect herself – but how could she explain such a mad start to her aunt, or hope to persuade her to agree to it? They had arrived only yesterday, and she knew that it was Louisa's intention to remain with her friend for well over a week. There was to be a ball in a few days' time, Lady Blanche had revealed last night, a grand affair that would be attended by all the families of rank in the neighbourhood, and far beyond. By unfortunate chance, a party was coming from Castle Howard, and remaining for a night or two. These were people with whom her family was exceedingly well acquainted. Lady Georgiana Morpeth, wife of the heir to Castle Howard, did not share her Christian name by accident: she was the daughter of her mother's great friend, the late Duchess of Devonshire, and someone she had known since childhood. Impossible then to persuade Louisa to depart, impossible to leave alone, and even if it were possible, it would surely occasion a great deal of comment and gossip, which was just – at this ridiculously late date – what she wished to avoid.

Miss Spry commented on her pallor, and Georgie said she had the headache, a little. She wondered if they might be able to walk out later and take the air. It was barely raining at all. 'Yes,' said Jane. 'If we wrap up warmly, I am sure it will do us both good. I do not ask you, Louisa, for I know it to be futile.'

'Of course it is futile. Let us go down,' Louisa replied. 'I will sit with Blanche by a good fire, and we will talk like civilised beings, while you two crazies court an inflammation of the lungs. "Take the air", indeed! The air is far more likely to take you! I swear I saw a seagull blow straight past the window just now with an expression of panic upon its face.'

They squabbled amiably as they made their way down the staircase, to find Lady Blanche in one of the saloons with her daughter. 'Gabriel and Bram have taken a party of ladies out riding,' she said. 'Although Lady Debenham did not go – she is feeling sadly bilious and is confined to her chamber, is it not a pity? Eleanor and I stayed behind, with the arrangements for the ball as an excuse. But in truth we hoped for a comfortable gossip with you.' When she learned that Miss Spry and Georgiana wished to go for a walk, and wondered if the beach could be reached without too much difficulty, she rang the bell for a footman. 'Charles will show you the way down,' she said. 'I am sure Eleanor would gladly accompany you if she were able, would you not, my dear?'

Miss FitzHenry said that she certainly would, and told them with shining eyes that the stair down to the sea was an extraordinary thing, such as did not exist anywhere else in her experience, and that she would gladly have gone with them, and would have enjoyed seeing their faces as they beheld it for the first time. She looked at her mother as if pleading to be allowed to do so, but Lady Blanche was firm in her refusal.

'Eleanor, I cannot accede to such folly. You know you are just recovered from an epidemic cold, and it is not the easiest of stairs, especially not the climb back up, so I cannot permit it until you are fully recovered. But as long as you are in the best of health, ladies, I can see that you are both energetic and will not regard it in the least.'

The pair promised they would not, and after putting on their outer wear followed the footman Charles deep into the bowels of the Castle, curious to see what had so impressed Miss FitzHenry, for it must surely be something quite out of the ordinary to deserve such a panegyric. Their attendant had provided himself with a lantern, and they exclaimed at the sights it revealed as they travelled deeper and deeper through the cellarage. This was the most ancient section of the Castle, he told them, and at least a thousand years old in parts, as they could well believe from the massive blocks of stone that made up much of the walls, and which Miss Spry thought might even be Roman in origin. At last they reached a massive iron-banded oaken door, and Charles produced a huge key and inserted it into the lock. It turned with ease, and he pushed the door open and stood aside to let them pass, telling them that he would await them here if they required no further assistance. They would be quite safe alone, he assured them, for the beach was effectively private and nobody would disturb them.

They had no need of the lantern now, for there was daylight enough. They found themselves on a rough landing at the top of a flight of natural stone steps, which led down to the smooth sandy floor of a large cave. Its entrance was tall, a cleft in the rock, and through it they could see the open beach, and the wild waves. The unmistakeable scent of the sea tickled their nostrils, and they smiled at each other. What a surprise! Their companion recommended them to go down slowly and carefully, and hold on to the thick rope that had been slung as a guide rail between stout iron hoops. The steps were slippery towards the bottom and some of them perilous underfoot with strands of seaweed and shells, he told them, as they were covered by the sea at high tide.

Miss Spry made her cautious way down, and Georgie followed her. When they reached the bottom they looked back, and Charles, sitting in a niche on the landing, raised a hand in encouragement. 'I suppose it is a sort of postern gate,' said Georgie thoughtfully. 'The inhabitants might have used it to enter or to leave in secret, even if they were besieged, and surely kept a boat here for the purpose. An escape route, if one were needed.'

'And even if some enemy did come this way, it would be impossible to climb the stairs and take the Castle if even a very few defenders held them. Two or three resolute men in armour might do it. Imagine coming up that narrow, slippery staircase in single file, knowing that armed men stood waiting at the top to push you back. A single misstep and you would fall to your death. How terrible, and how thrilling!'

Georgie agreed that it was both thrilling and terrible, and they made their way out onto the beach. The cave had been sheltered, but the wind outside was coming straight off the sea, loaded with spray, and literally took their breath away. They set out along the firm golden sand, glad that on Lady Blanche's recommendation they had tied scarves across their bonnets to prevent them blowing off and halfway across Yorkshire.

They walked briskly for a while in silence, their cheeks flushed and loose strands of hair whipping about their faces, and occasionally one of them bent to pick up a curious shell or gleaming stone that caught her eyes. Eventually Miss Spry stopped, and turned to look out to sea, and Georgie stood beside her, eyes watering. 'Magnificent!' she said.

'It is,' assented Jane. 'And now there is not the least danger of being overheard, even by seagulls, and I hope you will tell me just exactly what is going on between you and the Duke.'

11

His Grace the Duke of Northriding shut his study door behind him with a sigh of profound relief. He was alone at last save for his dogs, Tam and Nico, and they settled into their accustomed positions either side of the fire. He wished he could be so relaxed and at ease. Easier to be a dog than a duke, he sometimes thought, and then reproved himself for preposterous self-indulgence and maudlin self-pity.

Although he knew that nobody would disturb him here against his explicit instructions – and he had given instructions quite explicit enough that even servants far less well-trained than his own would have been foolish to ignore them – he felt a strong impulse to lock the door behind him. His home, which had been his sanctuary, no longer seemed anything of the kind.

It was his own fault, of course. When his sister Blanche had suggested this misbegotten house party as a solution to the problem of his marriage, he should not have listened to her. In the past he had always been most careful what guests he brought here, and his displeasant sensations upon contemplating the assembled company over the last few days showed how right he had been, and how wrong to go against those deepest instincts at Blanche's urging. He should have conducted this ridiculous... this ridiculous, degrading – degrading for all concerned – parade of candidates for his hand in London, or at one of his other residences. Anywhere but here.

But Blanche had argued – and he was obliged to admit that her argument had carried some weight – that he was not only looking for a bride for himself, a mother for his children, but also a mistress for Northriding Castle. Any woman who looked on this ancient place with indifference or disdain, any woman who could not appreciate its special wild beauty, simply did not belong here. If a young lady disliked the Castle in July, even an inclement and unseasonable July such as this one, she would hardly wish to spend a day, a week, a month here in January or February, when the wind across the North Sea knifed at your skin, and howled and moaned around the walls and turrets with the banshee wail of a soul in torment. Did she shiver now, and pull her shawl about her? Only imagine her discontent when the snow lay on the ground for weeks at a time and icicles appeared inside the windows. It took a certain kind of person, his sister said and he agreed whole-heartedly, to appreciate such a place and accommodate herself to its occasional discomforts as the price to be paid for its glorious setting and enormous, ever-changing skies and sea. For everything had its price in life, as he knew all too well.

Blanche was right, of course, and it was a matter for serious consideration. He had not the least desire to marry, but he knew he must, and it would be foolish in the extreme to choose a bride who would be miserable here, in his ancestral home, the jewel of his inheritance, the place where Mauleverer children were always raised. The trouble was, most of the young women assembled here were so very anxious to be duchesses – not to marry him, he could not so flatter himself, for he was in himself no great bargain, but to be duchesses – that had he been Satan himself and this the chief castle of the infernal regions, they would have complimented him upon the fine situation and healthful airs, and declared that no prospect could be finer than the lake of fire and brimstone that they beheld seething and boiling in the middle distance.

This being so, the whole exercise took on the aspect of a gigantic waste of time, since it was all but impossible to ascertain how any of his guests actually felt about the potential future that he laid before them. Could any of them say in perfect honesty that they thought they might be happy here? He had taken several of them riding just now, he had listened to them sing last night and the night before – that was an experience he would be perfectly content never to repeat – had walked and conversed with them together and separately, and felt he was no further on in understanding the private feelings of any one of them. Did he feel the slightest partiality towards any of the group of women he had brought here as prospective brides, did he feel any desire at all to take any one of them in particular as his wife and companion at bed and board, as a mother to his children, God willing? He did not. Christ knew he did not.

He walked over to the window, frowning abstractedly, and looked down upon the deserted beach below. He had not, he realised now, so much as thought to propose to the young ladies that they should brave the Duke's Stair and go down through the bowels of the Castle to walk upon the shining sands and breathe in great lungfuls of salty air. He could all too well imagine their faces if he made such an outlandish suggestion, their unsuccessful attempts to dissemble and feign pleasure at the prospect. He made a small sound of disgust, of impatience with himself as much as with them, and it was at that moment that he saw that he was wrong; that some young ladies, two at least, had without any prompting from him descended the steep steps, and were striking out along the beach at a brisk pace.

Gabriel watched them walk – these were not feeble town-bred damsels, he saw, they strode out with a will and were plainly taking pleasure in the exercise – and then he watched them come to a halt, and engage in what appeared to him at this distance to be an intense and enthralling conversation, apparently untroubled by the strong onshore wind that was whipping their hair about their faces and their skirts and petticoats about their ankles. One of the ladies was excessively tall, and he recognised her without difficulty as Miss... Miss Spry, the authoress, Lady Louisa Pendlebury's Sapphic companion. He had previously come across pieces that she had written, and been impressed by them, by the mind and sensibility they revealed. But he had little attention to spare for her just now, or her literary attainments, because with a certainty he did not think to question he knew exactly who her companion was. Her, it was her.

She was not tall or short, she was not fat or thin, there was nothing obviously distinctive or unusual about her to make her stand out at this distance, and so there was no reason at all for such certitude, and yet he knew. Put her among a thousand others, masked and cloaked, conceal even her extraordinary bright blue eyes from him, and still he would know her. Blindfold him, he thought, and he would know her, by smell, by feel, by taste. God almighty, *that* most of all.

12

They had, of course, been extraordinarily intimate. He thought, had thought even at the time, even while it was happening, that he would never as long as he lived forget that night, their conversation, the instant connection that had sprung to life between them and led – inexorably, as if nothing else could ever possibly have transpired – to her kissing him with such passion, to her pressing her gloriously lithe body against his, and then to him falling to his knees and... God. God. He groaned and rested his suddenly hot forehead on the windowpane, welcoming its soothing coolness. Tam seemed to sense his agitation and raised his long grey head in enquiry, whining a little, but then subsided when no further sound was heard from his master.

Gabriel was forced to admit that, while he had in all conscience been uncomfortable enough with his bizarre situation before the Pendlebury ladies had arrived, the recognition of just exactly who had come into his home had disturbed him more than he was able to articulate, even to himself in his most private of thoughts. It had been difficult at first to comprehend what she was doing here, but he had known even in that first instant that she was horrified to see him, and had had not the least idea who he was prior to that moment. She had lied to him once, for reasons he only partly understood even now, but there was no trickery in her. She had not come here with any ulterior motive. God knows she had betrayed no desire to use the secret that they shared as any kind of leverage. Very much the opposite, and most unflatteringly so, in fact.

And her presence had thrown all his plans into confusion.

Gabriel was still not entirely sure why he had opened the secret panel in the cupboard at the base of the tower and climbed up to see her last night – what he had hoped to achieve by it. He wanted her, of course. Still wanted her. It would be futile to deny that. His attention had been piqued as soon as he had set eyes on her, so out of place and yet so stubbornly refusing to leave, and he would not have been human if those long legs in the clinging red breeches, that expressive little face and tempting mouth beneath the lace mask, had not intrigued him. A girl, a beautiful blue-eyed girl in boys' clothing – what man would not want to know more? But he could see that she was not safe in that house, did not belong there, and he would have been happy – he told himself he would have been perfectly happy – to help her make her escape and never see her again. One virtuous action in a life that had been full of sin: a feather on the scale.

That was not what had happened: she had refused the chance to escape when it had been offered to her, and for that she must take some share of the responsibility. At least he could comfort himself with the undeniable fact that he had not so far lost his senses as to do anything that she had not asked of him, despite the desire for her that had almost overmastered him. And what she had asked of him...

It did no good at all to think of that now. He had spent enough nights reliving every word, every expression, every nuance of their kiss, every hesitation and sigh, the feel of her finger in his mouth, her bravery when at last she had let him know what she wanted from him. And then most of all, most of all, the sight of her on that sofa as she waited for him to pleasure her, still masked, half-naked, lips parted in desire and anticipation. And then when he had put his mouth on her, good God... the softness of her skin, her exquisite responsiveness, the little gasp of surprise and arousal she had let out when he had bitten her tender thigh, and the delicious wetness of her most secret places when he had buried his face in her and felt her opening to him like a flower, like... like a revelation.

He made a soft noise of disgust at the tenor of this thoughts. He was no poet. He despised high-flown sentiment, always had. One of the main aims of poetry, as far as he could see, and his classical education had confirmed as much, was to persuade women into your bed who otherwise might not agree to go there, and make everyone think you were a devil of a fine fellow, rather than a hopeless libertine, while you were doing it. A clever trick, or a cheap one, he was not quite sure. Both, perhaps. He'd never experienced the urge to versify. He had made love to women before, more women than he cared to count, and never felt a need to describe the lips, the hair, the eyes, the breasts, the taste of any one of them. He did not want to describe it now; he wanted to experience it. To taste her again, to kiss every inch of her body and caress the parts of her he had not yet seen and burned to see. If he must be crude – and it really did seem that he must – he wanted to be inside her, for his cock to follow where his tongue had so unforgettably been. But first he wanted to make her come again so gloriously, for her tenderest and most private places to quiver uncontrollably and then soften and relax deliciously because of what he, he alone, could do to her. And he wanted that almost – *almost* – more than he wanted to spend himself in her in his own unstoppable climax. And then he wanted to do it again, and again, and again, until he tired of it, or she did. Which, he had already known that night and knew now, would not be soon.

And she had been right, of course, hideously so; it was unconscionable to feel such powerful desire for a woman who was staying under his roof and still contemplate even for a moment wooing, proposing marriage to, announcing his engagement with, any other woman in the world. It was much worse than unconscionable – he had done unforgivable things before and probably would again – it was bloody stupid. And it was unnecessary.

Because there was an obvious solution to all of these difficulties.

13

Down on the beach, Georgie's head whipped round and she gazed at her companion in astonishment. 'How...?'

Jane smiled. 'I saw the way you looked at him; I saw the way he looked at you. And last night, very shockingly, I heard voices.'

'Oh, God help me,' said Georgie involuntarily. 'Does Louisa know?'

'She was asleep and heard nothing, and I haven't told her. I don't enjoy keeping secrets from her, and generally I do not do so, but if I tell her she will feel obliged to tell your brother. How could she not? He is "the head of the family" and your guardian. And I don't like to see myself as the sort of woman who informs another woman's brother or father of matters that they consider private. You're not a possession, though the law says you are.'

Georgie looked blindly out to sea. 'Last year Cassandra found out I was thinking of running away with Captain Hart, and she did tell Hal. He didn't reveal to me that she had, but she confessed to me herself later, and asked for my forgiveness. And I was happy to give it, because what she did forced Hal and me to talk to each other, which we badly needed to do. I knew she was only acting out of concern for me; she feared from her own bitter experience that Adolphus was a fortune-hunter, and I was too naïve to see it, and she was horribly right.'

'So are you saying that you would be happy for me to tell your aunt what I have discovered? You want me to do so, perhaps, just as Lady Irlam did?'

'No! No, I don't. This is different. Or if it's not different, this time it's too much. I've caused Hal and Louisa more than enough trouble in the past. What could he do – challenge the Duke to a duel? Try to force him to marry me? It would just make my poor brother unhappy and anxious about me again. Enough! I need to disentangle myself from this new mess that I have created, not drag others into it.'

'That does seem the best plan,' said Jane. 'But can I help? If you don't want me to tell Louisa, I won't, but I can listen.'

'You'll be shocked,' Georgie warned. Jane looked at her expressionlessly for a moment, and then she said, 'Very well, you won't be shocked. What happened was...'

Miss Spry listened in silence as Georgie recounted her story, and when she had finished said, 'I see...'

'I don't,' said her companion despairingly. 'I don't understand why I keep doing these stupid, reckless things. I could blame the Duke – that would be convenient and easy – but it's not true. It was my fault, all of it.'

'I'm sure that isn't quite correct. He must bear at least an equal share of the blame; he could have let you be, could he not? But have you considered,' said Jane with a slight grimace, 'that the solution might lie before you?'

'What do you mean?'

'I can't believe that I of all people am saying this, but if you have... this connection between you, then one option is to enter the fray, as it were. Might marriage to Northriding not solve all these problems for you? And I don't know why you would say that he would need to be forced to wed you, since apparently he must marry someone, and why not you? Although,' she added hastily, 'if you do not choose to participate in this most degrading competition for his hand – for that is what it amounts to – I could certainly not blame you! Every shred of self-respect must revolt at the thought.'

'I... I had not considered it at all. I was so shocked to see him here, to learn who he was... but I suppose in all honesty I should.' And then, abruptly, 'Shall we walk on? I'm feeling chilled suddenly.'

'Of course.'

They strode on in silence for a few minutes, and reached the far end of the cove, where the jagged rocks curved in a little and offered some small shelter from the wind. Miss Spry and Georgiana turned and looked back the way they had come, along the beach unmarred by any human footsteps save their own, and took in the full view of the Castle at last. It stood tall on its cliffs, its towers and battlements seeming to have grown out of living rock rather than by any work of the hands of man. There was not a touch of warmth or softness to be seen, not even a single tree. They could just see the cave opening from whence they had come as a darker cleft at the base of the cliff. It was undeniably impressive, but also stark, Gothic, intimidating, a place out of legend rather than real life.

'It is all very well to talk of the sublime,' said Jane, 'but I do not know if in truth I would care to live here. You must consider that too as you decide what to do. Louisa was right – it must be grim indeed in the depths of winter. And for all we said earlier, anyone trying to put a boat out would surely be dashed to pieces in an instant on those terrible jagged rocks.'

'Are you being metaphorical?'

Miss Spry laughed. 'I don't know. Perhaps. Forgive me – I should be the last person to suggest to any woman that marriage represents a solution to all her difficulties. Even if it might appear to do so, it surely raises so many other problems. It is merely that the state of matrimony is rather on my mind at the moment.'

Georgie looked at her curiously. What could she possibly mean?

Her companion went on, 'I have a decision to make, and it is a difficult one. By the very nature of it, I can share it with very few people. Well, since it seems we are trading confidences and telling each other shocking things... I want a child.' She looked about her at the deserted beach as if checking to see if they were overheard, then laughed as she realised what she was doing, stretching her arms wide and yelling at the top of her voice into the wind, '*I want a child!*'

Georgiana looked at her blankly. Aware that her mouth was open, she closed it, and said feebly, 'A child?'

'Yes. A child of my own. It has come to be almost an obsession with me in the past months. You may recollect that Louisa and I lived apart for a while last year, when she was with you in Brighton and I went travelling in the Lake Country alone. We had... not quarrelled, we did not do so, but we could not agree, and I went away to clear my mind, and give her space to think, too.'

'I suppose adoption is a most serious step...'

'That's not what I want. I know I should, but I do not. I want a child of my own,' Jane said again.

'But how...?'

'Marriage. One of our friends – a very dear friend, a widower with grown children – has offered to marry me. To make a child with me. Or at least to try.'

Georgie was silent, and Jane said, 'Now it is your turn to be shocked.'

'Oh, no,' she hastened to say. 'No, of course not. I have no right to be shocked. I was merely surprised. That you would consider leaving Louisa...'

'I will never leave her. I would stay with my husband for... as long as it took, or until it became clear that there would be no child, and then return to her, and take up our lives together, with or without a child. With, I hope.'

'Have you decided, then? I thought you said you had not.'

'I suppose in truth I have.'

'And Louisa – how does she feel?'

'She has come to realise that I will never be happy until I at least make this attempt. She supports me, and I will always be grateful to her for it, since she has no great longing for a child herself and so cannot truly enter into my feelings. But it is a great step to take, is it not? To disrupt our peaceful, ordered life together, that is one thing, and quite serious enough. But to put myself, even nominally, in the power of a man, to make myself his chattel in the eyes of the world, that is what I struggle with – not the rest of it, though you may find that hard to believe. I balk at that part, the legalities, the conventionalities, the involvement of the Church, even though he is a good man, and I trust him.'

'Is there no other way?'

'There you hit the bull's-eye. Obviously there is. I could conceive a child with him without marriage, and refuse to submit myself even to notional masculine authority. Others have done so, after all: my mother's friend Mrs Godwin was one, when she gave birth to her first daughter. And I applaud her courage. But it turns out, despite all my fine words, that I am not brave enough. That is what it comes to, though I can give excuses aplenty. Louisa urges me to think of the child, growing up in this society as a nameless bastard, made that way entirely by her mother's choice. And she is so far right in that I find I cannot do it.'

'I suppose... No, I do understand. And I cannot criticise you. You know what you want – I wish I were so sure.'

'You do not blame me, then, for contemplating taking a man I do not love to my bed with the set purpose of conceiving a child?'

Georgie laughed. It was exhilarating somehow to talk so honestly, and so very rare. 'How can I blame you or judge you? I of all people can hardly be so hypocritical as to censure anyone else's behaviour, in the bedroom or out of it. I who let – no, who begged a stranger to give me pleasure. And it is quite the done thing in society, what you propose, is it not, though it is never talked of in such a way?' She gestured back towards the Castle. 'Those women up there, is that not precisely what they hope to do? And not because they so badly want a child, either, but for much more worldly considerations, at least for many of them. And the Duke – have you not given an exact description of why he has summoned them all here? To marry one of them, a virtual stranger as she must be, without love, without even the trust and respect and honesty that you have with your friend, for the purposes of going to bed and getting an heir? And this is fully understood and sanctioned by society, is done every day, and nobody has the least issue with it.'

'That's perfectly true, of course. It is all a matter of conventional morality. But where does that leave you? You already know, if I understand you correctly, that you and the Duke are... physically compatible. You are attracted to him, and he to you, that was quite plain to me, at least, before ever you told me your secret. You could marry him on that basis, on the basis of powerful mutual desire, and though it may not be much to build a life on, it is still more than many men and women can be sure of as they enter matrimony. Might that not be enough for you? And if not, why not?'

'I cannot assume that he wants to marry me above all the others, Jane.'

'Never mind what he wants. I am sure he will make it clear; he does not strike me as a diffident sort of a man. What do *you* want?'

'I suppose that is the question, is it not?'

14

The tide was turning, and Miss Spry and Lady Georgiana made their way back to the cave, increasing their pace as little waves with white edges began nipping at the soles of their boots. They found Charles the footman sitting snugly in an alcove on the landing, warming himself at a brazier set in the rock. When he saw them approach, he doused it, and they followed his lantern slowly up the steep, winding staircase to the inhabited parts of the Castle. By the time they had climbed the further sets of stairs that led to their private tower, they were both out of breath and weary, glad to part to their respective chambers so that they might rest a little before they must change for nuncheon.

The entire company was there, the ladies exclaiming over the beauty of their ride earlier that morning. It was clear that Miss Debenham, a fine, showy horsewoman, considered that she had restored herself in the Duke's good graces, and scored a point over all the others. 'She took up a position at his side,' said Alice Templeton in low tones to Georgie, 'and refused to budge or allow him to converse with anyone else. And look at her crowing now, in the most displeasant manner imaginable. She truly is an odious creature!'

Georgiana turned to her friend and regarded her with interest. She had been so preoccupied the previous day with her own secret that she had not thought to wonder what Alice's feelings might be about the situation in which she found herself. Had she come here willingly – did she actually wish to be chosen by this man she hardly knew? Or had she been brought here at her mama's behest, indifferent or perhaps even reluctant? No one else was near; they could perhaps converse a little if they were discreet. 'Alice,' she said quietly, 'do you *want* to marry the Duke? I have not had a chance to ask you. But of course I know...'

'Why we are all here in this horridly undignified way?' whispered Alice with a conscious look and a blush, pushing the food around her plate with a small silver fork.

'I did not say...'

'You did not need to. I know *you* are not here for that purpose, but the rest of us plainly are.'

'And?'

'And... I don't know, Georgie. I admit I would enjoy putting Mary Debenham's nose out of joint, but I can quite see that that isn't a terribly good reason to marry someone.'

Georgie smothered a laugh. 'Oh, it may not be noble, but it is understandable!'

Alice grinned in response. 'No, it isn't, not really. But my portion is not large, you know, and I expect I must marry somebody. Mama says I must. At least he's not old, with hairy ears. I suppose, too, it would be a fine thing to be a duchess; that's what my mama thinks, anyway. And not to have to live with my mama any more, that is quite an attractive thought. But I don't think I'd like to be obliged to marry him. My mama can marry him, if she likes him so much. He scares me a little, Georgie.'

'Scares you?' Georgiana could not understand how it could be so; she had her own reasons to distrust Northriding, of course, but Alice could not know of them. And it was not as though she feared he would do her harm... or not precisely.

'Yes. He doesn't speak to me or even look at me very often, but when he does, I don't like it. Those eyes... And of course he has a terrible reputation, that's what everybody says, though nobody seems to want to tell me exactly what he does. I expect he is a wicked seducer, or something of that nature, and ruins ladies by the dozen. I wonder they should care for it; I'm sure I wouldn't. But I am glad to say that he shows no interest in me, or very little. There's no sign at all of his even contemplating seducing *me* even slightly, thank heaven. Because if he did seem as though he might want to ask for my hand, I'm sure Mama would make me marry him, even if I begged her not to. But hush! He is observing us! Talk of something else.'

Georgie too was conscious of those ironical silver eyes upon her, and they fell to talking of indifferent matters until the nuncheon was over. It had come on to rain hard by then, and the carriage excursion that had been planned for the afternoon had perforce to be called off.

Most of the party drifted into the library, and disposed themselves about it, listlessly leafing through books and periodicals, or frankly settling into one or other of the comfortably battered leather armchairs and closing their eyes in slumber. Lord Debenham was soon snoring by the fireside, and the noise was neither musical nor conducive to concentration on reading. Georgiana was restless, and wandered to the far end of the room, where she settled herself in a cushioned window seat that was built into one of the turrets with which the Castle abounded. Because of the curvature of the walls, she could not be seen, she realised, by any of the other occupants of the larger room, and so she set aside the book that she had picked up in a pretence of interest, and gazed out across the rain-lashed landscape. She could not see the sea from this side of the Castle, but she thought she could hear it.

A moment later she was surprised to find that she was no longer alone – one of the Duke's dogs had followed her silently, and when she smiled to see him he laid his great shaggy head on her lap, and looked up at her meltingly with appealing brown eyes, visibly begging her to stroke him as though he were the littlest pup and not a creature the size of her first pony. Her father had had dogs just like this when she was small, she recalled. She petted both enormous ears at once and he closed his eyes in bliss, and nuzzled at her, as if to say, That is quite pleasant, thank you, madam – I beg you, do not stop. The motion soothed her too, she found, and so she continued, to the satisfaction of them both.

'In a brown study, Lady Georgiana?' said a silky voice behind her. The big dog stirred at his master's voice, and wagged his long tail lazily, but did not move away from her.

She had indeed been so lost in thought that she gasped and started; she had thought herself alone save for her canine companion. 'Do you never enter a room like a normal person?' she hissed, aware that although they could not be seen, they could surely be heard if they spoke loudly.

'Almost never,' said the Duke amiably, seating himself beside her and making himself at ease. The turret, which had seemed a cosy refuge a moment ago, now appeared all too small and intimate to Georgie. The only previous occasions on which they had been in such close physical proximity had ended disastrously for her, she was all too well aware. But surely here, with the rest of the house party a bare few yards away, able to hear everything, able to see everything that occurred if they but rose to their feet and walked across the library, he would not...

He could see alarm on her face, as his words made clear. 'I

refuse to believe that you – unlike that little mouse of a friend of yours – are nervous of me,' he purred. 'Admitting always my reputation, and the fact that Tam is hardly an adequate chaperon – are you, boy? – what could I do to you here? Once again, and most tediously, you have only to make some loud noise and half the damsels and mamas of England will run to your rescue.'

'Leaving my good name in tatters,' she said bitterly.

'Oh, I would not be so sure of that,' he replied, eyes glinting. 'The ones who each cherish particular hopes of marrying me would surely not like to hear it spread abroad that I have been dallying with another, under their very noses. Would not that risk making the previously favoured lady a trifle ridiculous?'

'I would not care to wager my character on Mary Debenham's discretion!' she shot back.

He smiled a little grimly. 'I can understand that. Nor would I, if had a character. She is quite poisonous, is she not?'

'She is. And I am sure the "unfavoured" ladies would be all too glad to spread scandal abroad, if you reject them. As you said last night, you are not the Grand Turk – you cannot marry all of them!'

'Alas.'

She snorted, and Tam snuffled as if in agreement. 'I think not! Mary Debenham would smother you as you slept if it was to her advantage!'

'Adorable,' he said softly. 'The way you wrinkle your nose when you are being disapproving. Quite adorable. Tam agrees, I am sure of it. Look at his face: the hopeless adoration. He has excellent taste, of course.'

Georgie thought she ought to be beyond blushes where this man was concerned, but she was not, it seemed. 'Nonsense,' she said firmly. 'You need not trouble to make up to me.'

'No...?' he asked softly. 'It occurs to me that I was a little uncivil last night, when I kissed you and left you so abruptly. I owe you an apology, I believe.'

'For kissing me, or for leaving?' As soon as the words had left her mouth, she regretted them.

His eyes sparkled silver in appreciation. 'Very nice,' he said. 'Neither, I suppose. For disingenuity, though I accused you of it most unfairly. For taunting you with a desire which you must be fully aware I too feel; for implying that you alone experience this curious and very powerful pull between us. And for not kissing you properly. Kissing you should not be undertaken carelessly. It merits care and attention. Time.' He put out his hand and brushed her lips with one long finger. 'Privacy.'

'We should never be alone again!' she whispered shakily, the sensitive skin of her lips tingling at his touch, light though it had been. 'Indeed, we are not alone now, and I am not referring to your dog! And that reminds me – before you leave, as you must realise you should without loss of time, I need to tell you that we were overheard last night!'

'Really?' he said easily. He did not seem in the least concerned. 'By whom?'

'Miss Spry! And I have told her everything.'

'Everything?' He was smiling in a most disturbing way.

'Yes! I have no secrets from her now. She does not mean to tell my aunt, thank goodness. But it shows you that this must stop – we must be careful and never be alone together again!'

'It shows me,' he said, rising to his feet, 'that next time I pay you a nocturnal visit, I will be much quieter. You are quite right to reprove me. Tam, stay!'

And before she could reply, he was gone, though his dog, obedient to his master, remained behind, and looked up at Georgie with expectant eyes, clearly hoping for another caress.

They were quite as bad as each other, she thought, and both of them in their very different ways difficult to resist.

15

It seemed to Georgiana that the Duke's final words to her in the library turret had been little less than a promise that he would come to visit her chamber again soon. Tonight, probably. She should, she thought, be anxious at the prospect – Alice would have been terrified – but if she was honest with herself, she was not. She should, of course, have repeated her demand that he close up the secret stair that led to her room, or show her how to do so herself. She had done neither of those things, had not so much as mentioned the matter, despite having had several opportunities to do so. The idea that he was still free to come and go as he pleased should have appalled her. Not excited her.

Miss Spry's suggestion on the beach had set all manner of thoughts and fancies roiling in her brain, and the Duke's brief caress in the library had electrified her body. She was still tingling at the memory of his touch. She dared not look at him for the rest of the day for fear of what he might read in her eyes. The afternoon and then the evening passed – she could scarcely say how, what she ate, with whom she conversed – and she found herself in bed at last, curtains open to admit the fitful moonlight, with her eyes fixed on the section of the panelling that she knew concealed the hidden stairway.

It was a little after midnight when he arrived. The panel did not creak this time; perhaps he was more careful, or perhaps he had oiled the mechanism as he said he would. She could easily believe it of him. He set down his lantern on the tallboy and regarded her thoughtfully. 'You were expecting me. That's encouraging.'

He crossed the room and sat on the bed, very close to her. 'I saw you walking on the beach earlier today with the poetess,' he said very low. 'She is uncommonly tall, of course, and unmistakeable, but you are much of a height with most of the other young ladies, and yet there was no way I could mistake you for another. You looked quite at home there, I thought. And I began to realise as I watched you, and later when we talked I became sure of it: there is not the least need for all this heart-burning and worry about your reputation.'

'How so?'

'Marry me.'

He had said it, and her heart pounded in her chest at his words. But he was not done. 'I have the finest flower of English womanhood here, do I not? Or nearly so, for we must exclude any fortunate damsel whose parents have too great a care for her to let her marry such as I. But here they all are, at any rate, and I must confess that I find them dead bores, every last one. But you, you are not a dead bore. You are a constant surprise to me. And after all...' His voice was a caress, always, but his words held a sting. 'After all, the main requirement of me in this proposed marriage is somewhat... functional.'

She must have betrayed some small sign of distress or disapproval, for he said, 'I need an heir – you must surely know this. I would not have involved myself in this farrago otherwise. Until my younger brother and then my cousin died, I had no thought of marriage. I was lucky – I did not need to think of it, and Lord knows I did not want to. But now I must, for the sake of the estate and all its people. The next heir now, my man of business has informed me, is the elderly grandson or great-grandson of some distant great-uncle of mine – I confess I was not attending to the precise details – and lives a blameless life as professor of Greek and Latin in distant Massachusetts. A blameless unmarried life. The heir after him, his nephew, though they are apparently not on visiting terms, runs a low tavern on the dockside in Boston, and is married in a casual sort of way to a lady who rejoices in the name of Leaky Sue. There's a parcel of grubby brats about her heels, nominally his, though it is by no means clear if he is indeed their father. So you see...'

Still she did not speak, and he said with a twisted smile, 'I am sorry it is not a very romantic offer, Lady Georgiana. A sadly clumsy one, I fear. Put it down to inexperience, if you please, for I have never asked a woman to marry me before. But setting Leaky Sue aside for a moment, and setting aside too the fact that I am apparently to be the prize bull of the North Riding, I think we could deal together rather well, you and I. Looking at you now, I am sure we could. I promise you, it would not be such a terrible life, the one I could offer you. Not terrible at all. The status of a married lady is no small thing in our world, and I would strive to be a charming, undemanding sort of a husband most of the time – except of course where demands might be... appropriate and necessary. On both sides, my dear.'

He reached out and stroked a stray strand of hair back from her cheek. 'Will you not answer me?'

She found her voice at last. 'Such a flattering proposal.'

His eyes sparked silver fire in the lantern light. 'Hardly that. If I am the prize bull, what does that make you, or any woman who marries me? There, I have spared you from saying it. But I am sure we could enjoy ourselves more than a little, both of us, while we engaged in our... agricultural endeavours.'

She did not know whether to laugh or cry, and so did neither, nor did she speak. 'Would a kiss help you make up your mind?' he said softly. 'I seem to recall I made you something in the nature of a promise earlier.'

'Perhaps,' she said, as she had said once before. His words could not be described as flattering, but they were undeniably honest – had she not told herself she wanted honesty? – and she craved his touch, had been craving it all day. All week. All month.

'Well, it seems "perhaps" is good enough for me this time.' As he spoke he moved closer, and bent his lips to hers. He was not forceful, his mouth did not claim her ruthlessly, but the gentle pressure of his lips was irresistible to her, and she opened herself to him. He fixed his hands in her short hair and they melted together. It did not seem to matter what the circumstances were: when once they began kissing each other, the urgent impulses of their bodies would take over.

After a little while he withdrew from her slightly and said against her mouth, his voice less controlled than was usual for him, 'I told you that kissing you was something that deserved a great deal of time and attention, did I not?'

'Oh,' she said breathlessly, confused, uncertain, a little disappointed by the brevity of his kiss. 'Are you done, then?'

'I have barely begun.'

He was lying on the bed with her now, her face held between his big hands, and very slowly he acquainted himself with the contours of it. He took his time. He kissed her eyelids and feathered his way across her cheeks. When he came to her soft pink earlobe, he sucked on it and bit it gently, and she gasped. He explored her mouth again, and then the line of her jaw, and then her throat, as much as was revealed by the high neck of her nightgown. There were buttons fastening it, and he undid one – just one – and pressed a hot, lingering kiss on the tender skin he had revealed, where her pulse beat hard in the hollow of her throat. Then he raised his head again, and returned to her mouth, and now he was more assertive, and his tongue found hers, and hers came to meet it eagerly. She wrapped her arms about him and pulled him close, closer, and his body covered hers; the weight was welcome, and she shut her eyes and surrendered to sensation, pushing away any thoughts of right or wrong, or of how practised he must be in the arts of seduction and how easily she succumbed to him.

Presently he said, between kisses, 'Another button?'

'Yes!'

An electric moment later, 'Another?'

A while later, Georgie's gown was undone to the waist, and the Duke's lips were at her breast. He teased her with his tongue and with butterfly kisses for a long time, until she moaned in frustration, then finally he relented and drew one erect nipple into his mouth and sucked on it, while his clever fingers found the other, and tweaked it, gently and then a little harder. One of her hands was tangled fast in his silky hair, and the other clutched at the bedclothes. The sheets and blankets that had covered her had been pushed aside, and his body pressed hers to the mattress, a delicious pressure. She wondered in a sort of daze if he intended to continue his exploration; if he would kiss his slow, tantalising way down her belly and once more drive her to the edge of madness with his tongue and his lips in her most secret places. In that moment she hoped he would, it was all she wanted in the world, and she did not care what came after. Or, if she was honest, she knew what came after, and she wanted that too as she had never wanted it before.

He raised his head and smiled up at her, his eyes dark with desire. 'Christ, Georgiana, I want you, and I know with every fibre of my being that you want me just as much,' he said, his beautiful voice low, infinitely seductive, just a little ragged. The less controlled edge to it did not reduce the power it had over her: quite the opposite. 'Even if you thought to deny our mutual desire in words, and I notice you do not, your body always gives you the lie. Say you will marry me as soon as it can be arranged, and there will be no reason in the world for us to stop. I can stay here with you all night if you want me to, and we can share such pleasure...'

There was triumph in his tone along with the hunger, and something about it made her feel suddenly cold, though her body still yearned for the fulfilment she knew only too well he could provide. She was aroused, but she was also afraid, not of him, she realised, but of herself. 'No,' she heard herself saying, and she let her hand drop from his head.

'No?' There was no indignation or anger in his tone, just a sort of bewilderment, and his possessive fingers, which had begun to make their tantalising way further down her body, to pull up the hem of her nightgown, stilled, withdrew.

'I do not deny that I want you,' she said unsteadily. 'It would be foolish to do so and expect you to believe me.' She saw that he was about to speak, and put her finger to his lips, trying not to make it a caress. 'Perhaps what I mean to say will make no sense to you, but I need to say it none the less.'

He lifted his weight from her, and moved so that his body no longer touched hers. It made her want to whimper in instinctive protest, but she repressed the impulse, determined to continue. He lay at her side and looked at her, and she could no longer read his expression. 'If I marry you, I see two ways my life might be,' she said. 'Indeed, I had thought about this before, when I did not know who you were and believed I would never see you again. I can imagine – no, I am sure – that we would give each other a great deal of pleasure, as you say, and perhaps there would be the child or children that you need, but after a while, when you tired of me, I begin to understand my own nature well enough to know that I would continue to want... this, and I am very much afraid that I would seek it elsewhere, as, of course, would you. I fear I would become like Lady Oxford, or Lady Jersey, or one of a dozen ladies in society.'

'You would take lovers,' he said, his voice entirely expressionless.

'Are you saying I must not? Yet *you* would!'

'I suppose I would. But please, madam – you said there were two ways your life might be. What is the other?'

'I might fall in love with you,' she said. 'I'm sure a hundred women have before. And that terrifies me even more. I do not want to be that sophisticated, immoral woman – the duchess whose lover passes her husband on the stairs, and they greet each other with a smile, as though it is a sane and decent way to live when it is not. But much more than that, I do not want to be the woman who sits in this castle breaking her heart because the husband she loves has left her for another woman, or another dozen women. I do not want to lie alone in a cold bed missing you, or welcome you back, all the while hating myself because I need you so badly, even though you have come from someone else's arms, and will go back to them directly.' She fell silent, and he did not answer her. A long moment stretched between them, and at last she said desperately, 'Can you understand me even a little? Does anything I say make sense to you at all?'

He let out a great gust of breath, and lay back on the bed beside her, gazing up at the canopy. His face in profile had the stark beauty of a knight on a Norman tomb, of the marble face of one of his distant ancestors. That hard man, she was sure, would have seen her words as madness, would have entirely refused to accept her rejection. Would have taken what he wanted, merely because he wanted it. But he was different, as she had reason to know.

'You could use my body and its needs against me,' she said. 'I'm sure you know that. You have so much experience and you know exactly how to make me desire you. If you came back to me again now and put your hands on me, I do not think I would refuse you. I do not think I would refuse you anything at all, even knowing the danger I would be placing myself in if we risked conceiving a child. But it would not change anything. I still would not marry you.'

'I wish…' His cold voice dropped the words like poison into the quiet room. 'I wish I had never laid eyes on you in that house. Or, seeing you, had left you there to your fate.'

'I can't agree,' she said, and she wondered that she had the strength to speak. 'I needed to realise this about myself, however painful it is. You said I was spoilt – well, I am. But it is past time I grew up. As my brother said to me once, people's lives are not playthings. My own life is not, nor yours – we should take them seriously. Lust is not a good enough reason to marry. Or it should not be.'

He rose to his feet in one fluid movement and stood looking down at her, frowning, icily controlled. 'I can only be delighted, Lady Georgiana, to have provided a lesson that you feel you have profited by.'

'I know you are angry, and I cannot blame you, but thank you.' She had not covered herself, but lay exposed to him still, naked to the waist. She was oddly calm, and saw the remnants of desire warring with other, less easily read emotions on his face. Reluctant amusement was one, she thought.

'I do not think I want to know what you are thanking me for. I may be a rake, but I am still, I hope, a gentleman. Even as I wish profoundly that I had never met you, I must admire your resolution and your courage. You realise, do you not, that since you have refused me so very decisively, I must persist, and woo one of the other ladies? I know it is in poor taste to do so, but all my urgent reasons for marriage still remain. The people who depend on me, the estate. Leaky Sue, you may recall.'

'I know they do. I had not forgotten Leaky Sue. We will go away straight after the ball and leave you to your wooing, even if I have to tell Louisa all in order to make her understand.'

'Will you dance with me there, though, just once?' he said softly, and there was no anger in his tone now, only what she thought must be regret.

'Of course I will.' He smiled, as enigmatic as he had ever been to her, and turned to leave, and as he did so she spoke again. 'Can I ask you one thing?'

'I hate to think...' he said over his shoulder without turning.

'Please don't marry Mary Debenham.'

He looked back at her, silver eyes glittering. 'That is a promise I believe I can safely make. Goodnight, Lady Georgiana.'

'Goodnight...' she whispered, as the panel closed silently behind him.

16

The next day or so proved to be a species of nightmare for Georgie. That she had brought this entirely on herself was no consolation at all.

It began the next morning, when the postponed carriage expedition took place. They visited the impressive ruins of Whitby Abbey, just a short drive away, and while they were there the conviction that the Duke was beginning to court Alice Templeton began to grow in Georgiana's mind. He had, as Alice herself had admitted, paid her very little attention before – barely more than common courtesy required – but now it was different. He rode beside the carriage in which she travelled, his dogs keeping pace easily with his horse, and by the time they reached their destination Mrs Templeton was wreathed in smiles, and Mary Debenham and her mother were looking sour enough to curdle milk. Alice, by contrast, appeared dazed, and perhaps a little frightened.

As they walked amid the ruins – Tam and Nico close at their heels, Alice with her hand on His Grace's arm, although she looked as though she would rather be anywhere else in the world with any other companion – Miss Spry drew Georgie aside on the clifftop and hissed in her ear, 'What in heaven's name is he about? I had felt sure he was determined to pay his addresses to you. Did he not follow you into a private section of the library yesterday afternoon?'

'He did,' she replied dully. 'Then last night he came to my room again, and asked me to marry him. And I refused him.' She shrugged. 'He warned me that he would be obliged to court one of the other ladies directly, despite what had passed between us. I told him I understood.'

'Well, that is more than I do! Was he angry that you rejected him, and does this to punish you? I own I had not thought so poorly of him.'

'I don't know,' said Georgie slowly. 'I don't think so, but I can't be absolutely sure. Sometimes I feel I know exactly what he is thinking, and sometimes I cannot read him at all. After all, he must marry somebody; he has always made that perfectly clear. I asked him not to marry Mary Debenham, so I suppose I cannot blame him for this...'

'You have the most extraordinary conversations!'

'I know. He made me an offer, and began making love to me, and though I liked it excessively, all at once I knew that it would be sheer madness to accept him. I told him so. I told him that I feared if I accepted him I would either become a woman who was ruled by sensual pleasure and took lover after lover while her husband did the same, or – worse – I would fall in love with him, and his infidelity would destroy me. I don't want to be either of those people, Jane. Both paths lead to deep unhappiness and regret. I know that when I think of my mother, and what she would say to me if she were alive. I'm not sure he understood me, but do you?'

Miss Spry regarded her shrewdly. 'I think I do. And I agree with you. You cannot live your life with someone who makes you lose a part of yourself, or whose seductive influence turns you into a woman you do not want to be. It would be madness, as you say.'

'Thank you. May we talk of other things now? I know it was the right decision, but that does not make the results of it any easier to watch.'

'Very well. But you do not think in all honesty that you are a little in love with him already? Otherwise why does it hurt you so?'

Georgie had asked herself this as she lay sleepless after he had left her last night, and had reached no conclusion beyond the obvious truth that to fall in love with such a man would be nothing short of utter folly. 'I hope I am not. I certainly don't want to be. I told him there was nothing but lust between us; perhaps I was lying to myself. But does that not go to prove that I am right to reject him while I still have the strength to do so? Please, Jane, enough!'

'I suppose it does. Well, I will not speak of my own affairs to distract you, for nothing has changed for me and nothing can be done while we remain in Yorkshire. Shall we talk of the weather, or take out our books and begin sketching these most imposing ruins, like the correct young persons we most emphatically are not?'

Georgiana said something extremely unladylike about the prospect of engaging in artistic pursuits just now, and her companion laughed and consoled her. 'You must only endure this for a little longer. I understand we are to leave Whitby betimes and return to the Castle, so that Lady Blanche can help us sort out our costumes for the ball.'

'Oh, God, the ball,' Georgiana blurted out. 'I promised I would dance with him!'

'It will present a very odd appearance if you do not,' said Miss Spry with robust good sense. 'I do not care so much for the conventions of society – although, as we have established, I care more than I thought I did – but reflect on the fact that Miss Debenham and her mother are poisonous toads who plainly dislike you already, and if you give them the slightest reason to gossip it will cause you acute discomfort. If they thought you were avoiding the Duke, you know they would think to ask why, and who knows what conclusion they might leap to? You are uncomfortable enough as matters stand. It is only a little more to endure, and then it will all be over and done with. You need never see him again.'

'That's true,' Georgie replied with rather a wan smile. The idea of never seeing the Duke again was somehow no great consolation. 'We must leave the Castle as soon as we can after the ball, Jane. Even if I have to tell Louisa all in order to make it so.'

'There will be no need. I will make sure we go just as soon as we are able to do so without appearing uncivil. I am impatient to return to London, and she knows it.'

'Impatient to... to marry?'

'Yes – well, no, to set my plan in motion, before I lose courage and change my mind, or he does, and repents of his very generous offer.'

'I must admit I still don't fully understand why he has made it.'

Miss Spry said, 'I can see why you might not. But he is a friend, a very rare and special friend to both Louisa and to me. We have found ourselves, the three of us, able to discuss things that I dare say not one in a thousand other people would ever find themselves speaking of. I do not love him, not in a romantic way, but I trust him completely. Or else I could never contemplate such a course for a moment.'

'Trust,' said Georgie a little wistfully. 'I can see how important that is.'

17

On their return to Northriding Castle, Georgiana and Miss Spry enquired as to the whereabouts of their hostess, and were directed to a room in some distant part of the building, previously unknown to them, where they found Louisa and Lady Blanche, surrounded by open trunks and piles of rich fabric.

'The ball,' explained Lady Blanche. 'It is to be a masked one, as always, and it is generally understood that guests wear black and silver if they are able to do so, with perhaps a touch of white if they cannot, as that is always easy to find for young ladies. Our Northriding colours, you know, since ancient times, taken from our hair and our eyes, as you may see from many of the portraits going back for centuries. Some of the older people do not trouble themselves to follow the theme, or perhaps think it unlucky to wear black when not in mourning, but the younger people always seem to enjoy participating. It does make a great show in the hall, when everyone is masked and dancing, and the silver lace glitters in the candlelight. I have already helped some of our other guests choose costumes from our store, if they did not bring anything suitable, but now I think we must find something for you. Louisa has a silver ballgown with her that will be perfect, but she tells me you both need our aid?'

Georgie had not been able to repress a shiver at the thought of being masked, and seeing the Duke masked again – she was bound to recall all that had happened between them on their first meeting, and how he had told her just a few hours ago that he bitterly regretted it now. But that was a disturbing train of thought, and she pushed it aside with deliberate effort, and tried to lose herself in looking over the gowns that Lady Blanche pulled out for her inspection.

Miss Spry pronounced herself satisfied with a costume some thirty years old that had once belonged to the late Duchess – Jane declared that she had always thought the slightly raised waists and full skirts of the time following the Terror in France to be most becoming. The silk was striped in black and silver, and the low bosom would be filled with a white fichu, and her blonde locks piled up on her head to be dressed with grey powder and feather plumes. 'It will be like seeing my mother in the mirror, I am sure, at the age of my earliest recollections,' she said with a smile. 'I wish there were some means of preserving the impression, so I could show it to her when next I see her, for I am sure she would be most amused.'

Georgiana considered several gowns, oddly indecisive when surely it did not matter in the least what she wore, and at last with her hostess's encouragement settled on one of black velvet embroidered with silver thread and brilliants, which Lady Blanche thought might have belonged to her grandmother, a French lady, when she was newly married. The skirt was not set on an exaggerated frame, in a fashion which looked ridiculous to modern eyes and must have made it nigh on impossible to pass through doorways, but was nevertheless wide and full, supported by numerous stiffened petticoats. The black velvet skirt opened in a wide vee over these petticoats, which had been designed to be visible and were heavy with rows of silver lace. The same costly material also showed in a cascade from the elbow. The bodice was low, and Georgie would have to be trussed into it with some force. 'It should really be matched with a wig,' said Louisa, raising her glass to inspect it, 'for your hair is too short to look quite right in powder, but I hardly think you will care to wear one even if one can be found. Horrid, insanitary things. People in the past were so peculiar, I declare it makes me shudder to think of it now. One's own parents, even! But perhaps we can find a false curl, a ringlet of some sort, to attach to your own, to make it appear longer?'

'I have the very thing!' said Lady Blanche. 'I will be sure to have it sent to your chamber, and some pins along with it. I am sure your maid will contrive something. And do you have a mask...?'

Georgie had a mask. She scarcely knew why she had brought it to Yorkshire, though it took up little space in her luggage, but she had it none the less, and would wear it. A servant was summoned to carry the chosen gowns to the ladies' rooms, and they set about packing away the items they had rejected. The ball loomed large in her mind, but she told herself that this was folly; she would be prudent, treat it as any other social engagement, and as soon as it was over they could leave, and if she was lucky she would never set eyes on the Duke again, for he would be married to another woman, and presently, she was sure, she would succeed in banishing him from her thoughts and from her treacherous dreams.

18

Gabriel was beginning to fear that he would never succeed in banishing her from his waking thoughts and from the dreams and fantasies that tormented him. He sat in his study, having had enough of the majority of his guests for now, and he must have been betraying some unusual agitation, for the dogs sat there regarding him with what he could have sworn were anxious expressions. He stroked them both, and talked to them in the foolish way people, even dukes, spoke to their dogs when they were alone with them, but it scarcely helped his inner turmoil.

To his consternation she had refused him, in no uncertain terms too, and in his hurt – he didn't know why it should hurt, but there was no doubt it did – he had warned her that he would be obliged to woo another. This was, of course, nothing less than the truth. He had set about that wooing today, under her very nose, her beautiful little nose, and if a part of him had rejoiced to think that she would see what he was about and be hurt in return, a greater part had always known this for the ignoble and unworthy folly that it was.

But it was worse than that. He had seen her watching him as

he walked among the ruins at Whitby with her friend, and saw her look away with a poorly concealed expression of frozen misery when his gaze caught hers and challenged it. Her distress shook him, and he realised with a jolt of unwelcome certainty that if she was suffering, he was too. She was unhappy, that was plain, but no more than he was. He could call it a Pyrrhic victory, but that would be mistaken, for it was no sort of victory at all.

He didn't want to marry any other woman. Not the little mouse Alice who squeaked and trembled whenever he addressed her, not any other of the debutantes Blanche had assembled. He would previously have said – would have said a bare two days ago – that he didn't want to marry anyone at all, so it made no odds which woman he chose, but most curiously this no longer appeared to be true.

Fate was a damnably cruel jade. It was almost amusing, but he was not just now in the humour to be amused. He had proposed marriage to a woman for the first time in his life and she had refused him. There were any number of young ladies at the Castle who would have accepted him without a moment's thought and with every appearance of delight, but his cursed erratic fancy must light on the one who would say no. Who could find the strength to say no even when she lay in his arms, her pupils dilated with desire, her perfect breasts still tingling from his touch, her delectable little pink nipples still swollen with arousal, still slick from having his lips, his mouth on them. His hand had been on the hem of her nightgown; a moment later he would have... She admitted she wanted him, she even admitted – Christ! – that she would give herself to him willingly, completely, if he persisted. But she would not marry him whatever he did. It was refined torture.

To refuse him was of course her privilege; he hoped he was not such a coxcomb that he had expected her to weep with delight when he proposed the solution to both their problems. God knows it wasn't his masculine pride that was offended. He feared it was much more than that. He was trying very hard, as he smiled and conversed with others with perfect civility though he had hardly the least idea what he was actually saying, not to dwell too much upon her reasons, for they created a storm of confusion in his head – and not just in his head – that he found himself singularly ill-equipped to deal with. The picture that she had painted of him, passing his wife's lover on the stairs, that stung. The picture of him leaving her crying bitter tears when he left her bed bound for another's, that stung too. Her talk of mere lust, that was a barb in his flesh, though he had no idea why it should be when he'd never had the slightest problem with lust in the past; quite the contrary, in fact, he'd been an enthusiastic advocate of it. He didn't want to think about any of these things, to consider whether there was any justice in what she said, and what he could do about it if there was. He refused to.

He knew he had been damnably clumsy in his approach to her, babbling of bloody Leaky Sue like an imbecile. It must have been the most unflattering proposal of marriage that a young lady had ever received – Leaky Sue herself would have laughed, no doubt – and yet he was famed for the suavity of his address, his powers of persuasion, known across Europe as a man who could seduce a nun out of her convent, though it wasn't something he'd made a habit of, or at least not lately. (Venice had been the place for that, as for so much else, once upon a time.) He had lain awake last night rehashing every word, every gesture, every damn thing that had occurred in her chamber, and it had gained him nothing except a painfully intense erection and the conviction that he was very possibly losing his mind.

And there was no point to any of it, and it didn't matter whether he was touched in the upper storey or not, because she had refused him, and he was obliged to woo another. And he would. He would not go to her chamber any more, he would not attempt to shake her resolve or dwell on the thought of her lying there warm from his embrace; no, he would woo another, be accepted – for why else were any of them here? – and allow himself to dance his one dance with Georgiana at the ball, the only dance he would ever dance with her in both their lives, and then put her out of his mind for ever.

He also refused to dwell on his fear that this would be very, very hard to do. He wanted to lie on the floor with his faithful companions and whine like one of them, but of course he did not. Dukes did not do such things, even in private. Instead, he composed himself and left the room, to resume his distasteful wooing, all the while conscious that he was making a huge mistake and there was nothing he could think of that would mend matters.

19

Gowns chosen, Georgiana and her companions rejoined the rest of the party, and for the remainder of the day she was treated to the spectacle of the Duke staying close by Alice's side. He was not so uncivil as ever to meet Georgie's eyes again while he was doing so; his behaviour was impeccable, and he never overstepped the bounds of propriety, but the mere fact of his attention lighting on her seemed to make Alice extremely uneasy. Her mother, by contrast, was delighted, while Mary Debenham and her parents were trying and to a large extent failing to conceal their great chagrin at this new turn of events. Mary's sharp tongue, which had on previous days been largely employed in acid comments directed at Georgie, was now engaged in criticising every detail of Alice's dress and deportment. She spent much of the day giggling behind her hand with her crony Miss French, in a blatant way that made Georgie, rising above her own turmoil, itch to give her a set-down. Alice could hardly be oblivious to such behaviour either, and, after a particularly poisonous after-dinner sally set her friend blushing, Georgie drew her aside for a turn about the room.

The weather was a little better than it had been of late, the warmth of a fire was no longer necessary, and this evening the ladies were gathered to wait for the gentlemen in the long picture gallery that led off the great hall. It had French windows at one end that opened onto a sheltered little garden set into an angle of a turret, and Georgie, not stopping to examine any of the portraits of Mauleverer ancestors that held the other ladies' attention, took Miss Templeton's arm and ushered her outside. They found themselves alone, in a small, secluded space of low box hedges, stone statues and climbing greenery; an antique fountain in the shape of a wolf's head tinkled in one corner. She closed the door behind them and said, 'Now we can speak in private!'

She saw that tears stood in Alice's eyes. 'Oh, Georgie!' she almost wailed. 'I am in the most terrible coil! Miss Debenham's odious behaviour is the least of my concerns, horrid though it is. No! Mama is convinced that the Duke means to offer for me – perhaps at the ball! And she is delighted. She is writing to Papa this evening to tell him the wonderful news!'

'I do not think you can yet be sure that the Duke has any fixed intention of making you an offer,' said Georgiana. 'It has only been today that he has paid you any particular attention, and he seems to me to be... capricious. Perhaps his fancy will alight somewhere else tomorrow, and somewhere else again the day after.'

'I hope you're right! But that will be almost as bad, because then Mama will blame me, and say that I should have done something to secure his regard when I had the chance!'

'Like what?'

'I don't know! She has counselled me strictly never to be alone with him, and of course I would not in any case – it's not as though I *want* to, for heaven's sake! – but she has already reproved me for not appearing to be delighted whenever he deigns to notice me. She says I look like a frightened rabbit when he addresses me. And I expect I do! I am not stupid, Georgie, as a general rule, but when he speaks to me I can think of nothing rational to say. He is so very intimidating, is he not? Even when he doesn't have those terrifying beasts with him!'

It could not be denied that there was a certain awkwardness to this conversation, which Georgiana had not considered when she led Alice aside in a well-meant attempt to save her from Mary's spite. She found herself reluctant to discuss the Duke with her friend; it would be improper, wrong, and above all unwise to do so. But she was obliged to give her some answer. 'I confess I do not find him so, nor his dogs, for that matter,' she said with an effort at lightness.

'You do not freeze when he addresses you? No, you do not, for you are not scared of anyone, are you? Not even of men, or large dogs with huge, sharp teeth! I have noticed that, and I cannot tell you how I envy you for it. I expect it comes of having such a great quantity of brothers,' Alice said thoughtfully. She seemed to be fast regaining her composure now that Mary Debenham and the Duke were absent.

'I expect it does,' said Georgie with a weak smile. Alice looked at her fixedly, and as Georgie observed her with unease, an idea plainly occurred to her.

'I don't suppose that *you* would consider marrying him?' cried Alice in sudden inspiration. 'You're not scared of him at all, and I am sure you would make a perfectly splendid duchess! You are quite accustomed to all this...' She waved her hand expansively at the stone walls and many casement windows of the Castle, the sea and sky and dukes and dogs of Yorkshire. 'You have lived your whole life in the very first circles, you are on excellent terms with all those terrifying Howard and Cavendish ladies, when I cannot always distinguish them one from another. I can imagine it so clearly!' she said fervently. 'You will be very grand, and witty, and host splendid dinners which the Regent will attend. Quite apart from the Duke, though he is bad enough, the thought of all that horrifies me. If the Prince Regent or his brother of York, say, were to speak to me, I would... I would die of mortification!'

'But...'

Alice had the bit between her teeth now, and was not to be cut off or diverted. 'And what's more,' she said, eyes sparkling, 'Mama and Papa could not possibly blame me if it turned out that Northriding preferred *you*. Because you are an earl's daughter, and it is entirely natural that he should choose to marry one of his own rank, or nearly so. That is why horrid Mary Debenham was so catty to you before: because she thought that the Duke was bound to choose you over the rest of us. Indeed,' she said naïvely, 'I wonder that he has not. But I suppose you are not here for that purpose, after all, but as a friend of the family. I expect that accounts for it.'

'Alice,' said Georgiana, conscious of a bubble of wild laughter rising within her, clamouring for release, 'are you truly asking me to marry the Duke to save you from that fate?'

'Yes! I only wonder I had not thought of it before. Oh. Oh dear. I suppose it really is a great deal to ask of a friend, is it not?' Her face fell in a comical fashion, and Georgie was obliged to bite her lip quite hard to prevent mirth from overwhelming her. 'I'm sorry. I cannot expect you to do such a thing. I had not thought... But now I realise I was being foolish.'

'Not foolish, Alice, but... it is, as you say, a great deal to ask of me. I would help you if I could, if I could only think of a way, but...'

Miss Templeton pressed her hand fervently. 'I know you would! You are the best of friends. But I understand that if you agreed to take him instead you would then have in the end to actually marry him, to be alone with him, and... and allow him all the liberties that a gentleman must...'

'Yes,' said Georgie in hollow tones. 'Those.'

'I am sure you would mind all that every bit as much as I would. How could you not? I cannot ask you to sacrifice yourself to save me. To submit to... that. No,' she said with a dolefully little sniff. 'I see now that it was selfish of me, and I must endure it. Do not regard anything I have said, I beg you. And perhaps it will not be so very bad, after all. When I tried to tell Mama of my fears, she said that I was a silly girl and that I would learn to accustom myself to that aspect of life, as every married woman must. She said she counts linens – in her head, naturally, not out loud, which I expect a gentleman might not like, after all. And while I know she was trying to be helpful, probably, I must admit that is a thing I am sure I would have preferred never to know. But there is always death in childbed, I suppose. Even Mama,' she said with a spark of spirit, 'could not blame me for that, and if she did, I would not be here to see it! That is a consolation.'

'Is it?' said Georgiana wildly. She simply could not bring herself to discuss such intimate matters with Alice, nor to suggest to her that it was at least possible she might find pleasure in the Duke's embraces. It was not her place to offer consolation, and the reply that occurred to her – that the Duke was reputed to be a man of great experience, who might well know how best to set his nervous bride at her ease – was not something she felt any desire at all to put into words. Indeed, she wished she had not so much as thought of it. All this strayed, she felt, far too close to most dangerous territory. She also detected in herself a new and alarming tendency to feel slightly sorry for Northriding, faced with the prospect of a wife who shrank in horror even from the contemplation of being alone with him, quite apart from... No. That train of thought must cease.

'Will you forgive me, Georgiana?' said Alice now, her small chin wobbling a little. 'You are a true friend, I know, but I cannot ask so much even of you. I hope you will stand by my side, and be my bridesmaid, though, if I am permitted to choose one and do not have some grand lady whom I do not know forced on me. That way at least I will have one kind face beside me in my time of trial. And when I am dead, which I suppose will not be very long, if I'm lucky, perhaps you will have a care for my poor motherless child, left alone with his cold, unloving father – and his savage companions – in this bleak wilderness!' She gestured dramatically at Yorkshire once again, and Georgie was obliged to stifle the urge to applaud and cry, Brava! Her friend's soft brown eyes were overflowing with tears now at the deeply affecting picture she had painted of her brief but tragic future.

'Have you been reading Mrs Radcliffe again, Alice? I believe you must have been, and it has lodged Gothic ideas in your brain. Do try not to dwell on them. I cannot think the Duke so very bad, or your prospects so very dark, you know.' Georgie scarcely knew what to say, and did not think that Alice would appreciate being laughed at. Who did?

'No!' said Alice nobly, her head held high. 'You are very kind, but do not attempt to comfort me. There is no comfort to be had. My fate is sealed, I know. I will go back inside and reconcile myself with it. There is no use repining for a life fated to be cut cruelly short!' And on this excellent curtain line – not easy to say, either – she left, her bearing and gait very much those of a queen tragically and unjustly condemned to the scaffold, but resolved to meet her untimely death with courage.

Georgie remained outside, having no taste for the role of chief lady-in-waiting to Lady Jane Grey, and succumbed to the slightly hysterical laughter that she had been holding at bay for the last few moments, but when her mirth subsided she began to feel ashamed. She might think Alice's fears ridiculously melodramatic and overwrought, but it was still true that her friend dreaded the future that had been laid out for her without any regard for her own wishes, and shrank from this marriage with repugnance, hard though it was for Georgie to understand this.

Alice's case was very different from her own, and it would be unjust to fail to recognise it. *She* was fortunate indeed to be surrounded by close relatives, male and female, who would never think to force her into a match she did not want, however advantageous it might appear in the eyes of the world. Last year when she had made her come-out and gentlemen had flocked to offer for her hand, her brother had consulted her as to her preferences in the matter, and listened to what she had said, even though her choice was one he could not approve. When she had entangled herself with Captain Hart... but this was old ground, and there was no profit in going over it again and flagellating herself anew. She was aware – and her recent resolution to be entirely and painfully honest with herself obliged her to confront the thought – that Alice had just offered her an excellent excuse to change her mind and accept the Duke after all, should she want it. Should she want it...

But if she seized the chance, by the same token she must not deceive herself into thinking that she was being noble. She had read the same novels Alice had, but if she chose to become Duchess of Northriding she would be doing it because she wanted to, and not in order to save her friend from the Gothic fate she had so feelingly described. And all the powerful reasons not to marry him that had seemed so clear to her last night still held. She might not be frightened of the Duke as Alice was, the idea of physical intimacy with him was a temptation rather than a terror to her, but the vision of the woman she might become if she accepted him must prevent her at last from making such a choice.

She sighed, and arranged her face, and went inside.

20

The next day, the day of the ball, was enlivened by the general air of expectation that pervaded the Castle. Amongst all the bustle of final preparation, Georgie hoped that her own uncertain mood might go unnoticed – as, indeed, might the air of saintly resignation that Alice had assumed. This hope was encouraged by the fact that the party from Castle Howard arrived that afternoon, along with some other slightly less distinguished guests who were also to stay overnight because they lived too far from Northriding Castle to travel home afterwards, even by moonlight. The Duke's wooing must be suspended while he received his guests and entertained them, and this gave both ladies a respite, for very different reasons. But Georgie was sure that Miss Templeton and her mother were right in thinking that the ball itself might prove to be the perfect setting for a formal proposal of marriage. If it were successful, as it surely would be despite the feelings of the prospective bride, it would be followed by an announcement, and then by general congratulations and celebrations; what better occasion could be found?

And I am to be bridesmaid, thought Georgie. Good God, was

there ever anything so preposterous? I would not believe it if I saw it in a play. I am to stand and watch a terrified, reluctant, coerced girl marry a rake who thinks she is a dead bore, a rake who came to my bedchamber in secret two nights since, proposing marriage to *me*, undoing the buttons on my nightgown and kissing his way...

It was a relief to her when she was obliged to push aside such perilous thoughts and pay heed to Lady Georgiana Morpeth, chief lady of the Howard party. That amiable lady was all affectionate attention to her late mother's godchild, and full of questions about the health and situation of her brother Hal, her sister-in-law and all her other siblings. There were, of course, numerous enquiries to be made in return, about that lady's interesting children (she was, she confided, increasing again), and her dear sister Harriet and her baby son. Georgie remembered Alice's piteous claim that it was impossible to keep all these noble, inter-related ladies separate in one's head, and smiled a little to herself, as she listened with half an ear to some tale of the doings of Staffords she barely knew, and with the ease of long practice made exclamations in all the correct places. By the time she went to change into her masquerade finery, she had the headache.

When she emerged from her bedchamber to join Louisa and Miss Spry, the expression on her aunt's face suggested that she too was feeling some pain. 'Good heavens, Georgie,' she said, surveying her. 'I had not thought you so...'

'So...?' enquired Jane with a grin.

'So... eighteenth-century!' said Louisa with an expressive gesture of her quizzing glass.

'It's the dress,' said Georgiana helplessly. 'It was a little too small for me, I fear, and it had to be laced tightly in order to fit.'

'We heard the screams.'

'I did not scream, Louisa! I may have cried out, perhaps. I am not accustomed to such corsetry. But I am in it now...'

'More or less,' said Jane drily.

'I am in it, and it is too late to wear anything else. If I am to go to the ball, it must be this.'

'I do not say it is not becoming,' her aunt sighed. 'It may in point of fact be too becoming for my peace of mind as your aunt and chaperon. And I suppose if you are to dance in such a full skirt and high heels, to neither of which you are accustomed, it is just as well that it is a little too short. You certainly will not catch your heels and trip. And your maid has done very well with the arrangement of your hair; it looks perfectly natural. But I am excessively glad that Hal is not here to see you in such a low-cut gown; I am sure he would blame me, and most unjustly, for I had no idea...'

Jane said, her voice unsteady, 'The heels do make you quite tall, Georgie. I think you should be careful in your dancing partners, and make sure, if any particularly short gentleman should ask to take you onto the floor, to sit out that set, or you will look like a satirical print by Gillray.'

Georgiana glanced down at her chest, which was indeed far more exposed than had ever been the case in public before. The tight lacing of the bodice had had an extraordinary effect. She crossed the room to the cheval glass that stood in one corner, and studied her reflection doubtfully. It was, as she had said, far too late to change. It was time to go down to dinner, or they would be late.

The woman she saw – for it was not a girl she beheld in the mirror – was a stranger. Her short hair had been given the appearance of length with the aid of Lady Blanche's false curl, which nestled against her bare neck. Her bright blue eyes glittered behind the lace loo mask she wore, and her maid had set a black velvet patch beside her right eye, so that the mask did not conceal it, saying that the other abigails in the servants' hall had shown her how to do it, and furnished her with the means. Many of the guests would be attired in the fashion of the previous century, and would also be sporting patches. She had dimples, ordinarily, but they were not in evidence now, since she didn't feel she had anything at all to smile about. She shook out the ruffles of silver lace at her elbows, and took a deep breath. Louisa groaned. 'Try not to breathe more than is strictly necessary,' she advised.

'It is a masquerade, after all,' Miss Spry consoled her. 'You, Louisa, are wearing a gown that is in the current mode, but most other people will not be, I dare say. Many of us will present an odd appearance. Look at *me*!'

'I think it suits you,' Louisa said. 'I agree that the bold stripes are... not quite what one is used to these days, but the overall effect is pleasing. Your hair looks well in powder, and matches the gown. And I like the fichu. At least *you* will be warm enough! The castle is quite draughty in parts, I have observed, and Georgie is like to catch her death!'

This seemed unjust to Georgiana, as her aunt had quite as much bosom on show as she did, and she said so. 'I am not a young unmarried lady!' replied Louisa. 'Our situations are quite different. Nobody is likely to attempt to draw *me* aside into a dark corner and seek to compromise me!'

'Oh, I don't know,' said Jane, brown eyes sparkling. 'I've always thought that gown most attractive, as I believe you have reason to know.'

'I think we should go down, or we shall be late,' Georgiana said firmly. She squared her shoulders, ignoring her aunt's moans of protest, and they set off gingerly down the steep staircase.

21

The dinner that preceded the ball was a grand occasion. The distinguished members of the Howard party were seated in the places of honour, so she was not obliged to be in any very close proximity to the Duke, a fact for which she was excessively grateful.

Everyone present had made some sort of effort to dress according to the prescribed theme, although most of the older guests had done so by the use of colour, rather than by donning any outlandish costumes. Alice was miserable in white and silver, and Mary Debenham glittered coldly in a priceless lace court dress of quite recent vintage, which, it must be admitted, suited her icy blonde prettiness very well. There were other ladies in low-cut gowns from the previous century – it seemed that the attics of Castle Howard had also been raided for the purpose – and as a result Georgie did not feel so very out of place, though she might have wished that her dinner neighbours would raise their gazes to her face occasionally. Yes, she felt a wild impulse to say, breasts! Two of them – a matching set! Clearly a novelty where you are concerned! I must not, she resolved, have another glass of wine. For several excellent reasons.

The Mauleverers had, as hosts, made a particular effort with their costumes. Lady Blanche had reserved for herself a striking silver gown in which, with powdered hair, she rather resembled Madame de Pompadour, and her children were both dressed chiefly in black, which flattered their pale complexions and striking dark red hair. Young Mr FitzHenry looked very handsome, and many of the ladies present were quite obviously conscious of the fact. Alice was seated by him, and seemed to find his attentions greatly to her liking. Georgie had the fleeting thought that if *he* instead of his uncle were of a mind to pay court to her friend, she would be by no means so reluctant or so frightened.

But Georgiana had no eyes for him. How could she? The Duke was in full court dress of black velvet heavily embroidered with silver, with white ruffles at neck and wrist, and his long hair, which he had not chosen to powder, was drawn back into a short queue. Perhaps he'd grown it for the purpose. His eyes were bright behind his plain black mask – a mask she thought she recognised – and when he saw her watching him his lips quirked, and he raised his wineglass to her with a courtly inclination of his silvered head. She feared she coloured as she responded, and hoped he did not perceive it beneath her mask. She was mortified that he had caught her staring, but he was so very arresting in the costume that she had not been able to stop herself. He was always handsome in modern dress, especially in evening dress, but the contrast of sensuous velvet and delicate lace with his powerful, athletic frame was something piquant, entirely new, and powerfully attractive. Definitely no more wine, she told herself.

He claimed her for the second dance, a fitting and in sober truth unavoidable tribute to her rank. Lady Georgiana Morpeth, conscious of her delicate condition, was not dancing. She sat to one side observing the throng and gossiping with Louisa and some of the other ladies past their first youth, several of them gently fanning themselves as the heat in the great hall increased with the press of bodies. The guests who came from close by had arrived, and filled the room, and as Lady Blanche had said the effect of so much black, silver and white by candlelight was enormously striking. Georgie had danced the first set with a young Howard or Stafford, who had flirted in a decorous fashion that did nothing to trouble her composure, but she feared that the Duke would be a very different matter.

He took her hand and bowed over it. 'Ma dame,' he said softly. 'Vous êtes ravissante ce soir.'

She closed her eyes briefly as she swept him a full curtsey, and prayed for strength. His voice was seductive enough in English; French was more than a woman could be expected to endure. 'I could say the same of you. You must be conscious of the effect you create in that outfit – it is as though Casanova walks among us again. I hope Miss Templeton is swept by away your charms this evening. Do you dance with her next?'

They took up their places. 'I can't remember. But I shouldn't think she would be: she has hardly shown any evidence of succumbing to my allegedly irresistible allure up to now.'

'She's frightened of you.'

His mouth thinned below the mask as the music began and they moved apart, and then together. 'You exaggerate, surely? She is merely timid and a little shy of me because we are not yet well acquainted. I have felt no temptation to overstep the bounds of propriety with her, nor done the least thing to cause her any alarm.'

'I do not exaggerate. She finds even conversing with you intimidating, and the prospect of being alone with you positively terrifying. Which might be a problem in the future you have planned, I'd have thought.'

'Did I choose poorly? Again? How maladroit I appear to be. You must bear a share of the blame, for I am sure Miss Debenham would have been more receptive.'

'Oh, I have no doubt of it.'

'It does make me wonder, could any of my prospective brides ever meet with your approval?' he said silkily. 'You are inconsistent, Rosalind. You do not want me for yourself – or you do, in truth, but you dare not – but you are so very quick to find fault with all my other choices.'

'That is unfair!' she hissed. 'I am not at all jealous, I assure you! Mary Debenham would be a disastrous match for any man of sense.' His mouth quirked again, and he made a graceful, ironical little bow in acknowledgement of the inadvertent compliment without losing his place in the dance. She ignored it and swept on. 'And I cannot believe that even *you* really wish to marry a woman who hates dogs *and* dreads intimacy with you so much that she plans to make it bearable by telling over household chores in her head all the while!'

He let out a little snort of incredulous laughter. 'No!' she said. 'I assure you, sir! On both counts!'

'Well, if I were truly to wish to live up to my deplorable reputation, I could say that I am confident such measures will not prove necessary. But I take your point, my dear – it's perfectly true that I have no wish to figure as an ogre in my own marriage bed. The picture you paint, dogs aside, does sound rather fatiguing, and not hugely enjoyable for either of the parties involved. And,' he added, his silver eyes glinting wickedly behind the mask, 'you have excellent reason to know that I am never selfish when it comes to pleasure.'

'Hush!' she whispered fiercely, though his words set the blood thrumming in her veins. She did have every reason to know it, and the pictures and sensations his words evoked were a delicious torment, at such a time and in such a public setting. She was sure he was aware of the effect he had on her, that was the worst of it, and he was laughing at her as the dance ended.

Alice was indeed his next partner, and Georgie was all too conscious of her white, rigid little face – the Duke's expression she could not read – as she took her place in the set close by them, and turned in the figures with Mr FitzHenry as her partner, thankful he appeared to have given up his previous attempts to flirt with her in the face of her obvious and consistent lack of interest. She could not help but feel guilty as she beheld Alice's barely concealed distress, knowing she could free her friend from the fears that haunted her with little more than a word. A significant glance, a nod would do it. But at what cost to herself?

It was all too much for her suddenly, and when the dance was ended she made an excuse to her waiting partner and slipped from the crowded room, rejecting his offers of assistance. She made her way through the empty picture gallery and found the door that she had used with Alice the evening before. Escaping into the garden, she crossed to a stone bench and sat, drinking in the reviving sea air and gazing blindly at the moonlit scene. But she was not left in peace for long.

'This was my mother's favourite spot,' said the voice she had been half-expecting to hear. She sat still and watched him approach, and thought as he did so that this was surely his natural element: the rhythmic sound of the crashing waves on the beach far below, the velvet darkness, the everyday objects transformed into something strange and eerie by the moonlight. Every fibre of her body was aware of his proximity and her blood sang in her veins at the prospect of his touch, however much she might tell herself that it should not be so. It was so; perhaps it always would be.

'I wondered if you would follow me.'

'That's not quite true, is it, if you are honest? You knew I would. Because I cannot keep away from you, and *you* do not want me to.'

'I should want you to,' she sighed, tacitly acknowledging the truth of his words. He was very close now.

'We never want what we should, have you not observed? How convenient it would be if we did. I think you and I are alike in that. The tantalising little patch you wear beside your eye is *La Passionnée*, you know, and it suits you perfectly. The rules of society are clear enough, and dinned into us from our earliest childhood, but you, quite as much as I, struggle to follow them, even though the penalties for transgression are all too obvious, for women so much more than for men. Perhaps you would find it easier,' he said gently, 'if you could make for yourself a way of life that allows you to blur such boundaries, rather than trying and failing to conform over and over again. Your aunt has done so, after all. I consider it admirable, though I am sure she would care nothing for my approval, the way she and her poetess manage to live entirely as they please, and do it with such insouciance that nobody even thinks to censure them.'

'They are not done yet,' she said drily, struggling to maintain her composure as she always did when he was close by. 'We will see if their latest start pushes them beyond the bounds of what society will accept at last. I hope not. Because it's dangerous, living as you please. Look at Lady Georgiana Morpeth's mother, the late Duchess of Devonshire, if you wish for an illustration.'

'I know,' he replied. 'Believe me, I do not mean to belittle your fears. Her life was undeniably tragic, and I understand why it preys upon your mind. But Devonshire piled cruelty on cruelty – to make her greatest friend his mistress, to keep her living under their roof... You do not need me to rehearse the whole sorry story. It hardly helps my case, I am well aware, as an example of what supposedly civilised men can do to the women they marry.'

Once again, she resisted his invitation to turn the conversation to more personal matters; she feared he was about to renew his suit and she did not know if she had the strength to resist him for long when she so craved his touch, his mouth on hers. 'I was not old enough to discuss it with my mama, naturally, but Louisa has told me that Mama believed her friend would never have involved herself with Lord Grey if Devonshire had not treated her so badly for so many years. She was very unhappy, and confided in Mama a great deal.'

She thought his face was unwontedly troubled behind the mask, though it was hard to be sure in the moonlight. 'Georgiana,' he said softly, 'I am conscious that I am making *you* unhappy by a lack of consideration. I am certainly all too aware that I made a sorry hash of my proposal. Babbling of Leaky Sue like a simpleton – I would not wonder if it gave you a disgust of me. I know what you fear, and my behaviour since we met has given you little reason to think me a man of sense, much less one of feeling or any shred of decency. But let me ask you this one last time – can we honestly not find some way to make things work between us?' He took her hand and drew her to her feet, and when she stood he did not release her, but raised her gloved fingers to his lips and kissed them with intense concentration. 'I must always make a sad mull of things when it comes to you. You make me nervous, you know,' he confessed with a wry smile, still gazing down at her hand where it lay in his, rather than looking up and meeting her eyes.

'Nervous, you?' she scoffed, clinging perilously to her composure, unbearably conscious of his nearness, of the sheer physical power of him, and how his body called out to hers, how the mere touch of his hand, the brush of his lips, left her wanting so much more.

'Something about your presence,' he said, releasing her, but only so he could cup her face and draw her closer, 'makes me lose my head and say outrageous things I do not really mean, or do not wholly mean. I beg you not to pretend you do not understand me, for I know you are affected in the same manner. Or you would not have told me you were a widow, on a certain memorable occasion, or as good as invited me to put you across my knee and spank you.' He was close enough to see the dark flare of desire in her eyes as memories flooded her, and he laughed, very low. 'Now, you see, the way things generally proceed between us, I would immediately add, "an invitation I look forward to accepting", or some such nonsense, and you would make pretence to be shocked, while all the while intrigued, and both of us aroused, and sharing that knowledge. And this is all very well – it is more than that – but Georgiana, please tell me, I implore you to tell me, how I am to marry another woman, any other woman, when this, whatever it is, this physical connection, call it lust if you wish, is alive between us? I must ask you one final time, before I commit myself to a course that I fear will lead to unhappiness and regret for many, would it be fair to that other woman, or for that matter fair to either of us?'

'I know it would not,' she admitted, shaken by the force of his words.

His hands were still about her face, holding her gently but inexorably as he looked deep into her eyes. 'I do not want to marry any other woman, no matter who she might be,' he told her. 'I do not commonly use words such as right and wrong, for I gave up that privilege long ago. But it seems to me entirely wrong to crash into another woman's life, uprooting her from all that is familiar and comfortable and asking her to put her future, her whole chance of happiness in my power, when all the while there is this madness in me, and I know that I would abandon her without a second thought to follow you across the world if you asked me to. Or even if you did not.'

'Would you?' she said wistfully. She could not help herself.

'Georgiana, you know I would...' It was almost a groan, and then their lips met. Her arms slid around his neck, and he released her face to clasp her to him, his big hands tight on the boned bodice of her gown below her breasts, holding her fast, holding her exactly as she needed to be held, as their mouths fused in mutual need. She pressed herself against him, wanting to be closer still, pushing her fingers deep into his silky hair and freeing it from its restraining band. 'Georgiana...' he whispered again against her mouth, and then he kissed his way along her jawline, and she threw back her neck, letting him take her weight, surrendering herself to his strong arms and inviting him wordlessly to explore her throat, her almost entirely exposed breasts, with his lips and tongue and teeth.

He was tasting her skin at the point where her neck met her bare shoulder when a sound behind them penetrated their reverie. The Duke raised his head, Georgie opened her eyes, and they saw in mutual shock that they were no longer alone.

22

The trouble was, she was too beautiful, too desirable, too... too *his*. She was in his blood and there seemed to be no way of getting her out, that was the bare truth of it. Gabriel had made all sorts of resolutions and had meant to keep them, but at the sight of Georgiana in that gown every single one of them had fled. He had intended, though the prospect had filled him with no joy, but rather a sick feeling of wrongness, to ask for Miss Templeton's hand in marriage that evening. He thought she and her mother were expecting as much, her mother being far the keener of the two. But of all the women assembled here, Alice Templeton seemed the most amiable, though undoubtedly shy. More than that, he did not think her home was a happy one, nor her wishes ever consulted by those around her, and he could at least offer her an escape to a better life, along with the status marriage to him would bring. She was extremely timid and presently a little nervous of him, but that was only because they were not yet well acquainted, and she was not, he thought, slow in understanding or lacking in character. Many marriages began, and went on to prosper, on flimsier foundations. They would marry, he would treat her with all possible consideration and afterwards bother her as little as was compatible with the reasons for their union, and he would have done his duty by everyone who depended on him. He had thought that he was reconciled to it all.

The trouble was, he could not find it in him to give a fig for duty when Georgiana appeared on the staircase in black velvet and silver lace, and their eyes met. She looked like a princess, a duchess, a queen from the previous century. His princess, his duchess, his queen. He understood now – and it was very late in the day for a man of his reputation and experience to come to such a realisation – how a man could become obsessed with a woman, and throw aside everything, all thoughts of duty, honour, family, obligation, in order to possess her. The very word 'possess' and all it implied could make him hard, could set his body and his mind on fire with longing for her. Just her. He'd fought a duel over a woman once, but he'd been no more than a foolish boy then. He couldn't even remember her face now. He couldn't remember any other woman's face.

Georgiana's feet were clad in high-heeled shoes that Blanche must have found for her, since they were very far from the current mode. He had never previously held a conscious opinion about women's shoes, but now he wanted to fling himself at those feet and kiss them. Her ankles were revealed, in white stockings clocked with silver. They were very shapely ankles, but God knows he had seen many, many ankles before and they had not affected him so. The skirts of the gown were full, black velvet over silver. His colours. His. She was very tightly laced, and his hands should be about her little waist, spanning it, holding her tight. Her bodice was low, and her beautiful breasts were revealed by it, nestled in silver lace. The areolae of her nipples were concealed, just barely, he thought, but he didn't need to imagine them because he'd seen them, had kissed them, and just now he would have given every single thing he owned in the world to kiss them again. He wanted to bury his face between her breasts. He wanted to eat her.

Her lovely, well-shaped head was carried regally on her long white neck, and that neck was circled with a simple black velvet ribbon, which he would very much like to remove, with his teeth. And she was wearing – this was the last straw where his composure was concerned – that damnably enticing black lace loo mask. He knew in his blood that it was the same one she'd been wearing on their first meeting. Her eyes were revealed, those beautiful, unforgettable blue eyes, and beside one of them, in order to push him right over the brink, she had set an alluring black velvet beauty patch, such as had been fashionable in his grandparents' day. Patches had their own language, and this one – it was the sort of curious thing he knew, though now he wished he didn't – was entirely appropriate for her, being the patch that conveyed the useful information that the wearer had a passionate nature. And he knew the truth of *that*.

He also knew in his bones that it was the sheerest insanity to contemplate marrying another woman when he felt like this. She could call it lust if it made her happy. He didn't really care what it was called any more.

What was more, when they danced together it was very clear to him that, however hard she tried to conceal it, she felt exactly the same. She did not want him to marry any other woman alive one whit more than he wanted to do it. She would find excellent reasons to object to any bride he might choose, while all the while refusing to admit why. Surely it must be possible to make her see...?

By the time the dance with her had ended, he was fixed in his determination to try again. He endured the next set with Miss Templeton with an impatience he was barely able to conceal. He did not even stop to worry how exactly he would contrive to get

Georgiana alone and make a last desperate attempt to convince her that she could, she should, she *would* marry him. He knew an opportunity would present itself, for it must, and was not in the least surprised when he saw her leave the room, her face pale. This was his last chance and by God he would take it. He followed her. He was not in a state just then to consider or to care whether anyone saw him go or not.

They spoke – he thought she came tantalisingly close to admitting that it would be the sheerest folly for them even to think of parting – and then, as he had always known they would be, they were in each other's arms. This was his best argument, surely, and it did not need words. It was perfectly clear that they could each of them have been married to another and it would not have mattered; it could even have been his wedding day, or hers, and still they could not be alone for five minutes without claiming each other. In sober truth, lust was far too feeble a word to describe it.

This time they were interrupted. He knew she was horrified – he felt her stiffen in his embrace – and he could have cursed aloud in frustration, for this did not suit his purposes at all, though he feared she would think it did. He had wanted her to admit, to herself as much as to him, that they should marry. She had not quite done so, and now he had no option but to put out the fire of scandal before it had a chance to flare up and ruin her. He saw in a lightning glance just exactly who he was dealing with, the worst possible news, and everything he said after that was preordained for him.

23

It seemed a veritable crowd of guests had been seized by the urge to take the air at this precise point in the evening, and to do so in what was still known as the Duchess's Garden. Blinking, Georgie beheld the appalled faces of her aunt and Miss Spry, and the unattractive mixture of shock and prurient fascination that warred for prominence on the sharp countenances of Mary Debenham and her mother. The only person present who betrayed no distress at all was Alice Templeton, who seemed nothing but delighted, and appeared to be repressing the urge to cheer and do a little dance of celebration.

All these impressions penetrated her dazed brain in a matter of seconds, but she would never know how she might have reacted to them if left to herself, for Northriding recovered his wits much faster than she did. Perhaps, she was later to reflect bitterly, he had practice in dealing with disasters of this nature, and worse.

He did not release her, though his hands slid imperceptibly down to her waist, and he gave the tight bodice of her gown a warning squeeze. 'Ladies,' he purred. 'So many ladies! This is unexpected, but what a delightful surprise nonetheless, as you may be the first to congratulate us. Lady Georgiana has just this moment agreed to do me the honour of becoming my wife. I beg you will forgive me for my ardour, but I hope you will consider it excusable, and even understandable, in a newly betrothed man. Will you not wish us happy?'

Lady Louisa rose nobly to the occasion. Her blue eyes were a little wild, but her voice was reasonably steady as she said, 'I suppose, sir, you should be censured for not applying first to Lord Irlam for his sister's hand, but we were, after all, aware that you were seeking a bride when we agreed to visit the Castle, and so perhaps his permission was implicitly given and your... ardour may indeed be excused. Please accept my congratulations, Northriding, Georgiana. I am sure I wish you very happy. And no doubt you will write to my nephew directly and set right your omission in formal terms.'

Miss Spry murmured approval, and Alice added her voice to the congratulations with enormous enthusiasm; from beneath her eyelashes, Georgiana saw the Duke's sculpted lips twitch appreciatively as he took in the full extent of Miss Templeton's most unflattering joy at the unexpected reprieve she had been given. She could see that he was amused, though she was not. Mary and Lady Debenham were obliged in common courtesy to express equal pleasure at the news, although it was obvious that it gave them considerable pain to do so. She could hardly doubt that they would spread the tidings of her indiscretion with lightning speed and lurid detail.

Georgie found she had recovered her wits, though she still dared not meet the Duke's eyes. By slow degrees she eased herself from his embrace, not without a pang of regret, if she were honest with herself, and stood by his side, fixing a false smile to her face. He took her hand and set it firmly on his arm, saying, 'Perhaps we should go in and announce the happy news to the assembled guests, and this ball will become an engagement celebration. What do you think, my dear?'

'Of course, sir,' she replied with tolerable composure. 'I am sure everyone will be delighted for us. Let us go instantly.'

The next few hours were a blur to her. She was the object of general interest, and found herself embraced and wept over by Lady Blanche and Lady Georgiana Morpeth, and showered with congratulations by many other persons with whom she was not yet perfectly acquainted. Even in her dazed state she could not help but notice that the Mauleverer family and their tenants and servants seemed particularly delighted at the news – they anticipated, she realised, an heir for Northriding and the security that would bring to all their lives. Mr Summerson, the rector, pressed her hand with especial warmth, and told her that he thought she would make a wonderful duchess. 'I am confident that you are just what Gabriel needs,' he said, 'and what the house needs, and the estate and its people, though I know it cannot be expected that you should care for all that yet.'

She was obliged to begin a celebratory dance alone with the Duke, though the very many pairs of avid eyes upon them as they did so precluded the possibility of much private conversation. 'So, you have your wish,' she said between gritted teeth. Her face was aching from smiling, and her head was pounding afresh.

He sighed. 'What else could I do, my dear?' he whispered, and she knew that to anyone watching it would give the appearance of a tender endearment. 'There was nothing else that could be said in that moment that would have saved the situation, and your reputation. I know you are angry, but do me the justice of admitting that.'

'Of course I admit it. I am not a complete fool, though so often I behave like one. But was it really necessary to announce the matter immediately to the assembled party – to your family, your tenants, and half the nobility and gentry of the North of England? Do you wonder I feel trapped?'

'I do not wish to trap you. No, do not scoff – I promise you I do not. How does it serve me? You know I have no taste for a reluctant bride, whether you or any other. But if I had not made the announcement that instant, it would have presented a very odd appearance – for what better occasion could there be to make the news public? – and given those two poisonous creatures a golden opportunity to spread damaging rumours about you. Now they cannot, or if they do nobody will regard it, for it would appear to be nothing less than sour grapes from a woman I have rejected. They will hardly want that, and so they must attempt to present at least an appearance of complaisance to the world.'

'As must I.'

'We can talk later. We must. You know this is not the time or the place, Georgiana. But for what it is worth, I am sorry. I hoped to persuade you to acknowledge the strength of what lies between us, not force your hand. Please believe me.'

And with that she was obliged to be content for now. When at last the ball was over and the guests had either called for their carriages or made their way to bed, and the last of the congratulations had been uttered with widely varying degrees of sincerity, His Grace was able only to whisper in her ear, 'Shall I come to you tonight? To talk,' he hastened to add as he saw her stiffen.

'No,' she replied. 'Please don't. I will now be obliged to suffer a homily from Louisa – she has the right, you must admit. And after that I want nothing more than to sleep. I am too tired for more words tonight, or for anything else, for that matter.'

He kissed her hand to signify that he understood, and they parted. When they reached their tower – and the stairs seemed steeper and more numerous tonight than they ever had before – Louisa told Georgie with a significant look that she would look to see her in her chamber as soon as her maid had done undressing her. 'Because I cannot have a serious conversation with you while you are still wearing that ridiculous gown,' she said. 'The way his eyes devoured you when he saw you in it, I am sure it is half the cause... But never mind that now. I will see you in half an hour, Georgiana.'

When Georgie tapped upon her aunt's door a little while later, she found her in bed, wrapped in a red silk robe of Chinese design. Her dark hair was braided and lay across her shoulders in long plaits, and she looked tired, and somehow older than she did in the day when her defences were up.

'I'm sorry, Louisa,' said her niece, sinking into the chair that sat beside the window, and resting her weary head against its back. 'Truly I am. But I've said that before, haven't I? There is no reason you should believe me this time.'

'What in heaven's name have you been about, Georgie? Has this been going on under my nose for all the time we have been here? I suppose it must have been, and I completely ignorant and absorbed in my own affairs, fool that I am! But good God, child, it has only been four days or so since we arrived! How have you travelled so very far so quickly?'

'Less than that – three, I think. I can't tell; it makes my head spin to think of it, but I agree, it does seem much longer.'

'However did you begin it? Has he been making love to you in secret since the very day you met him? How is that even possible? I do not understand anything! I knew you were reckless, but this...'

'It began before,' said Georgie, too tired now to dissimulate, and without expression she told her aunt all that had occurred since her first meeting with the Duke, though she did not reveal Miss Spry's knowledge of her actions. Louisa listened in stunned silence and when she had done said again, 'Good God. What Hal will say... Well, that settles it. You must marry him now.'

'I don't know. I suppose I must.'

'It's partly my fault, for if I had not followed you tonight... I saw you leave, and thought you seemed distressed; Miss Templeton told me you were seeking fresh air, and said she believed she knew where you would go, and offered to show me. Jane tried to stop me, said I should leave you be, but I did not heed her, and spoke sharply to her. I suppose those odious Debenham creatures scented some scandal when they saw us arguing, and followed us in that excessively ill-bred and inquisitive manner. What a catalogue of disasters. I did not know they were at our heels until it was far too late.'

Her niece shrugged. 'Perhaps Alice saw him come after me, and did it all on purpose. I know she had hoped I might marry the Duke instead of her; well, she has her desire. It hardly matters now, does it?'

'Don't you want to marry him? You certainly seemed happy enough in his embrace – we can all vouch for that! You said just now that he asked you to marry him yesterday, and you refused him, but you did not say why. Make me understand, Georgie, please, because at present I do not. We cannot allow this match to go forward if there is something you are not telling me that is greatly to his discredit. You know Hal would never insist upon that, whatever the scandal it might cause. Has Northriding hurt you, and you are too embarrassed to tell me? Are you in fact afraid of him? Has he coerced you in some manner?'

'No,' said Georgiana listlessly. 'No, I have told you everything that has happened. It's not all his fault, you know, Louisa – we share the blame. He has not done anything I have not asked him to. Begged him, practically. And that's what I am afraid of.'

'I warned you against his charm, did I not? Though God knows I had not the least idea how right I was!'

'I don't think it's even that. I could say he had mesmerised me, could I not, and lay off the blame on him that way? But I don't think it would be true. He has said himself that there is something dangerous in each of us that calls to the other, so that we cannot stay apart even if we try. And I have tried. Of course,' she said with a little constraint, 'he could have spun the same tale to every woman he has ever met, to get her into his bed. I expect it has worked a thousand times before, and certainly it has worked well enough now. I can have no way of knowing.'

'Do you fear he will be unfaithful? Is that why you refused him?'

'I fear he will, and for that matter I fear I will too, if we marry only to satiate our physical desires, however strong they may be. How can I know what I might do, what I might become, if I give in to this... this compulsion? It frightens me, Louisa, the strength of it! What would Mama say, or Papa, if they were here and saw me entering into that sort of marriage, so unlike their own? What would you think of me, or Hal, or Cassandra? They love each other! You love Jane! You are each of you very obviously happy with the person you have chosen as your partner in life. You would all be disgusted with me – oh, you would not say so, I dare say, but you would be. And when it came to it, so would I.'

'Love might grow between you, if indeed you do have this... this connection. Could that not be the case, do you think?'

'If I fell in love with him, the inevitable betrayal would be worse.'

Her aunt had no answer for this. 'I must write to Hal, you know, and send my letter by the fastest means possible tomorrow. And he will come here, I expect, as quickly as he can.'

'I know he will. I am sorry, Louisa,' she said again, 'for this fresh disruption I have created for you all.'

'Oh, go to bed, child!' said her aunt in fond exasperation. 'You must be exhausted – I know I am – and perhaps things will look brighter in the morning. It is not every family,' she added with a gleam of humour, 'that would see a betrothal to a highly eligible duke as a cause for heart-burnings. Most other people – witness the Debenhams – would be rejoicing at their good fortune!'

Georgie made no answer, but smiled wearily and bade her goodnight.

24

The following day was largely occupied in saying farewell to the Howard party, and to the other guests who were to take their leave. Much to everyone's unexpressed relief, this included the Debenhams, who had somehow discovered urgent reasons to be elsewhere. Nobody pressed them for more details; everybody was glad to see them go.

Louisa had instructed her groom to leave at first light, bearing a letter to her nephew; if he made excellent time and encountered no delays, he would reach Lady Irlam's home near Skipton at the end of a long day's travelling. If in turn Hal set off very early on the morning after he received the news of his sister's most unexpected engagement, and proceeded with similar reckless speed, he might arrive at Northriding Castle late that same day, at the cost of sprung horses, snatched meals and physical exhaustion. But he could hardly feel comfortable pushing on so hard if accompanied by his wife, so Georgie did not look to see Cassandra with him, and she was sorry, for she thought her sister-in-law might stand her friend in these trying times. She had had her own adventures around the time of her marriage to Hal, and all had not gone smoothly between them even after they had married. Perhaps she would be able to give sage advice, though Georgie doubted very much that any of it would really be applicable to her most peculiar and difficult situation.

Georgiana found it hard to cope with the affection shown to her by Lady Blanche and her daughter, which she was obliged to meet with answering warmth, feeling a fraud all the while she did so. Lady Blanche, who would presumably – if nothing happened to prevent it – be her sister-in-law too very soon, confessed that she had cherished half a hope that Georgiana and her brother might make a match of it even before the Pendlebury party had arrived, despite all she had said to the contrary. 'Louisa had talked about you a good deal in her letters, you know, my dear, and so the idea was already in my mind, though of course I said nothing of it to anyone. I could not imagine anyone more suitable on paper. And as soon as I set eyes on you, and, more to the point, as soon as I saw Gabriel set eyes on you, I could not help thinking that you would be perfect for each other! I knew he was interested in you from the outset, and you in him, dare I say? And I am delighted to be proved right!'

She was plainly more than happy to welcome Georgie into the family, and Eleanor in particular seemed glad to gain a relative so near to her in age, who would be able to chaperone her in society soon enough. She endured a particularly awkward conversation in which the girl – who would, how ridiculous, be her niece and might wish to call her Aunt – asked her innocently about her plans for the rest of the year, to which she was obliged to give evasive and unsatisfactory answers, saying that there had been no time to think of such things just yet. It was so far true: she had no plans, but was in an atrocious state of confusion.

Despite the happy news, everyone who remained at the Castle seemed a little lethargic and lacking in energy that day, no doubt as a result of their exertions at the ball, and it came on to rain hard as the afternoon progressed, a heavy, cold, drenching rain that depressed the spirits. The greatly reduced party did not linger downstairs long after dinner, and the Duke was sensitive enough to Georgie's mood that he made no suggestion of visiting her later, and did not appear in her chamber unannounced, as he so easily could have done. She lay awake a while, wondering if he would come, unsure if she wanted him to, wondering what she would say to him if he did. But he did not, and at last she fell into a restless sleep, plagued by unquiet dreams.

She slept late the following morning, but rose in time to bid goodbye to Mrs and Miss Templeton – formally, in the case of the older lady, whom she had never liked, and affectionately when it came time to take leave of her daughter. They embraced, and Alice whispered a fervent, 'Thank you!' in Georgiana's ear. It seemed unlikely that Georgie would ever be able to convince her friend that she had not sacrificed herself for her sake, and she certainly did not feel equal to attempting the task now. Her feelings about the prospect of marriage to the Duke were complex, and seemed to change by the minute. She did not think Alice would understand; how could she, when Georgie did not understand herself?

Georgiana, Lady Louisa and Miss Spry were now the only guests in the Castle, and an air of greater informality prevailed, along with a certain lessening of tension. When the Duke suggested that he and Georgie took a walk together after nuncheon, nobody suggested that any supervision was necessary. The expression on Louisa's face showed all too plainly that she considered it rather too late for that.

They made their way down through the depths of the Castle to the beach, dispensing with any aid on this occasion, His Grace carrying the lantern. The dogs had wanted to accompany him, but he had called a footman to hold them back and make sure they did not follow, though they whined piteously at being left. The descent was made largely in silence, and the pair did not speak of anything but commonplaces until they were outside on the strand. The tide was out, and a large expanse of gleaming beach was revealed, without so much as a human footprint to mar its perfection. The rain had stopped during the night, everything was as fresh and clean and shining as it could be, and fitful beams of hazy sunlight struck silver from the waves.

'What an extraordinary place this is. It's so beautiful,' said Georgie, anxious to keep the conversation upon such unexceptionable topics as the scenery and the weather.

'I have always found it so. Miss Spry would agree with you, I imagine, since she is of a literary bent, but I doubt many others among our recent party could be persuaded of it.'

'Mary Debenham would have gone into raptures over a pile of mouldy sacking if she thought it would curry favour with you!'

'True, but she would have been quite obviously dissembling, and you are not. And you forget, it would have been a pile of mouldy *ducal* sacking.'

'That makes all the difference.'

'To her, certainly.' He stopped, and turned to face her. 'Georgiana...'

She looked up at him, stray curls blowing across her wind-flushed cheeks, her expression troubled, and he pulled her close. She had no will to resist him, but warned him feebly, 'We can be seen from every window on this side of the Castle, I dare say.'

'I am not proposing to throw you down on the wet sand and have my wicked way with you, my dear, tempting though the idea may be. Although I should tell you that, if I did, I imagine any spectators at Northriding would probably feel impelled to cheer us on rather than to disapprove.'

'Of course – the heir.'

'The heir. But that is a cold and impersonal word to use, is it not? Our child, Georgie. I believe I should ask you, though perhaps it is unwise of me to do so: how do you feel about that; about the prospect of motherhood, perhaps quite soon?'

'It is not that I mind. I do not think it's that. I was raised in the expectation of becoming a mother, and my own family life has been a very happy one, unlike so many, unlike the Cavendishes, for example. It is the fact that we hardly know each other that disturbs me,' she said suddenly, feeling the truth in her words as she spoke them. 'We are discussing making a child together, yet we really don't know the least thing about each other. I don't think that we have had a single conversation that has not consisted mainly of outrageous flirting, and ended in kisses rather than confidences.'

'It is the way our society is arranged. Not the kisses, of course, but all the rest. The lack of acquaintance, certainly. If I were not standing here with you now, remember that I would be talking in some superficial fashion with Miss Debenham, Miss Templeton, or one of the others, if indeed I were permitted to walk with any one of them unchaperoned.'

'It's barbaric.'

'It is what we have.' He sighed. 'You know I agree with you. It is barbaric, for many reasons. I am sure you think that as a man I have a great deal of freedom, far more than you have or ever will have, and of course this is true in many ways, but not in all. I must provide this estate and all its people with an heir. I have a duty to them that can no longer be shirked, and my own inclinations are of no importance. If I were one of those men for whom the female sex holds no attraction whatsoever, if I cared at all for duty and family, I must still persuade some woman to marry me, and we must go to bed together and contrive to make a child between us, however much we both hated every minute of it. A miserable prospect for both, I am sure you agree. We are not farm animals.'

'How fortunate that you are not such a man,' she said bitingly. 'Quite the reverse, in fact.'

'I suppose you have no reason to believe me, Georgiana, but I have never been indiscriminate in my amours, which have in any case not been as frequent as rumour would have you believe. I swear to you that I have never pressed my attentions on anyone. The prospect of making advances to a woman who had agreed to be my wife through parental pressure or even her own ambition, yet shrank at the prospect of my touch, was always distasteful to me. It could not be anything else.'

'At least she would have explicitly agreed.'

'Where you have not?'

She made no answer, and he swore violently. 'I don't know what to do,' he said at last. 'I have never known such uncertainty. I can release you from our betrothal – of course I can. Today, or in a week, or a month. We can insert a conventional announcement of our engagement in the papers directly, and then another a while later, saying that it has been called off. It will be understood that you have jilted me, and I can live with that if I must. I could say... Georgiana, this is an impossible position to be in. If I say your reputation may suffer some damage as a result, if you reject me after the way we were seen together at the ball, you will reply that of course it is to my advantage to point that out. That is so, but it does not make it untrue.'

'I do not know that I care so very much for my reputation just now. My brother may feel differently, of course.'

'Let us not bring others into this any more than we need. I do not give a fig for your brother's feelings, or your aunt's, or even my sister's. But Georgiana, if you mean to refuse me, that is of course your right, but you know I must look elsewhere, and quickly. However much I sicken at the thought of it.'

'I have ruined everything for you!' she cried as sudden cold realisation hit her. 'Oh, God, but I have. Your house party, all your arrangements, all of it wasted. And if I did as you suggest, you would be obliged to court another woman immediately. But what decent family would want a man who has so recently been betrothed to someone else in scandalous circumstances, and then soon after jilted for mysterious reasons that surely could not be to his credit? It would mean that your choice of bride must surely be made from those who are solely concerned with your position and your fortune. And you will be tied to such a woman for life, and it will be my fault!'

'How can I possibly answer you?' he said, his voice constricted. 'Whoever should own the blame, or even if there should be no blame to apportion, everything else you say is true. And yet you know I desire to marry you and no other woman in the world. Just you. Beyond that bare fact, what on earth can I say?'

She was crying now, salt tears pouring down her face and making her eyes and lips sting in the sharp breeze. He swore again when he saw, and took her by the shoulders. 'Georgiana, I could say I do not want you as a sacrifice. Christ knows I do not want you to marry me for some noble and misguided reasons against your will. I have said a dozen times that I do not want an unwilling bride, and least of all if that bride is you. I would prefer you come to me of your own free choice. But if I must be completely honest with you, now that we are speaking of it, I know that for my part I do not have the strength to be noble. Do not expect it of me, I beg you, for if you expect it you will be disappointed.'

She looked up at him questioningly through drenched lashes.

He said bluntly, 'I mean that I will take you on any terms I am offered.'

'If my brother should force me – but he would not – you would still take me on those terms?' she sniffed.

'I fear I would. No – I know I would. On those terms, on any terms, as long as I can have you.' He took out his handkerchief and wiped her face, but the gentleness of his touch in contrast with the stark nature of his words just made her weep the more, until he took her in his arms and let her sob her distress and confusion out into his shoulder.

At last she drew away from him a little and tried to regain her composure. 'I can't do any more of this now. It is too exhausting. I will have my brother to face soon enough.'

'I am sorry for it. I am not in the least acquainted with him, though I believe I know him by sight. He is tall, is he not, one of the younger Corinthian set, with the dark hair and striking bright blue eyes you Pendleburys all seem to share? I have always thought, if indeed I thought about it at all, that he seemed amiable enough. My poor girl, is he in truth so very terrible and stern? I will protect you, if I can. If we engineer matters so that he sees me first and has his fill of abusing me – as he is entitled to do – before he has a chance for a private interview with you...'

Georgie laughed at the picture thus presented to her, glad of the lightening of mood after so much intensity. 'He's not terrible at all, and anything but stern. He is the best of brothers, and even when I got myself in a terrible tangle last year he barely censured me as almost any other man would have done. It's not that I'm afraid of him in the least. The idea is ridiculous. I'm just ashamed.'

'Of what we have done?' His face was closed now, unreadable to her once more. 'Of being caught, and exposed to public embarrassment? I suppose that is reasonable.'

'Not that, or not exactly that. Of the trouble I have caused him, now and in the past. You know that we were orphaned eight years ago, and poor Hal – who was barely one and twenty then – was obliged to take care of all five of us, at an age when most other young men care for nothing but their own pleasure. Bastian has always been well-behaved, but I have been a constant trial, and the younger boys are monsters. It would take me all day to tell you of the mischief that they have caused.' She gave a little hiccup of laughter. 'Jonathan and Hugh once tried to stow away on a ship of the line, and almost caused an international incident.'

'You have four brothers?'

'Five, and no sisters. Alice Templeton thinks that's why I am not scared of you.'

'Perhaps it is, at that. I imagine growing up with five brothers could have that effect. I only had one myself, two years younger, and a much older half-sister.'

'I did not know you and Lady Blanche were not full siblings.'

He shrugged. 'It makes no difference to us. We have always been as close as our age-gap permitted. I have visited her every year in Ireland, or she has come here.'

'Sir...'

'I think by now you may be allowed to call me Gabriel, you know, my dear.'

'Gabriel, then, I am sorry. I cannot repeat it often enough, I think. For saying that I had lost a husband at Waterloo, that whole ridiculous story, when you had lost your brother and your cousin there. It was unforgiveable of me.'

'How could you know? I do not regard it, I assure you. You meant no harm.'

'I never mean any harm, but still I cause it. It's just another example of my thoughtlessness. I have sworn a hundred times to do better, but still I keep on making these reckless errors.'

'You think our marriage is another such? No! No, it is my turn to apologise. Do not answer that. I know you are weary of these endless discussions, and you have more to face later. Let us walk on, and talk of something else. You will catch cold if we stand here any longer.'

She agreed readily, and they walked on across the lonely beach, her arm through his, and talked of lighter matters for a while, to the relief of them both. One could not live at such a pitch for ever, and there would be more challenges to face soon enough.

25

Henry, Lord Irlam, arrived at Northriding Castle, driving his own racing curricle, well after the dinner hour, his tall, imposing African groom Jem Oldcastle at his side. He descended stiffly from his two-wheeler, Jem took the reins, and a footman came out to climb up beside him and direct him to the coach house and stables. As Hal handed his beaver hat and mud-splashed many-caped greatcoat to the butler, he saw his aunt Louisa descending the great staircase. She had obviously been watching out for his curricle from one of the windows that overlooked the courtyard. 'Hal!' she said. 'At last. Lady Blanche has asked me to tell you that a room is made up for you, and I am to say that the Duke awaits you in his study if you should care to see him tonight; if you are too tired now he will meet with you in the morning, when you have rested.'

'I would be glad of it, God knows,' replied her nephew wearily. 'That was an atrocious journey on frightful roads, and we were nearly overset half a dozen times. I've never heard Jem curse so in all the years I've known him, and I learned some terrible new words I was tempted to use myself. I am aching all over, and if my teeth have not rattled out of my head it is a wonder. But I should see Northriding now, much as I would rather not.'

'Let us talk first,' she said conspiratorially. 'I could not set down everything in my letter, for fear of it falling into someone else's hands. But not here! Come into the parlour where I have been waiting. I shall give you a glass of Madeira and you can warm yourself by the fire for a little while until you feel more the thing.'

She led him up the stairs and into a small candlelit room with a cosy and very welcome fire. She poured him a glass of wine, and he sat down heavily upon the red satin sofa and drained it with a sigh. He was not yet thirty, and his handsome, strong-boned face was of a naturally cheerful cast, but there was little sign of cheer in him now. 'Thank you! That is better. Now tell me; if what you have to say is worse than what you felt able to set down, I cannot for the life of me imagine what it might be.'

Lady Louisa began her tale with Georgiana's scandalous meeting with the Duke in London, and went on to describe subsequent events exactly as her niece had recounted them, up until the scene in the garden and the forced announcement of their betrothal. She spoke quietly, without excessive emotion, but if she had thought that this might temper her nephew's reaction, she was to be disappointed.

'Christ, Louisa,' he said blankly when she had done. 'Good God almighty. Has she run mad?'

'I don't think she has. Consider for a moment, Hal, as I have had time to these last days – is anything she has done so very different from your actions last year when you first met Cassandra? Do not tell me that nothing in the least improper happened between you before you wed her, for if you did, I would not believe you. There was a certain occasion – the night of the Windleshams' ball, as I recall, when the pair of you disappeared for quite half an hour...'

Her nephew blushed like a schoolboy, and did not meet her eye. He did not deny or admit anything, but merely said hastily, 'Yes, I take your point, but dash it all, that was Cassandra! It's completely different!'

'Why?'

'Because I love her, and she loves me. It's not the same as letting a complete stranger... I can't say it to you! I wonder you were able to say it to me, Louisa!'

She smiled a little ironically at her favourite nephew. 'You love each other now, and I am excessively glad of it. But can you honestly say that either of you felt such an overpowering emotion, or at any rate were fully aware of feeling it, when you first—'

He cut her off hastily. 'Let us set that aside, if we may, ma'am, and move on.'

'Let us, by all means!' she said drily. 'What I am trying to say is that you do not think any the worse of Cassandra for permitting you... whatever liberties she permitted you, I am sure I do not wish to know. And perhaps you can extend the same courtesy to your sister where Northriding is concerned. Hal, people of our rank in life have intimate congress with complete strangers all the time; to claim otherwise would be rank hypocrisy. Many men, of course, do so just as often as they are able, as far as I can tell, but both men and women do it as soon as they are married. It is quite usual for a couple to marry, with all that implies, when they have never so much as had a private conversation. Nobody thinks there is anything in the least odd about it. And do not try to tell me you are religious, and that is the nature of your objection to what has occurred, for I know you are not.'

'I suppose if the fellow had made her an offer in an ordinary sort of way, even after a few days' acquaintance, I would not think anything of it,' he said dubiously.

'As for that, you know he asked her to marry him the night

before all this blew up in our faces, Hal. As far as I can see he has been consistent in his desire to marry her more or less since we arrived here. But she refused him.'

Her nephew groaned. 'His reputation is very bad, though, there's no denying that. He's not what I would have wished for her, dammit. That frightful scandal when he was little more than a boy, people still speak of it now... And it's not as though he has reformed of late, as far as I am aware. Let's hope he means to! Or what was he doing at a cursed orgy, Louisa, I would like to know?'

His aunt sighed. 'What do you think he was doing, Hal? For that matter, what was she?'

'She was tricked there by that pestilential Aubrey woman, though I cannot imagine why. You told me so yourself!'

'But then she stayed, Hal. She did not flee in horror as another girl might. God knows what would have happened to her there if Northriding had not seen her, and taken her aside.'

He laughed incredulously. 'What happened to her at his hands – whatever, don't look at me like that, you know perfectly well what I mean – was not bad enough for you? How much worse could it have been?'

'Much worse. You know it could have been much worse. You do not need me to spell it out for you, Hal. He did nothing she did not want him to do. He has up to this date done precisely nothing that she has not very much wanted him to do.'

'That seems to be the root of the problem. If he's what she wants, and she wants him that badly... I suppose there is no point hashing it over endlessly, is there? The upshot of it all as far as I can see is that she must marry him. I do not see what else is to be done.'

'But she is not sure she wishes to. She is in considerable distress and confusion of mind.'

'What would you have me do, then? Of course I will help her if I can, but I have not the least idea how else to set this right.'

'You cannot make all of them happy, Hal. Not the boys and not Georgie. She needs to work this out for herself, with the Duke, as you did with Cassandra. And what a miserable time we all had of it, while we are on the subject, living in the house with you while you came to your senses.'

He had the grace to grimace. 'I know. I remember what an awful mess I made of things, thinking the worst, refusing to listen to her when she tried to talk to me. Loving her, torturing myself over it. Are you saying this is in some way the same, Louisa?'

'I think it might be. I can't be sure, as I don't believe Georgie fully knows her own mind yet, and nor does Northriding, though at least give him the credit for being absolutely sure he wishes to marry her and nobody else. He knows exactly what he wants, though perhaps not just why he wants it so badly, which is more than she does. Will you go and talk to him now?'

Hal stood, and stretched his long limbs. 'I suppose I must. Christ, what a day.'

26

The butler ushered Lord Irlam into his master's study, and left them alone. The two tall men – effective strangers – stood and studied each other critically across the space that separated them, tension in the air. If Lady Louisa had been there, she might have remarked that they resembled nothing so much as two big, handsome, stupid dogs who happened to encounter each other in the street, and were not quite sure if they should fight for supremacy or decide to be friends.

The Duke moved to greet his reluctant guest. 'Irlam,' he said. 'I'm glad you got here safely at last. Perhaps you might not care to shake my hand, after all that you have heard of me. But I dare say you would be thankful to sit down, and take a glass of wine. You have had a long and weary day of it on my account, and I am sorry.'

'I thank you, Duke, but my aunt gave me wine, and I do not wish for any more just now,' Hal said a little stiffly, very much upon his dignity. But he took the chair that his host had indicated.

'I told your sister that I would see you alone, so that you might have your fill of abusing me for my conduct, and spare her your wrath. She laughed at me. But please, begin whenever you wish. I shall not say a word in my defence, for I am not sure there is anything to say.'

'What is the point, after all?' said Lord Irlam, passing a hand wearily over his face. 'You are a good two or three years older than me, Northriding, and my aunt has just been reading me a lecture on the dangers of hypocrisy. It's not my place to jaw at you like a damned parson. I just wish it hadn't been my sister… but Georgie always had a talent for getting into scrapes, without any help at all from you.'

'So she tells me.'

'And out of them, in fairness to her. The last fellow… well, she hit him with a poker. My wife and I rushed to rescue her, but there was no need. Knocked him down, stood there kicking him where it would do him most good.'

'She did not tell me *that*,' said the Duke gravely, though his eyes were twinkling. 'I hope I never give her cause to do the same to me.'

'So do I, if it comes to that. But I shall not be the man to stop her if you do. You must know that I would knock you down myself without a second's hesitation if I thought you had hurt her.' The younger man's face was grim, his blue eyes oddly formidable, and his host could have no doubt that he meant exactly what he said.

'I would not blame you. How could I? God knows I have no desire to hurt her, or to see her hurt. I'd marry her tomorrow if I could, and try my best to make her happy. But she has not accepted me, you know. Not explicitly. And she said you would not force her to take me, though I am well aware, as is she, that almost any other brother would insist we wed, after all that has passed between us.'

'I probably should insist upon it. But then, if I was of that cast of mind, we would not be having this conversation, because she'd be married to the other fellow, Hart, by now, and he'd be making her life miserable and doing his best to play ducks and drakes with her fortune into the bargain.'

The Duke's mouth thinned, but he spoke lightly enough. 'Well, I won't do that. Waste her fortune, I mean. Her portion is a matter of complete indifference to me, I hope you are aware, and I will of course make generous settlements, though I doubt that is of any interest to you just now. I trust I shall not make her miserable, either. God knows it is far from being my intention, but I am not sure that is a promise anyone can make when embarking upon a life together, in sober truth.'

Hal regarded him curiously. He said, 'What would you do, if I were the sort of fellow to come the stern paterfamilias and force Georgie to marry you?'

'Take her, damn your eyes for it like a cursed hypocrite, and consider myself lucky to have her,' he answered shortly. 'Worry about everything else later.'

Like his sister on occasion, Hal found that at this moment he could not read his host's face. 'And if, since we have established that I am not the man to force her, she cannot be persuaded, what will you do then?'

'I do not know. It is enough to drive a man mad; it is driving me mad. Irlam, understand me – I do not have the luxury of infinite time at my disposal. Unlike you, I had one younger brother only, and one cousin to inherit Northriding if we both died without male heirs. But they both took mortal injuries at Waterloo – my cousin had in fact joined up in an excess of patriotic fervour without my knowledge, the young idiot. The heirs beyond them – well, it does not bear thinking of. I have a grave responsibility to others than myself; I must marry, and soon. I have already allowed a year to pass when I should not have done, when my duty was clear. But we have had some other family troubles, which I need not burden you with. And now this.'

'I had not realised. You are in the devil of a coil, are you not?' Hal had not thought to find himself feeling sympathy for Northriding, notorious rake and seducer of sisters, but he did now. He was all too familiar with the crushing weight of family responsibilities, having endured plenty himself in the last eight years. And he was exceptionally lucky, he knew, that he did not lack for heirs, but rather the reverse.

'I am, but I cannot – I will not – use the facts of my cursed predicament to put pressure on Georgiana. I have already told her too much of them, and I regret it bitterly. I find I am not always... clever where she is concerned, and say things I would wish to take back the moment the words have left my mouth.'

I remember that feeling, thought Hal. Well do I remember it. Perhaps Louisa is right after all...

He said only, 'I think I will take that glass of wine now, Northriding, if I may.'

'So will I,' said his host. 'More than one, I believe, if you will join me. There are other things I need to tell you, and they will go more easily with a glass of wine.'

27

Lord Irlam did not go to see his sister that night, but upon parting from the Duke in perfect amity made his weary way up to the bedchamber that had been prepared for him, and slept like a log for eight hours. When he arose, he found upon enquiry that the ladies of his family were taking breakfast in their private sitting room, and made his way there.

Miss Spry greeted him in a friendly fashion, and tactfully absented herself just as soon as she could do so without an appearance of discourtesy, leaving the three Pendleburys alone. Georgiana was looking tired, her brother observed, with dark circles under her bright blue eyes and a pinched look about her mouth.

'I'm sorry you were dragged away from Cassandra, Hal, and for such a reason,' she said quietly. 'I know talking pays no toll, but honestly I am.'

'I feel we've been here before, Georgie. I do not mean to ring a peal over you. There's no point, is there? And I'm damnably tired of it, to be brutally plain with you. But I think we have gone past the point where I can rescue you. I see no alternative but marriage, and swiftly.'

Her eyes leapt up to his in pained surprise. 'I did not think you would force me, Hal!'

'But I should not have to. You surely realise the gravity of what you have done. Setting everything else aside – and you have Louisa to thank for the fact that I am prepared to do that – you know that Northriding must marry. That was the whole point of the nightmarish house party he was obliged to host. If you jilt him now, he will find it devilish hard to do so – or at least, I suppose he could go into the common street and find all manner of bold hussies who would be delighted to take him on tomorrow, but not one of them would be the sort of woman he could or should make his Duchess. Unlike you.'

Louisa said, 'I don't think that's quite fair to Georgie…' She fell silent when her nephew shot her such a look as she had never received from him before.

'No, Louisa, I'm afraid it is perfectly fair. I know you're right, Hal,' said Georgiana, looking down, her face pale and drawn. 'Believe me, I do. I said as much to him yesterday, and told him how sorry I was that I had overset all his plans. I did not mean to.'

'You're always sorry, Georgie. Unlike the twins or Fred, you never mean to do it. But it's not enough this time. You can't run away – you have to put it right.'

Her voice was a little cracked, and wobbled as she answered him. 'I do not even know if I can give him the heir he needs so desperately. And then what will I have done to him in all my thoughtlessness?'

'Nobody knows that,' said Louisa. 'It's impossible. He doesn't know if he can either, for that matter, as far as I am aware. You can't worry about that now. You have quite enough to think about without tormenting yourself over things no one can ever give guarantees on.'

'You're right,' she said listlessly again. 'Both of you. I'll go and make myself ready, then find him and tell him I will marry him. I am sure he will be delighted to hear it. Will you come with me? It is better I am not alone with him, for when we are alone you know what happens...' They both nodded without saying anything more, for they had every reason to know, and she stood – she had not touched her breakfast – and left the room, closing the door softly behind her.

Louisa raised her glass and looked at her nephew through it, a question on her lips, and saw to her astonishment that he was smiling broadly now. He winked cheerfully at her. 'Pour me a cup of coffee, would you, Aunt?' he said.

'I suppose you know what you are about?' she said drily as she did so.

'To be honest, I wasn't sure until I opened my mouth whether I was going to command her to marry him unless she wanted to be cast off, or strictly forbid her from doing so. I thought in the end the effect would probably be much the same whatever I said, but I felt sorry for the poor fellow last night, and so I thought this way would be kinder to him. If I'd said I meant to forbid the banns, we'd have had to leave here directly, which would have caused complications. I couldn't be sure just how long it would take her to convince herself she "owed it to him" to elope with him, or some such Drury Lane nonsense, and all the while he'd be fretting himself to a shade over it. Besides, can't have a Pendlebury running off to Gretna, dash it all. Not the done thing. And damned bad roads for it, too, if it comes to that.' He took a gulp of coffee. 'Much less trouble this way, get them safely leg-shackled so they can sort it out between them and leave the rest of us in peace, as you said yourself last night. But d'you think I should have shouted at her like a Dutch uncle, made it more convincing, or would that have been laying it on too thick?'

'You've never shouted at one of the children in your life, Hal, under the worst provocation. This is no time to start.'

'You're probably right. Too late to start coming the stern brother now, you think?'

'Much too late.'

'Pity, but I dare say you're right.'

'I'd say I often am, but all this has taken me completely by surprise, so I shall not. Hush, she is coming. Wipe that foolish grin from your face, Hal, or she will suspect something!'

28

Her brother and her aunt accompanied Georgie downstairs, keeping their faces admirably straight and avoiding catching each other's eyes, and found His Grace busy with his steward. That gentleman took his leave at once, and when the door had closed behind him, Georgiana approached the Duke and said resolutely, 'I will marry you, if you still wish me to.'

He had risen as they entered, and took her hand, raising it to his lips and saying, 'Thank you. I hope... But this is not the time, perhaps, for such discussions.'

Their eyes locked, and though they did not speak or move they appeared to have forgotten that any other persons were present in the room; Hal was obliged to clear his throat to drag their attention away from each other. 'How are we to manage the business?' he asked prosaically. 'I think perhaps you should arrange for a special licence, Northriding – let's not wait three weeks for the banns to be read, shall we?'

'Please, God, no. I don't think I could stand it,' said Louisa to nobody in particular.

'I have, in fact, already sent to obtain one, a day or so ago,' the

Duke said. He met his betrothed's outraged gaze steadily, though his lips twitched, and said blandly, 'I thought it seemed like a useful sort of a thing to have to hand.'

Louisa snorted, and converted it to a cough, but Georgie paid her no heed. 'Is it possible merely to insert the gentleman's name, and leave the lady's blank, to be added at a later date?' she asked sweetly. She felt a spark of anger at his presumption, and welcomed the hot emotion; it was an easier thing to feel than the confusion that otherwise threatened to overwhelm her. 'That would have been excessively convenient for your purposes.'

'Wouldn't it? I don't believe it is, in fact. It seems a sad omission. Perhaps I shall raise the matter next time I speak in the Lords,' he replied with perfect composure. He was so calm, and that annoyed her further, perilously close to tears as she was. 'I imagine it might prove extremely popular.'

'I dare say it would. They are all men, are they not? But I am a woman, and I did not come here in the expectation of being married, so I will need clothes,' Georgie stated, refusing to succumb to his teasing and soften towards him. Did she even want to? She wasn't sure.

'Are you quite positive you shall?' he shot back outrageously in a low tone meant for her ears only. She coloured, and glared at him once more, but he did not seem to be in the least abashed. A little silence grew between them, stretched. He knows, she thought, that he can always win me over; even now, if we were left alone, he'd reach out, touch me, and I would welcome it with pathetic eagerness... But the power of the physical pull between us is not in question. It's everything else that is so difficult.

'We will be obliged to draw up marriage settlements without loss of time,' Lord Irlam ploughed on heroically. 'I have a lawyer in York now – it's been useful, with all the tangled affairs of my wife's estate. I presume you do too, Northriding?'

'Naturally,' said the Duke urbanely. 'I have business all over the North. And call me Gabriel, please, as we are to be brothers. Perhaps we could repair there in a couple of days, and I am sure, Georgiana, you will be able to find anything you feel you require in the way of trousseau. You will all be welcome as my guests – I have a house hard by the Minster which is most convenient.'

Georgie could only nod and attempt a smile. She fell silent now as her future – hers – was discussed. She had no objection to raise. She'd said she'd marry him, hadn't she? It would be weak and childish, she thought with sudden piercing clarity, to blame others – Hal, Louisa, Gabriel himself – for this situation she found herself in, to say that she was being forced. She wasn't. She must admit that a part of her, not just her body that always yearned for him but perhaps also her heart, urgently wanted this. If only she weren't so frightened – of her own feelings, as much as anything else. And as for his feelings... She had every reason to know that he was obsessed with her. He'd convinced her of the truth of that. What she could not know was whether it could possibly be enough to base a life upon.

'Oh, and call me Hal, naturally. Quite right. York races?' asked Hal with interest, though Georgie at least barely heard or heeded him.

'Of course. Not at this time of year, sadly. Next month.' If the Duke felt any fraction of her inner turmoil, he did not show it.

'Dashed nuisance, that. Could have combined the two things, you know.'

'That's all very well,' objected Louisa, with a brief roll of the eyes at the propensity of men to be distracted by inessentials, 'but must we all decamp to York then come back here again directly for the ceremony? It sounds most fatiguing and unnecessary. Could you not simply marry there, perhaps in the Minster itself?'

'I am sure it could be arranged without too much trouble,' said the Duke of Northriding drily. 'Many of my ancestors have married there in the past.'

'My wife can travel down from Skipton, then, to be with us,' said Hal. 'My brother Bastian is with her there, and will come too, I dare say. Make it a regular family affair, as is only proper, Gabriel. But I am *not* summoning the younger boys up from Hampshire. Well do I remember the chaos they caused in the days before my own wedding.'

'Thank God,' said Louisa. 'They are perfectly happy where they are, and Cousin Leo has charge of them and is – one hopes – keeping them out of trouble. If he can manage a ship full of rowdy sailors, presumably he can manage the three of them. Leave them be.'

Hal explained to his host, 'My late mother's sister, Mrs Winterton, is with my three youngest brothers at our home in Hampshire. Her son is a captain in the navy, and has been teaching them sailing this summer, heaven help him. Yes, we can well do without them, believe me. You don't understand why yet, but you will soon enough, I promise you.'

'I look forward to meeting them another time, of course,' His Grace said politely.

'"Ignorance is bliss",' Louisa said darkly. 'I recommend you put off that date as long as you are able. A year or so should do very well.'

'I suppose,' said Hal suddenly, 'that I should congratulate you both! Wish you very happy! Remiss of me not to, and forgive me for it, but the circumstances, you know...'

'Indeed,' said the Duke with an admirably straight face, 'it is perfectly understandable that you should forget. Thank you!'

Georgiana came out of her reverie with a start and murmured her thanks too, glad to have the conversation turn to less awkward matters. Upon discussion, in which again she took little part, it was thought sensible for the entire party to adjourn to York upon the following day, so that they could lose no time in setting about the various pieces of business that took them there.

The preparations for this hasty departure involved a great deal of bustle, and as a result Georgie saw very little of the Duke in the intervening hours, and they were not given any opportunity to be alone for the rest of the day. This rather unfortunately allowed her a great deal of time to brood upon her situation, but lessened her painful confusion not one jot, since there did not seem to be any conclusion that could usefully be reached, or if there were one, she did not reach it. As the day passed she became aware of a growing need, a compulsion almost, to be with him, to be held by him, even just to speak with him: a foretaste, she thought, and an unwelcome one, of what her future might so easily be, yearning for his company. She was in a sorry state, and chided herself for it. She knew he was busy, and she knew why; if nothing else, her pride would not allow her to seek him out. It was not until after dinner that they had the chance to exchange as much as two words, and that in public.

'Does your house in York also have secret stairs and passages?' she said with unconscious wistfulness as he bent over her hand to bid her goodnight. Just at that moment Hal was deep in sporting conversation with Mr FitzHenry, and the ladies were engaged in a civil but intense discussion over the best places to shop for fashionable apparel in York; Miss FitzHenry was decidedly of one mind, and her mother quite another.

'Naturally it has secret stairs and passages, as well as any number of priests' holes,' he said gravely. 'No Mauleverer would ever consent to reside anywhere that did not. We had to have them specially installed at great expense in Grosvenor Square when we bought the house. And in York they did not serve just for romantic intrigues, important though they undoubtedly are, but for much darker purposes. Guy Fawkes was a connection of the family, you know, and on many occasions one or more of us was in imminent danger of ending up with our severed heads displayed on Micklegate Bar.'

She shuddered at the thought. 'Such a rebellious history. Did your relatives go on to be Jacobites, then?' she asked curiously. She knew so very little about him, about his family, and this at least could easily be remedied, and might serve to calm her a little.

'It is a reasonable question. My grandfather was of that party, I believe, though it has not been talked of much in the family. He managed to keep his head and his possessions through his father's influence, my great-grandfather fortunately still being alive at the time of the '45 rebellion. The Sixth Duke was a man of great address and pragmatism, while his son at that point was very young and foolish, and came close to losing everything through his romantic enthusiasms. But we learned our lesson, changed even our religion at last to conform with the times, and have been stout supporters of the Hanoverians ever since. Although that does violence to one's feelings sometimes, with Prinny at the helm. He is shockingly bad ton even by my standards, I am sure you must agree.'

She had strong opinions of her own on the subject, and would have like to prolong the discussion, to remain in his company, but Louisa swept her off to bed. Georgie supposed that there would be time enough in the future to talk of such matters – they would have a whole life together in which to do so. It was a strange idea, and hard to encompass in her mind. She thought she would not truly believe that she was indeed to marry Gabriel, as she must learn to call him, until she stood at the altar with him, or perhaps later...

They left the Castle early the next morning: two travelling carriages for the ladies and their abigails, Hal in his curricle, and the Duke driving his own sporting vehicle and team of famous greys. Louisa expressed the hope that they would not engage in a childish sort of a race, as men were prone to do, so foolishly competitive as they were, but as Miss Spry wisely said, if that was their inclination there was nothing any of the ladies could do to stop them. When the slower coaches arrived at the respectable inn where it had been agreed they would meet to take nuncheon, the gentlemen were found toasting each other amicably in tankards of ale; it seemed there had indeed been a race, and His Grace had won it. 'I had perhaps an unfair advantage, as I know the roads so well,' he said with a deprecating smile. In some mysterious masculine fashion, the contest appeared to have cemented the bond between them, and the two men seemed to have resolved to be fast friends, despite the undeniably awkward circumstances of their meeting, which Hal at least seemed to be well on the way to forgetting.

After they had eaten, they set out again. The ladies' carriages kept pace with each other, and Lord Irlam slowed to stay with them, but Gabriel drove ahead to ensure that his house in Petergate would be ready to receive his family and guests.

It was late afternoon by the time the Pendleburys entered the city through the imposing turreted barrier of Monk Bar – Georgie craned her neck to look for severed heads, but not a one was to be seen – and made their slow way through the narrow, crowded streets to the Mauleverer mansion. The housekeeper and many of the indoor servants came to meet them, and Georgie could not help but blush, as she was well aware that they must know she was their master's intended bride, and as a result regarded her with a great deal of frank Yorkshire curiosity. Nobody was in any way discourteous, and she could not blame them for their interest; she supposed she would be obliged to accustom herself to it, as to so many things in her new life.

The house was quite large, though of course much smaller than the Castle, three red-brick storeys high, and of a symmetrical, modern appearance from outside, with an imposing stuccoed portico sheltering the door. Georgie knew from what Gabriel had said, however, that this classically regular façade concealed a much older, partly medieval building, and had stables and other outbuildings not visible from the street, all of which had been extensively remodelled by the previous Duke and his favourite architect John Carr many years previously.

She was shown to a fine panelled bedchamber with its own private sitting room furnished in costly silks and precious carpets; she thought it was probably the Duchess's suite of rooms that had been prepared for her, so grand as it was, and she wondered if one of the doors led to where Gabriel slept. She dared not explore. The thought of him so close must set images moving in her head that made her blush and bite her lip even though she was alone: images of things they had done, pleasures they had tasted, and things they had not done, yet. She wondered too if the door would remain firmly closed, or whether her prospective husband would be impatient and think to anticipate their marriage vows. She was herself unsure whether she wanted to anticipate them or wait until convention called it decent – more than decent, necessary, vital, a matter of obligation rather than mere carnal desire. It seemed a foolish and arbitrary distinction: sin one day, duty the next. She also knew, more strongly with every passing day, that she sought more than sensual pleasure from his embraces, and that to have him here holding her would bring her a deeper comfort than simple physical release, and soothe, at least for a while, her roiling thoughts.

But that night, at least, she remained alone in the high four-poster bed. She lay in the darkness in her virginal nightgown and let her hands drift down her body as she thought of him, and despite all her fears and ever-present uncertainty she could not deny the treacherous little spark of excitement that had been kindled deep inside her when they first met, and that would flare to a flame with a word, a look from him. If he came to her now to claim her... But he did not, and she slid into sleep, to dream of him and wake unsatisfied.

Bastian, and Hal's wife Cassandra – tiny, red-haired and green-eyed – arrived from Skipton the next afternoon, much to her husband's delight; one would have thought, Louisa observed, that they had been separated for a month rather than a day or two. The succeeding week was a whirl of activity, which combined visits to dressmakers with the signing of legal documents, and much consultation with the officials of the Minster. As His Grace had slightly cynically predicted, these gentlemen were delighted to be asked to conduct the wedding of one of the senior noblemen of the North. There would be a choir, and all the ceremony of which the Church of England was capable at a few days' notice.

There was little opportunity to talk privately with her sister-in-law – when the gentlemen withdrew, Lady Blanche was always there, and her daughter, not to mention Louisa and Miss Spry, that lady only imperfectly concealing her impatience to return to London and advance her own affairs. Cassandra was accompanied by Kitty, who was both her own maid and Georgiana's former nurse, and Georgie had thought that one or both of them might take her aside and ask her how she felt about the enormous change that was about to overtake her life and set her on a new path. She was half-expecting to be questioned particularly on her feelings for the Duke, by Kitty if not by Cassandra, but rather curiously she encountered no such interrogation, and she was glad of it, for she had at this delicate moment no desire to examine her emotions more deeply than she was obliged to. The questions she anticipated never came, and in the bustle of preparations she did not have time to stop and ask herself why. What Hal said to Cassandra or even to Kitty in private, of course, she could not know.

Despite the Duke's words, Georgie could see no evidence of secret stairs and passages in the mansion in Petergate. The formal rooms at the front of the house, the dining and withdrawing rooms, all presented a modern appearance, consistent with the aspect it presented to the street, and apart from her bedchamber she had not yet penetrated to the family's private quarters. In any case, whether there were indeed passages or whether he had been teasing her, she received no nocturnal visits in those days before her wedding. Perhaps, she thought, he was constrained by considerations of propriety or merely of good taste, now that his family and a great part of hers were gathered together in such proximity, for the house was inevitably crowded with so many visitors. For a while she told herself that she was unsure if she wanted him to come to her in secret or not, and when upon reflection honesty compelled her to admit that she did want it, that she desperately missed being alone with him, missed his conversation just as much as his touch, she resolutely pushed away the idea, and refused to dwell on its implications. There was, she told herself, no need to brood over the matter. They would be married soon enough.

But still she lay awake each night for a while, waiting, thinking of him and wondering if he was thinking of her, lying just a few feet away in his own lonely bed. She wondered if his imagination was running riot, if his hands, too, sought a sweet release he would rather have gained from touching her, from her touching him... She tried very hard not to wonder if he might ever want more than that from her, if he were open to such feelings, or would even acknowledge them if they came. He'd known so many women intimately, or so she had heard, though she knew frustratingly little detail of his apparently scandalous past. All those women... Had he ever loved one of them? Been faithful, even for a while? Such thoughts were not conducive to restful sleep, she found.

There was little time for introspection or serious conversation with anyone in that hectic week, but one afternoon, when it happened for a wonder not to be raining and no appointments presented themselves for an hour or so, Georgiana's brother Bastian told her very firmly that she must put on her bonnet and pelisse and come out for a walk with him. They would explore the interesting ruins of St Mary's Abbey, he said; it would be a crime not to do so when they stood just a few hundred yards away from the house, and furthermore he expected that some air would do her good. She agreed that it would, and they set out, passing the glorious façade of the Minster on their way, before anybody could stop them or find some urgent matter that required her instant attention.

They were a handsome pair, very alike, with the glossy black hair and shockingly bright blue eyes that characterised all the Pendleburys. They attracted a good deal of attention as they made their way towards the Abbey, and Georgiana was a little surprised to be greeted warmly, by name and title, by several persons of all ranks as they walked. She smiled at them all, and made the appropriate responses, but she did not stop.

When they had admired the impressive remains of walls, windows and doorways, and wandered under the ivy-covered arches for a while, Bastian said, 'I am glad to have seen it, of course – Matthew told me I should on no account neglect to do so – but what I really wanted, Georgie, was an opportunity to talk with you alone.'

This could hardly be news to his sister, and she thought she knew what he was about to ask her. She supposed it was inevitable that someone would, after all, though she had not expected it to be

Bastian. 'Do you truly want to marry Northriding?' he said now, frowning. 'Something my aunt said in passing the other evening made me think that Hal is in some sense forcing you, though I could scarcely believe it of him, and indeed he laughed the idea off as nonsense when I charged him with it. But I could not be easy in my mind until I had spoken to you and made sure. What in the devil's name is going on?'

'I… It is complicated, Bastian. Hal is not forcing me, precisely. He did point out to me that I must marry Gabriel, that I owed it to him after my recent actions and their consequences, but in truth he was not telling me anything that I did not already know.'

'My God, Georgie, are you with child? Has he—?'

She cut him off, with a wry smile at the sudden recollection of Hal asking her the same question a year ago, during her entanglement with Captain Hart. It was not entirely flattering to be the object of such repeated enquiries; nor was it entirely unjust. She had not been quite so reckless, not quite, but she had come perilously close, and she feared that any self-control that had been exercised in recent days had been on the Duke's part and not hers. If he had come to her bed here in York, would she really have turned him away, or denied him anything? She knew the answer.

'I am not with child, and I promise you he has done nothing to me against my will, nor has he hurt me or offended me in any way. But it is true that I am compromised – Gabriel and I were discovered in a highly awkward situation, by Louisa and Jane, and more to the point by others who do not wish me well, and he had no option then but to announce our engagement.'

'That does not mean that you must go through with it,' Bastian said hotly. 'I am surprised at Hal, and sadly disappointed in him too. I did not think he was a man to place the proprieties above his sister's happiness. You know he has never shown such petty concerns before. He has been nothing but understanding where my own situation is concerned, and has accepted Matthew without question, when not another brother in a hundred would have done so, but would instead have cast me out and forbidden mention of my name. Is it because you are a woman? Because if so, I am—'

'You do him an injustice,' Georgie said swiftly. 'The matter is more complicated than you know. What has passed between Gabriel and me is only the half of it, though I know that for almost any other guardian it would be more than enough. It is not that at all, Basty. Gabriel is obliged to marry, to secure an heir now that his younger brother and his cousin are dead. The next heirs are quite ineligible, and the future of his estate and all its people depends on him siring a son. And through my foolishness I have made it almost impossible for him to win another bride of suitable birth and breeding.' She saw the doubt still lingering on his sweet, loving face and went on urgently, 'You must see the truth of this. He announced our betrothal to half the noble families of the North at his family's grand ball; he had no option because of the compromising situation in which we were discovered. And if I jilted him now, what would people say? His reputation is bad enough without that. Hal says that in common decency I cannot do it to him, and he is quite right.'

'He gained his bad reputation over many years, and quite without your help! And if you behaved improperly, so did he, and he is a man of great experience, and a good deal older than you! I do not like to see you made a sacrifice of, even if you have been foolish. We all do foolish things, but are not made to suffer such lifelong consequences for them.'

Georgie laughed. 'Most people would stare to hear you say that marrying one of the most eligible men in the country made me a sacrifice of any kind.'

'We are not most people! You have no need to marry for wealth and social standing, thank God, and when have we ever truly cared what people thought of us?'

'Have you not been listening? It is not a matter of reputation, of what strangers think, but of taking responsibility for my own actions at last. I owe this to Gabriel, and as for compromising me, he had already asked me to marry him once before we were... surprised in each other's arms.'

'And you refused him? And still he forced his attentions on you? Good God, Georgie, I begin to think his reputation is not near as bad as it should be!'

'He forced nothing on me, Basty, I promise. He never has.' She sighed, and set out to spell out something of the true nature of her situation once more. 'When we are alone together, we cannot seem to prevent ourselves from... from giving way to passion. It is a sort of madness that possesses both of us. So in the end it must be for the best that I marry him. If I am honest with myself, and I am trying very hard to be, I simply cannot endure that he marries another, even if someone suitable could indeed be found. I would suffer the fiercest torments of jealousy if he so much as glanced at another woman; I know, because I already have before we were betrothed, when he was obliged to court another because I had refused him. I hated it! And you must see that it would certainly be unwise for me to wed another man, when he has only to look at me and I lose all sense. I think, I fear, that if I married someone else, or he did, and if he came to me after and asked me to run away with him, I would go. No – speaking of it now, I know I would, without hesitation. And I am quite sure he feels the same. So if this, this spark that is between us is unique to us, and endures, very well. We may have a chance of happiness. If it is not, if it has revealed some defect in my character, then better I am married, I suppose, to a man who has no illusions about my nature, before some other worse disaster overtakes me. I only hope I can indeed give him the son he needs.'

'You make no mention of love,' her brother said tentatively.

'I do not, and nor does he. And I beg you will not, Sebastian. Seriously, please don't. I couldn't bear it.'

He took her hand, and squeezed it warmly. 'I think I understand. When did life become so complicated, Georgie?'

'When Papa and then Mama died, I think.'

'You must be right. Oh, my dear, I wish I could help you. I hope...'

'I know. Let us not talk of it any more. We should go back, for I am sure there must be a thousand things still to be done.'

Bastian was still troubled in his mind, but he accepted Georgie's evident wish to turn the subject, tucking her arm through his and leading her back towards the busy streets of the old city, and the uncertain future that awaited her.

29

A day or so earlier, a most curious and – if anyone concerned had known of it – excessively disturbing scene had taken place in a rented house on the edge of fashionable London.

A lady in her thirties was sitting over breakfast, wrapped in a lace peignoir of scandalous design. The vision of her ample charms thus revealed was, however, wasted on the gentleman opposite her at the table, or one would hope so, for he was quite plainly her brother, half-brother, or some other close male relative: they were both handsome, if a little dissolute in appearance, with glossy chestnut-brown hair and wicked dark eyes. She looked clever, though he perhaps did not; they neither of them looked kind. The boudoir in which they sat was sadly disordered, with piles of feminine clothing intermixed with trinkets and what appeared to be a large number of unpaid bills. The pair seemed inured to the chaos around them, and the gentleman addressed himself in silence to a large tankard, while the lady flicked through her correspondence in a desultory fashion. But presently she chanced upon something that interested her enormously, and as she read on, she sat up straighter, her fine black eyes flashing with concentration, her dark brows furrowed. Her companion was oblivious to her change in attitude, until she said, in a voice rich with triumph, 'Adolphus, put down your ale and listen to me. I believe I have discovered something that may change our fortunes at last!'

'Well, I'd like to hear it, though I can't imagine what it might be. I think we're at point non plus, myself, and it'll be the sponging house for us next,' he said, without any noticeable signs of excitement.

'You're wrong! Only listen to this from Fanny Trent... No, it is too long to read to you, for she is such a rattlepate it is a wonder nobody has throttled her yet. In any event, shorn of all her nonsense, she tells me that she met Selina Debenham and that sour-faced daughter of hers at a posting house somewhere or other on the Great North Road – it does not signify where...'

'Really?' he replied in accents heavy with sarcasm. 'Selina Debenham, you say? At a posting house? How fascinating! And you call your blasted friend, whatever her name is, a rattlepate!'

'Only listen! Selina was in a towering rage, Fanny says, because she'd dragged the whole family up to Northriding Castle in the hopes of snaring the Duke for the girl.' She saw he was about to interrupt again, and held up her hand. 'You will understand all presently if you will only be patient and listen for a moment. Selina failed in her scheme, and that is what made her mad as fire. She could not help but tell Fanny that Northriding has this very week announced his engagement, at some dreary provincial ball he held and she attended. And the woman he is marrying, my dear brother, is someone you know very well indeed. It is Lady Georgiana Pendlebury! What do you think of *that*?'

Captain Hart had been swigging his ale as she spoke, and now he choked on it, and his sister was obliged to pound him on the back, which she did in an impatient and ungentle fashion. It was a while before he recovered himself enough to speak. 'Georgie!' he croaked. 'Dammit, Caro, you should know not to spring her name on me like that! A fellow has feelings, you know.'

'Feelings!' she scoffed. 'It's her eighty thousand pounds you had feelings for, Adolphus Hart!'

He acknowledged that there was some truth in this, but added wistfully, 'She was a fine piece, though, sis! Marriage to her would have been no kind of hardship, setting aside the fortune. I was always sorry I never managed to persuade the minx to...'

'Never mind that now. I presume you still have a score to settle with her, after the atrocious way she treated you?'

Hart's fingers went unconsciously to his right temple, where he still bore the scar which Lady Georgiana had inflicted on him with a poker the last time they met. That she had been protecting herself from crude and unwelcome advances on his part was, naturally, not something that was very likely to occur to him. And he had been humiliated, too – knocked down in the dirt by a slip of a girl. It was not to be thought of, but he found that he did quite often think of it, and the memory, along with the wound, had festered. He swore now at the recollection. 'I'll damned well say I do!' he replied with some heat.

'Well, there is no denying that my last scheme to pay her back and put her in your power again did not work as well as I hoped,' said Mrs Aubrey, 'and you must take the blame for that, for I lured her to that house just as I promised, and it is not my fault you failed to take advantage of it!'

'I've told you a hundred times,' her fond sibling replied between gritted teeth, 'I could not see hide nor hair of the chit when I got inside. I searched the whole place from top to bottom, opened every door I could, and saw some damned interesting sights, including you, my dear sister, in a situation I could have well done without laying eyes on, but her I could not find.'

'We know why now, don't we?' Caroline said, with barely concealed impatience. 'You may not have been attending – perhaps you were drunk – but my dear friend Lucienne told me not a sennight ago that she saw the Pendlebury girl, who I had previously pointed out to her, going into a private room with some man who must have approached her, and emerging from it with him some considerable time later. Lucienne said it was quite plain from her demeanour just exactly what they had been about – and you must admit she would know if anyone would.'

Captain Hart did not quibble with this; he was too well acquainted with the lady in question. 'But you don't know who the fellow was, do you? You'd think your Lucienne could describe a man she saw twice, but apparently not. Perhaps *she* was drunk! I shouldn't wonder at it.'

His sister brushed this aside. 'She saw him only for a moment on each occasion, she did not get a good look at his face, and was in any case not particularly attending, as why should she be? She noticed only that he was tall, dark-haired, and well-dressed, and held the girl very firmly by the hand.'

'I dare say!' said the Captain coarsely. 'Don't suppose it's all he held her by, if your precious friend is right. Lucky devil.'

'And that is very much to the point. I could do nothing before – the chit thought she had me at an impasse, and she did, damn her, when she threatened to expose my role in her going there, as well as what I carelessly let her see of my activities. I admit that was a mistake on my part. But now, now things are different, thanks to Lucienne and also to today's news.'

'How so?' said her brother.

Mrs Aubrey sighed. She was, of course, fond of her only half-brother – was she not exerting herself even now to right the wrong that had been done him last year by the Pendlebury family? – but she admitted privately that he was often a trial to her, as there could be no doubt that he had not been handed his fair share of the family's brains at birth. If *she* had been present and directing matters in Brighton last summer when he had been in pursuit of his little heiress, he would not have made such a mull of the affair, and now would be wed to her and in happy possession of her extremely desirable fortune. No doubt Mrs Aubrey too would have had a share of that great bounty, as would have been only fair. It was regrettable, all that they had lost, but she was a gamester with a reckless streak, not a woman to dwell on the past, and it seemed to her that the future held new promise now. So she stifled her exasperation, and explained, 'We know that the girl visited a house of most dubious reputation...'

'You engineered that,' the Captain put in. No doubt he thought he was being helpful.

'That doesn't matter any more, Adolphus,' she said, with exaggerated patience. 'Because we now also know that, instead of leaving immediately, as any innocent should if she found herself in such a place because of another's trickery, she stayed, and went apart with some stranger, and stayed a long while with him in a private room. While we do not know what occurred there, I think we can imagine.'

'Damn right we can!' said her brother, his eyes bulging slightly. 'I suppose he might have forced himself on her,' he added thoughtfully, with no particular appearance of concern for one who had once been the woman he intended to spend his life with.

'That doesn't matter either.' Indeed, to Mrs Aubrey, it did not. 'Whether she was forced or went willingly, she is irrevocably compromised. And now that she is betrothed to the Duke, we can make use of it.'

'Terrible reputation, Northriding,' said Hart sapiently.

'I dare say. But who cares for that, when a man is as wealthy as he is? Such a great prize – I am sure she thinks she has done very well in snaring him, and is excessively glad she did not throw herself away on a penniless nobody like you! No, she is to be a duchess! The whole pack of them must be delighted, especially after the dance she led them last year. They were almost forced to welcome Captain Hart into the fold with an appearance of complaisance, but now they will be allied with one of the oldest and richest families in England.'

'When you put it like that, it does seem damned unfair.'

'Of course it is. But however much of a rake Northriding might be, I am sure he would not take a woman with a past as his bride, and such a past. An affair of the heart he might forgive perhaps, if he is taken with her, but to marry a woman so reckless that she went to that house, and met a stranger there, and... Well, I need not say more, need I? Men are such hypocrites where a woman's reputation is concerned,' said Mrs Aubrey. She had a great deal of bitter experience to back up her words, and they rang with conviction. 'He would worry that she might foist any passing stranger's brats upon him and swear they were his. These old families are terribly proud, it is well known, and obsessed with the purity of their lineage. So I expect that Lady Georgiana would pay a great deal, a very great deal – and not only in gold, Adolphus, I am sure – to have us keep her secret, so that she may still marry her precious Duke and take her position at his side.'

'Not only in gold...' said Hart slowly. She perceived that he understood her at last. To give him his credit, he was slow, but sure. 'She is damaged goods already, so it cannot matter to her in the least what she gives me. I care for the money, naturally – I feel we have a right to it – but much more than that I will be very glad to have the opportunity of paying her back, the little vixen. You see if I do not make her suffer for what she did to me. You may rely on me for that. And if I can foist a brat of mine on Northriding as his precious heir, why, so much the better. That would be a pretty revenge indeed. Caro, you're a genius!'

'I know I am,' said Mrs Aubrey. 'I never had the least doubt of it.'

30

Ignorant of these schemes to do her grave injury, Georgiana stood in silk and lace before the altar in the cathedral of the North and took Gabriel to be her lawfully wedded husband. Hal gave her away, and Cassandra and Miss FitzHenry were her matron of honour and bridesmaid. Hymns were sung by small boys with angelic voices, and a surely superfluous number of clergymen in their best robes officiated. Nobody would ever be able to say later that the Ninth Duke and his bride were anything other than legally bound one to the other. Half the inhabitants of York and a fair number of fortunate visitors had crowded in to witness the spectacle; the cavernous building was large enough to receive them all with room to spare. Small girls threw rose petals, and all the ladies present cried, apart from the bride herself, who smiled mechanically or looked suitably serious at the appropriate moments and felt numb through it all, as though someone other than Georgiana Pendlebury were participating in the ceremony. The Minster was populated by a great number of stone statues, silent witness to the important event taking place beside and below them, and Georgie felt herself to be one of them, rather than a living, breathing woman. It was possible, she thought in a disinterested fashion, that she was behaving slightly oddly, for she could not help but see that her brothers and her aunt occasionally shot worried blue glances at her, and at each other.

She endured the ceremony in some type of trance, and in a trance received the congratulations of her family, and of the assembled strangers of all ranks of society. Her daze took her through the crowded streets – the distance to the house in Petergate was too short to require that carriages should be brought up, and it was barely raining at all – and up to the steps of the mansion, where the assembled servants awaited them with beaming faces and hearty congratulations.

It is possible that the new Duchess would have floated through the rest of the day in this peculiarly detached state of mind, had not a disturbance before the doors of her new home caused her preternatural calm to crack, and then to shatter into a thousand pieces.

A small crowd had gathered outside the building to see the newlyweds enter. Among them was a most respectable-seeming couple in their middle years, and a young lady who appeared to be their daughter, for she resembled the older lady greatly in her honey-blonde prettiness. The couple seemed embarrassed, or in some other manner distressed, and plainly they were attempting to persuade the young lady to quit the place in some haste and come away, but she refused, growing visibly agitated, and it could be seen that in fact tears were pouring unheeded down her pale cheeks. Georgie's attention was drawn most particularly to the group when she heard Lady Blanche exclaim, in low but deeply anxious tones, 'Good God, Gabriel, it is Isabella and her parents! What can they possibly be doing here, and on such a day?'

The last of her detachment deserted her when she saw her new husband's demeanour change as he took in the sight; he was always pale, but she could have sworn she saw sweat break out on his brow, and an expression almost of horror cross his face. It was a fleeting impression, and then it was gone, and he assumed a masklike appearance. He was silent for a pregnant moment, and then he said, 'We must greet them, Blanche – ask them to come in and join us. They are family, after all.'

'I suppose we must,' said his sister, moving forward and saying in tones of welcome that rang entirely false in Georgie's ears, 'Lady Ash – Isabella, my dear sister – Mr and Mrs Richmond! What a surprise to see you, but how fortunate! You find us celebrating my brother's marriage; we are just come from the Minster this instant. Duchess, may I present to you my dear sister-in-law and yours too, Lady Ashby, and her parents, Mrs Richmond, Mr Richmond, from Harrogate?'

Georgiana gathered her wits together and said all that was proper, and the Richmonds bowed and curtseyed, and pressed somewhat incoherent congratulations upon her. They had not had the least idea – they were so sorry to intrude – such a happy day. All this was to little effect, as their daughter paid not the least attention to any remark addressed to her, but continued to stand silent beside them, tears still running unheeded down her face, staring at the newlywed couple with an expression something akin to horror. She was suddenly possessed by a strong conviction that Lady Ashby was about to fall in a dead swoon at her feet, and she thought that Blanche was aware of it too, for she became urgent in her insistence that the trio come inside and made themselves comfortable. Surely they would at least take a glass of wine? But the Richmonds were equally firm in their refusal to do so; they could not possibly intrude on such an occasion, they said. They did not mean to be discourteous, but they hoped that Lady Blanche and the Duchess would understand that they must instantly return to their inn, as their daughter had sadly overexerted herself in walking about and was somewhat unwell. Gabriel gave some almost imperceptible sign to his sister, and she shot him a glance of complete comprehension, then drew the little family away, taking Lady Ashby's right arm firmly in hers as Miss FitzHenry took the left. The Richmonds followed helplessly behind in their wake.

A small, uncomfortable silence threatened to develop, but it was mercifully broken by Lord Irlam, who suggested in a practical fashion that they ceased standing about in the street like so many stocks for people to gape at, but instead went inside, for the rain was coming on stronger every second.

Before Georgie well realised what he was about, the Duke lifted her into his strong arms and carried her across the threshold, to the cheers of the household. A moment later she found herself alone with him, in a room she had never entered before but which she supposed to be his study. He was still looking white and shaken, and said, 'Well, that was an edifying spectacle to grace our wedding day. Take off your wet things, Georgie, and I will explain. I fear it is not a pretty tale.'

31

'I had no idea that your brother was married,' Georgiana said blankly, as she struggled to undo her damp pelisse with stiff, cold fingers that did not want to obey her. 'Nobody has ever so much as mentioned the fact, or named his wife, his widow, in conversation.'

Her husband came to help her, and once done drew her close to the fire that burned in the grate, and urged her to sit. 'I do not suppose we have. Ash had been married for a little less than a year when he died,' he said in expressionless tones. 'He was wounded in a skirmish before Toulouse, and came home to recuperate; he met Isabella Richmond in Harrogate, fell deeply in love with her, and they married quickly. They were very happy together in the short time they had. They lived at the Castle while he recovered from his injury – they had their own apartments – but of course when Bonaparte escaped from Elba, my brother was obliged to return to service. I asked him not to go, said he had done his duty and more already, begged him to think of Isabella too, but he would not listen to me. He'd always been damnably stubborn; we all are. Isabella found she could not endure to be parted from him, and of course in the peculiar circumstances of last year there was no need for it; her parents travelled out to Belgium to be with her. And thank God they did. They were in Brussels at the time of Waterloo.'

Georgie thought she might have an inkling of what Gabriel was trying to tell her. 'She saw...?'

'After the battle, poor Ash lay on the field alone and in agony for a night – it pains me greatly to think of it, and his wife's anxiety at that time can only be imagined – but when he was at last found and identified he was brought to her lodgings, very gravely wounded, and died in her arms a short while later. There was no chance that he could have survived such an injury. My cousin was taken there too, and she and her mother did their best – I imagine it was chiefly her mother, poor lady, for Isabella was in a state of collapse by then, I am told – to nurse him, but he too died a few weeks later.

'I travelled out to Belgium as soon as I realised that my cousin John had signed up upon some foolish patriotic impulse. He was no kind of soldier, he was just an impulsive boy. I was there for his death, though not in time to see my brother alive again. It was... a difficult period for all of us.'

She reached out instinctively to him, and he took her cold hand in his. 'I am afraid there is more, and when I have told you all perhaps you will understand why I have waited until now to marry. The Richmonds brought Isabella back to Yorkshire at last, with my assistance. They thought it best they take her home to Harrogate – the Castle was full of painful recollections, and my presence was in no sense a help.'

'Do you resemble your brother so much?'

'I did not think so, in all truth, but we were close enough in age, he was just two years younger, and certainly the similarity was enough to cause her distress, as you saw for yourself today. I suppose it is that, and also perhaps the fact that a worthless fellow like me is still alive – is married, now – while poor Ash is dead and in his grave. But in any case, after a few weeks had gone by Mrs Richmond wrote to me and told me that Isabella was with child. *Said* she was with child, perhaps I should say, for that is how her mother put it.

'I think you must be able to divine the confusion of my feelings. We were all happy for her, and hoped that the news would give her reason to live, and time to rebuild her shattered life and look to the future once more. And for our part... Not just the possibility of an heir when we had thought that chance entirely gone – that was a great deal in itself – but that something of my brother should survive. To see a child of his growing up and taking his place as my heir... Of course I was uneasy, we all were: Isabella had been very ill, and to think that everything should rest on such a fragile hope. It was almost a form of torture as the months passed, I found...' He trailed off, and passed his hand over his face.

'She lost the child?'

'I am not sure there ever really was a child. Her mother certainly believes that there was not. She began to suspect as much as time passed, and around Christmastime at last she felt obliged to speak to Isabella on the subject, despite her natural reluctance to do so. Mrs Richmond meant well, and I do not see what else she could have done in the circumstances. She felt that her daughter could not be allowed to live in delusion indefinitely, that it was unhealthy to allow it to continue. The result of her intervention, though, was that Isabella collapsed entirely, and for a long time her reason and even her life were despaired of. She has been under the care of a medical gentleman here in York for several months; they make a speciality of such afflictions here, using the most modern and humane methods. I would have gone to visit her, as would Blanche, but it was thought best by her physician that we did not do so, as it might give her pain. She has been better lately, we were told, and evidently now has been discharged from medical supervision. I cannot think that her parents brought her by the house against her will, for they have always been most careful of her wellbeing. I can only imagine that she must have expressed a wish to visit us, or just to see the place where she stayed with Ash on her honeymoon. Perhaps they thought it progress, and were glad of it.' He smiled bleakly. 'It did not look like progress to me; did it to you?'

'No,' she said quietly.

'I am sorry,' he said at last, 'that you were subjected to such an encounter on your wedding day. I wish I could have spared you that.'

'It's not your fault,' she answered with conviction. 'Poor lady, her poor family. It was just an unfortunate coincidence that they should be passing at that moment among all others. How could you predict it?'

'I wrote to them,' he said. 'I did so as soon as we arrived here. I thought they should know I was to be married, rather than hear it from strangers, when if things had turned out otherwise their daughter might have been Duchess of Northriding one day. I owed them that. It has always preyed on my mind: the fact that news of my marriage could not be kept from her for ever, and would undoubtedly cause her distress. It is one reason among many that I delayed seeking a bride till now. Perhaps you can understand why I did not have the heart for any of it for a long time, though I knew in the end I must do so. It was not by any means an easy letter to write to her parents, though I knew that they at least would understand my situation. But I directed the letter to their home in Harrogate; I did not know they were here.'

'How could you?'

'I suppose you're right. But I should have told you of Isabella's existence before. The shock to you would not then have been so great.'

'I do not suppose the whole tragic tale is something you enjoy recalling.'

'It is not.' He smiled a little more naturally this time. 'Thank you for listening and uttering no reproaches. Enough of such sadness, on this day of all days. What would you like to do now, my dear? I am entirely at your disposal.'

She rose, and he rose with her. 'I think we should go to bed,' she said.

32

Amusement, surprise, and something else warred within his eyes. 'Well,' he said, 'I see you mean to be a bold sort of a duchess from the outset. I own I had not expected it, but I am not in the least displeased, Georgiana, I assure you. On the contrary!'

'I think you know perfectly well that that is not what I mean,' she replied, flushing. 'You look exhausted; I too am tired. It has been a hectic few days, with this latest shock on top of all the rest. We do not dine and make our celebration till later, and I think we should take the opportunity to rest now, and recover our composure.'

'I must tell you,' he murmured, 'that although you obviously think me a poor creature, I am not yet in the habit of taking to my bed in the middle of the day for such a reason.'

'Maybe you should be. At your advanced age…'

She meant to shock him, to tease the set look from his face, and it seemed she had succeeded. He laughed, and took her loosely in his arms, resting his forehead on hers. 'I can think of many responses to that pert remark, and none of them in the least conducive to – what was it you said? – recovering our composure.

But with great age comes patience, or so I am told. I will willingly go to bed and rest, my dear, if you will come with me. I will ask no more of you just now than the comfort of your embrace.'

His words, and the warmth in his eyes, brought a lump to her throat, and she could do nothing but nod, and climb the stairs with him to his oak-panelled bedchamber. They could comfort each other, she thought. He seemed to need her, at least in this moment, as much as she needed him, and surely that must be a good sign?

It was not as though they had not lain on a bed together before. They had done all sorts of things under cover of darkness, after all. But somehow to go openly together to the suite of rooms they now would share, to take off her shoes and lie down with him on his big four-poster in broad daylight, felt different. Felt serious. Everyone in the house would likely know where they were, from Lady Blanche and Louisa to the servants, and would make understandable assumptions about what they were doing. They were very thoroughly married, and all the world knew it. There was nothing secret, nothing illicit in their union – quite the reverse. They were supposed to be making an heir. Duty demanded that they do so, and as soon as possible. But when she gave herself to him at last, she knew it would not be with any thought of duty.

She had a coronet of damp white roses and a precious Point de Malines lace veil on her head, and plainly it would be ridiculous as well as uncomfortable to lie down in such a thing; Gabriel explored with gentle fingers, found the pins that held the whole confection in place and pulled them loose, then carefully lifted it away and set it down upon a side table. 'There,' he said. 'Perhaps you will feel more like yourself without it.'

'I don't know that I will. Maybe I never will. I am a duchess now, apparently.'

'You are. My duchess. But you are still Georgie.' He saw the doubt and confusion on her face and said, 'You're weary too. Come and lie down, and perhaps sleep a little. I think we both need it.'

The Duke shrugged off his corbeau coat and tugged ruthlessly on his cravat, then tossed both aside on a chair. 'Let me unfasten your gown for you, or you will crease it horribly.' He was right, of course, and she stood as his patient fingers worked at the tiny silk-covered buttons that ran down her back. When he had finished, he stepped aside; he did not further help her to put off her gown, nor make any comment as she did so, and she was glad of it, conscious of an almost overpowering sense of shyness that, God knows, she had never felt in his presence before and had not looked to feel now.

Slipping off his shoes, he pulled the velvet coverlet and linen sheet back and lay down. Before she allowed herself to think about it too much, she crossed to the bed, and climbed onto it to lie rather stiffly at his side. He put his arm about her, and she settled her head on his chest. This was new. Under the silver-embroidered wedding waistcoat and the thin lawn shirt, she could feel his heart beating steadily. Somehow it, and the warmth of his body, calmed her. She sighed unconsciously, and snuggled closer. His hand came up, almost hesitantly, and stroked her disordered curls with great and unexpected gentleness. 'You were right, Georgie,' he said softly. 'I did not know it, but this is exactly what I need. Thank you! Now let us try to sleep if we can.'

Georgie had imagined she could not possibly relax into slumber; her mental state was agitated, confused, and the Duke's arms, holding her with no trace of amorous intent, unfamiliar. She had never been held in just this way before. There was nothing in the least lascivious in the way he embraced her, but his nearness, the masculine scent of him, the weight of his big hand on her head, were all subtly disturbing as well as comforting. It was an extraordinary combination.

But, exhausted as she was, she must have slept despite everything, for when she next became aware of her surroundings the light coming through the tall windows had changed, and so had her situation.

Gabriel had pulled up the bedlinens to cover them both. She was exceedingly warm. Hot. Her face was pillowed comfortably on his chest as it had been when she fell asleep, and his strong arms were still secure about her, but everything else had altered. At some point in the afternoon she had turned into his embrace, so that her leg now lay across him and her body was pressed to his; his thigh had inserted itself between hers, or she had wrapped herself around it, and it seemed to fit very snugly there. Their proximity did not feel quite so innocent any more. Did not feel innocent at all.

She raised her head a little and saw that he was awake, his glinting silver gaze regarding her from under his heavy lids. There was a world of meaning in his eyes. 'Georgiana...' he said, his voice deep and caressing, and at the mere sound of it all the fine hairs on her skin stood on end.

She felt sure that her face was creased from sleep and unbecomingly flushed from the heat of the bed, and from their closeness. But her dishevelment did not seem to have given him a disgust of her. 'Would you care to kiss me?' he said simply.

'I should like to.' It was true. She knew all her confusion, all her unanswered, unanswerable questions still remained. She also knew, or feared, that physical intimacy between them would not resolve anything. But God, she wanted it. Wanted him. It would have to be enough.

Georgie wriggled into a more upright position, lying on his chest now with her breasts crushed against him, a delicious pressure. His hands came tight about her ribcage and pulled her a little higher, so that she was able to reach him, and take his face between her hands, and brush his lips with hers. She was only tentative for a moment; it seemed a long time, far too long, since they had tasted each other – they had not been properly alone since the night of the ball – and it felt so right that within seconds their mouths were locked together in mutual and growing hunger. She fastened her fingers in his hair and pressed every inch of her body close to his, and his hands slid down her stays and over her petticoats till they found her buttocks and cupped them through the flimsy layers that covered her. He pulled her tighter still against him, and she gripped his hard thigh between hers. She wanted, needed there to be no space between them, for his flesh to touch hers.

But they were still largely clothed – her long-sleeved embroidered lawn habit shirt and all her undergarments, his waistcoat, shirt and pantaloons. She put a finger to his lips and drew away from him reluctantly, so that she could sit up. She unbuttoned her shirt with impatient fingers, pulling it off and flinging it away so that her arms, shoulders and upper chest were bare. He followed her lead, shrugging out of his waistcoat, dragging his shirt over his head and letting it fall. She had not seen him shirtless before, despite all their intimacy; his torso was far more strongly muscled than his habitually languid demeanour would lead one to imagine. She had no time to admire him, though, for he lifted her without the least effort and set her astride his body, and her knees came up instinctively so that she could set them on the bed either side of him and steady herself. He was partially sitting now, so that they faced each other, breathless, panting. He seemed to understand what she needed; his clever hands pulled her white petticoats ruthlessly up so that her naked core could settle against the bare skin of his abdomen. In his haste, fragile muslin ripped. She did not care. She gasped at the intimate contact, and he smiled.

They stayed still for a moment, skin to skin. Through the thin fabric of his pantaloons she could feel him hot and hard beneath the back of her thigh. His left hand came down to clasp her buttock once again and tuck her more tightly into him, and she welcomed the pressure with a tiny moan. The tips of his fingers grazed her most sensitive skin, and now his right hand moved to cup her face. She turned into it and pressed her lips to his palm, and then her tongue came out and tasted it.

He said, his voice unsteadier than she had ever heard it, 'I came to look for you, Georgiana. It seems important somehow that I tell you that now.'

Her hands were on his chest, tangling in the soft whorls of dark hair that grew there; she could not get enough of touching him. 'How can that be? When, when did you do this?'

'In London, after... we first met. I couldn't get you out of my head, and so I went to ton parties in search of you. I never go to such parties now. I am invited to some, but I don't like them much, and so I never go. I went looking for you wherever I thought you might be, but I did not find you. Of course, I had not the least idea who you were and could think of no way to find out.'

He laughed softly. 'I could hardly go about asking people if they knew a beautiful girl with extraordinary blue eyes and short dark curls; I had not quite lost all self-control. Not quite. I even procured a voucher for Almack's – Sally Jersey has a soft spot for me still. You should have seen the tabbies stare. You were not there.'

'I easily might have been. What would you have done if you had found me?' she whispered. His right hand had left her face now, and his fingers were tracing idle lines down her throat, and across her shoulders, and lower. His other hand was similarly occupied where her buttock met her thigh. It was increasingly difficult to form coherent thoughts. She was aware of heat kindling where her sex was pressed against his bare skin, and could not resist moving a little in response to it.

'Solicited your hand for a waltz, perhaps. God knows I had no wish to dance with anyone else, and I did not. If I had walked up to you and claimed you and you alone as I wished to, that would have given the chaperons something to chatter over.'

'I might have panicked and refused you.' She scarcely knew what she was saying. He had found the ties of her chemise and undone them, and was pulling the thin material down so that her breasts were exposed, offered up to him by the boning of her stays. Her nipples were engorged and aching for his touch; with an inarticulate murmur he bent his head and tantalised her with long, slow licks around them and across them. The contact was wonderful, but it was too brief. She arched her back in mute appeal and ran her hands up the corded muscles of his back, and his fingers tightened on her bottom in response, kneading the sensitive skin.

He spoke against her flesh, between tantalising kisses, and his feathered breath tormented her further. 'You might well have publicly spurned me. What a scandal that would have caused among the haut ton. And even more if I had put you across my shoulder and carried you off out of the place so that I could ravish you immediately in my carriage, which was one of the fantasies I entertained at that time. One of the many fantasies...'

His right hand held her tightly under her breast, splayed possessively across her ribcage. She felt taut as a bowstring in his grasp, and acutely conscious of his strength, and his desire, and hers. And hers.

'I simply could not get you out of my head,' he said raggedly, 'your fearlessness, the sight of you there on that couch baring yourself to me, the taste of you, the fact that I might never see you again, and yet my tongue had explored you so intimately and brought you to...'

'Oh, God, please, Gabriel!' she said wildly. His lips closed on her nipple and sucked it at last, gently and then harder, and she moaned aloud, and dug her nails into his flesh, and writhed against him.

He pulled away after a long moment, and the air was cold on her slick, sensitised skin, and then his tongue went out again to taste her. She could feel the short stubble on his cheeks against her breasts as he moved his attention from one erect nipple to the other, and she welcomed the friction. She was wet against him, and although the ridged muscles of his abdomen were hard and the contact delicious, she needed more.

'I could not get you out of my head,' he said again, 'and now I do not need to. Can I lose myself in you again, Georgie, and give you pleasure as I did once before, as I have been desperate to all these long weeks?'

She moaned assent, and he turned her on her back and moved away a moment, to drag off his pantaloons with impatient hands before returning to her. 'Shall I undress you?' he said. 'Would you be more comfortable?'

'The only thing that would make me more comfortable,' she said, 'is you setting about fulfilling your fantasies, and mine!'

'Yours too? Do you say so?' He was smiling, teasing her, as he smoothed back her ruined petticoats with exaggerated care.

'Do not pretend you did not know it!' And then his hungry mouth was on her, and she could no longer speak, nor did she wish to. He did not tantalise her any longer, did not kiss his slow way upwards to her core as he had once before. There was no need, and it was not what either of them wanted. There would be a time for slow exploration and sophisticated pleasures, but this was not it. She was in a high state of arousal before ever his eager tongue touched her most secret places, desperate for release. God, she had missed this, had dreamed of this too every night.

Within a few moments she was clutching the bedcovers and gasping as the waves of pleasure built and then broke over her, and he devoured her and prolonged the pleasure ruthlessly until she saw stars behind her closed eyelids.

This time there was no need for him to move away or let her go. He came to lie close beside her, took her limp hand and kissed it, and said, 'Georgie...?'

She could only murmur yes, and welcome him into her arms as he came back to her. He was above her now, and she wrapped her legs around him and clung to him. He kissed her neck and her breasts, whispering endearments, teasing her sensitised skin, and then a moment of discomfort, but no more than that, and she knew that he was inside her.

'Oh, God,' he gasped. 'How I have longed for this. Let us be still a moment.'

They lay panting, their bodies slicked with sweat, and he touched her face with gentle, wondering fingers. She captured one between her teeth and bit it, then sucked on it, and he traced the moist, tender flesh inside her lower lip as she had done to him once before. She whimpered in response to all the sensations his touch, the pressure of his body on hers and in hers evoked in her, and he laughed shakily. 'Very well,' he said, 'very well, my eager Duchess.' Slowly at first he began to move in her, with her, and before long they found a rhythm together, growing harder and faster. His hands found hers and clasped them, and she arched her back against him and raised her hips to meet him as he thrust into her, her legs locked around him and her heels pressing into his buttocks. This was the forbidden action at last, the thing women talked of, if they talked of it at all, behind their hands, and her thoughts were fractured, almost submerged as she was in the physical moment and all the new sensations it brought, but some small, detached part of her brain was glad that she was experiencing it with him, and no one else. No regrets, in this moment. Whatever came of it.

He cried out her name as he spent himself in her, and she held him as he shuddered in release. Their hands were still tightly clasped. He lay with his full weight on her for a moment, but before she could become aware of any discomfort he rolled over, taking her with him so that she lay on top of him once more.

'Georgie...' he said again after a moment. 'I am afraid to speak and break the spell. I know that sometimes I am damnably clumsy where you are concerned, I have always been guilty of talking too much when I should keep silent, and I do not... But thank you.'

'Thank you...?' she murmured distractedly, her head buried in his neck, drinking in the spicy scent of him.

'Thank you for marrying me when I know you still have doubts. Thank you for all you risk in doing so. I promise you I am more than conscious of it.' She stiffened a little in his embrace; he felt it and said ruefully against her curls, 'You see? I will always be talking when I should learn to be quiet and hold you.'

'No... You have been avoiding me, have you not, these last few days? I thought you might come to my bed, but then I realised why you did not. It must have been because you did not wish to discuss my doubts any further. And I did not either, so I did not seek you out. And...' she said, with a little catch in her voice, 'and... I don't want to talk about them now. Like this.' She shivered a little, and he pulled the covers up over them, not speaking until he had done so, wrapping his arms around her again.

'God knows I will not force you to speak of something that brings you distress, now of all times. I suppose that's partly true, the reason I was avoiding you. I'm sorry, Georgie. The plain truth is that I was afraid, I think, that if we spoke again on the matter your obvious reluctance might compel me to behave as a true gentleman would and let you go. And I knew I would regret it for the rest of my life if I did so. I am aware that that's not very creditable and I am not excessively proud of myself for it. "Selfish" does not even come close to describing my actions.'

'You have others than yourself to think of.'

'That's kind of you, but it's not really true. I owed it to many, to marry and... all the rest of it. But you must know that I lost sight of that a good while since. For many days now I have been aware that I wanted you, I want you, for myself, not for the damn dukedom or the estate or any of that.'

'Well, you have me.' So much still lay unspoken between them, and she felt she had exposed herself enough. But this much was true: he had her. As to whether she had him, could ever truly... But she must not do this to herself now.

'I hope I never give you cause to regret it, my dear.'

'So, do not!'

'If it lies in my power...'

She sighed. 'I was being childish; do not regard it. We both know that you cannot make those kinds of promises. Nobody can. But something has been tormenting me, Gabriel. When I speak of it to anyone, they tell me I am being foolish.'

'I doubt that. You are no fool.'

She shook her head. 'Never mind that. You do not have to pay me compliments; this is serious. I worry that I will not be able to give you the son that you need.'

'If that were so – and there is no reason to make such an assumption – I do not see how we could ever know if the fault, though fault is not the correct word, were yours or mine. This sort of thing is out of our hands, is it not, and always must be? And the same would be true whomever I had married.'

'You do not have natural children here and there, then?' She spoke with studied lightness – he might have a dozen, for all she knew, a man of his reputation, and if it were so she supposed she must accept it – but he answered her seriously.

'I do not. I have always been careful, whatever people have said of me. No bastard children, no need for mercury cures. I should have told you both these things before, perhaps. I did tell your brother in our first awkward interview, once the bottle came out.'

'I think you should have said. But everything has been so fraught and peculiar these last days... I am glad, on both counts.'

The conversation had strayed into uncomfortable territory, and she was glad when he said, in what she thought must be a deliberate attempt to row back into safer waters, 'I cannot imagine what time it might be, but surely it must be not far off the dinner hour.'

'I think I heard the clock striking six a little while ago,' she murmured without thinking, and then blushed when he laughed at her. He seemed to be genuinely amused rather than offended.

'I will take good care to distract you better next time, madam! You put me on my mettle. But if you are right, we should get up and dress for dinner, should we not?'

She agreed and they parted, but he gave her a long, lingering kiss before he let her go. 'Till later, Georgie,' he said, and the gleam in his silver eyes told her that he was back in the ironical mood that was so familiar to her.

33

In a surprisingly short space of time, the newlyweds found themselves alone in the mansion in York, save for the discreet and admirably trained servants. They had celebrated with their assembled families that first evening, Georgie trying her best to ignore the odiously quizzing looks both Louisa and Miss Spry gave her when they gathered, rather later than had been planned, around the dinner table. Hal and Cassandra left for Skipton the next day; they would remain there, he told her, for at least another few weeks before they returned to London. 'Do you think I need you nearby?' she asked him half-jokingly as they parted.

'I don't know if you do, Georgie, but I will be in any case.'

'My disasters are no longer your concern,' she said, suddenly a little tearful.

'I hope there will be no more disasters, but if there are, you know where I am.'

They embraced, and Cassandra and Bastian both hugged her too, and whispered, 'Write to me!' in her ear, and then all three of them were gone.

Louisa and Miss Spry took their departure the next day.

Georgie had seized a moment to walk alone in the garden with Jane before their departure, and had asked her what her immediate plans were. 'Marriage,' she had replied, with a smile that tried for droll and landed instead on uncertain.

'You are resolved on this course?'

'I am. We are. We have been in correspondence, Lord Carston and I – there is no longer any need for discretion, I think, for my news will be public soon enough – and he is still of the same mind. I will be married soon, just as soon as it can be arranged.'

Georgie blinked at the news. Lord Carston was very well known to her; he was a close friend of Louisa's, as he had been of her own father. He was Hal's godfather, and hers too, a distinguished widower in his late forties with children grown. A handsome, lazily humorous, infinitely tolerant man. And one with hidden depths, clearly. 'I… Life is so much more complicated than I thought it was, just a few short months ago,' said Georgie. 'I see the truth of that more and more with every day that passes. I wish you well.'

'Thank you. I hope you will stand my friend.'

'I will. I will be godmother to your child too, if you will have me.'

'Thank you, Duchess!' said Miss Spry with a wry smile. 'That is a generous offer, and I am happy to accept it. There will be rumours swirling about us, I dare say – if not at first, then certainly if I do conceive a child, and then go back to live with Louisa, and remain there. It may involve your family in scandal, certainly in gossip, and so I am grateful that you do not mean to distance yourself from us.'

Georgiana laughed with genuine amusement and shook her head. 'A scandal, and not caused by me! How can I be anything but grateful?'

'I suppose that is true! But it is kind of you none the less. Perhaps you and I will be mothers together.'

'Perhaps.'

Jane looked at her shrewdly. 'Has anyone thought to ask you how *you* feel about the prospect of motherhood?'

'Gabriel has. I did not know how to answer him. It seemed theoretical then, whereas now, of course, it is not. Do not think that I am instinctively averse to the idea...'

'That is just as well!' her companion snorted.

'I suppose it is. It's just... I feel as though I am changing. I'm not the person I was a month ago. In a month's time, or in six months, I may be different again. I may have a child growing inside me already. I honestly do not know how I feel about that. If I knew, I would tell you.'

'You are under a great deal of pressure. My situation is different – if I do not conceive, it will matter to nobody in the world but me. Lord Carston, William, does not require an heir from this marriage.' She saw Georgie's face and said quickly, 'I am sorry! You do not need reminding of your situation, I am sure. That was insensitive of me; please forgive me.'

'Nonsense. It is no less real merely because we do not speak openly of it. One thing I do know – I want to do this for Gabriel if I can, and not because of some notion of duty. I know how much it means to him. I am sure enough of that.' It was true; she'd come to realise it over the last few days. She would give him everything she was capable of giving, no matter what she might receive in return. And not just her body. She had burnt all her bridges now.

'I cannot question you. The world is hard enough for women, even women of your class. And more and more I think that it does not matter why people act, or what they say, but only what they actually do to hurt or help each other. Even though things can still go horribly wrong, however well one means by one's actions.'

'The road to hell is paved with good intentions?'

'Let us hope not, on this occasion, or we are all bound for ruin.'

Jane stopped her restless pacing and turned to look Georgiana in the eye. 'I think when we meet again both our situations will be clearer. I hope so. Shall we wish each other good luck?' They embraced, and then it was time to leave, and in any case there seemed nothing more to be said.

Georgie's new sister-in-law Blanche and her children also departed that day; they had formed a plan to visit Harrogate, and perhaps take the waters there. It was obvious that this was the merest pretext to leave the newly-weds alone, but they could not be dissuaded, and it was possible that neither the Duke nor Georgiana tried very hard to change their minds. The trip would also give Lady Blanche, she told the couple, an opportunity to visit the Richmonds, who had now returned to their home, and form some more balanced judgement of how Isabella did when she saw her in a calmer, more familiar setting, free, she hoped, from the effects of the severe shock she had received. 'I will write and tell you how I find her, and what her mother says if we are able to converse in private,' she said. 'Do you mean to stay here, or return to the Castle, or...? You could even go abroad, I suppose, if you would care to do so.'

His Grace smiled at his sister. 'I do not know; we have not had a chance to make any firm plans. I will let you know, of course, Blanche, if we decide to make some change.'

Gabriel was responsive to Georgie's moods in these days, and gentle except on occasions when gentleness was emphatically not required; he seemed to sense that the sudden departure of all her family and his had left her feeling cast adrift. 'Would you prefer to go away – to Paris, perhaps, or London?' he asked her the next morning as they lay in bed. 'I can't help thinking that to be entirely alone with me might not be to your taste. There is no earthly reason why it should be, of course.'

It was one of those occasions when Georgie could not read him; if she had been forced to guess, she would have said he seemed subdued, and perhaps a little hurt, but that was ridiculous, of course. He'd given her no reason to believe she held such power over him. She sat up and leaned back against the pillows, trying to formulate her thoughts, for her own sake as much as his. They were not three days married. 'It's not you, Gabriel, or being alone with you,' she said. 'The truth is, I am not used to being alone with anyone. I suppose it is only natural – I have five siblings, as you know, and when we are all together there is a bustle such as you cannot conceive. My aunt Sophia has always been there too, and sometimes Louisa, and now Cassandra, of course, Miss Spry, and Bastian's dear friend Matthew, whom you have not yet met. And in London or in Brighton, when the boys have not always been present, we have been caught up in a constant whirl of social engagements – this was also the case when we travelled abroad last year, and we had companions on our journey too. I do not think I have ever been in just one person's constant company in my life before. You must make allowances while I accustom myself to it.'

'I understand,' he said. 'I suppose my situation has been very different. I envy you, I think. I have certainly led a solitary and selfish sort of existence as an adult. I was always with Ash when we were young, but Blanche was married when I was ten or eleven, and then my father bought Ash a pair of colours when he turned sixteen – I was at Oxford then, though only briefly. My brother was my father's obvious favourite, or so I thought at the time, which was perfectly understandable. I was always a disappointment to him, and then of course I embarked on my sadly unsteady way of life, about which the least said the better, I think.'

He had not spoken so frankly of his family before – there were hidden depths there, she was sure, and she would have liked to know more if he felt able to tell it, but perhaps he regretted his openness, for he now moved to distract her in a most effective manner. 'There are, of course, certain advantages to being alone in the house without family or guests to entertain that I think we both can recognise and appreciate,' he said silkily, and he reached out one lazy hand and laid it on her inner thigh, then began to stroke her sensitive skin with the lightest and most tantalising of caresses.

He was lying on his side, looking up at her as he spoke, and she became aware that she was naked, exposed to the waist, and that he was regarding her with a glint in his eyes that she had come to recognise. His expression, and his touch, called an instant response from her, and under his gaze her nipples hardened into taut peaks and her skin flushed with heat, a heat that began to gather between her legs and demand attention. She did not attempt to cover herself, but reclined against the pillows, her eyes holding his.

'No need to get up for breakfast?' she said, a trifle breathlessly. He had the power – had always had the power, ever since their first meeting – of arousing her with a word, a glance. When that was combined with his touch, she had no hope of resisting, and no desire to do so. Whatever else they had, or did not have, might never have, they had this.

'No need to get up for luncheon or dinner, if we do not wish to!'

'I do not wish to,' she declared.

She pulled back the coverlets and moved to straddle his body, and he shifted to accommodate her, steadying her with his big hands either side of her hips, smiling up at her and waiting to see what she would choose to do. She reached forward and took hold of the headboard with both hands, a movement which brought her erect nipples close to his face. He murmured, 'So damn beautiful...' and the words as much as the whisper touch of his breath caused her skin to pucker and tighten even more. But still he did not put his mouth on her.

She leaned a fraction closer and brushed his lips with one hard peak. 'Must I beg, sir?' she said in a low tone, almost a growl.

His clever tongue teased her, circling her aroused flesh for a split second and then withdrawing, and she whimpered in frustration. 'A gentleman should never make a lady beg,' he said, close against her breast, and she could hear the smile in his voice. 'But it is so very enjoyable, I do not think I can resist the temptation, sinner that I am.' He blew on her gently, and she gasped and writhed against him. 'Does the touch even of my breath excite you so much, Georgie?'

'You know it does!'

'Imagine, then, the sensations if I took your lovely little pink nipple in my mouth and sucked on it, gently at first and then harder.'

'I am imagining them! But I would rather feel them!'

'Will you beg me, then?'

She moved again, and brushed the aching bud of flesh across his lips, and his mouth opened a little, to give her a hint of its heat and its wetness, but it was just to tantalise her, no more. 'Very well,' she said, 'I beg you, Gabriel, to take my nipple in your mouth and suck on it.'

His tongue came out again and tasted her for a precious second. 'More!' he whispered. 'Beg harder. I'm not yet sure you really mean it.'

His hands were gripping her hips, holding her to him, and she could feel his member aroused and hot against her core. She was astonished, always, by his control; she did not share it. She was wet and lightheaded with desire, and ground her pelvis against him. She could feel his instant physical response, but still he did not relent and give her what she so desperately needed. 'Gabriel,' she moaned, 'please, please, take me in your mouth and suck on me. I'm aching for your touch. Kiss me. Bite me. Eat me up till there is nothing left. I fear I could die from wanting it!'

And then at last he did. The sudden ruthless way he seized her made her cry aloud and arch her back, clutching at the headboard and pressing herself into his face. He sucked and nibbled on her aroused flesh and then opened his mouth wide and took in almost her whole breast, her nipple grazing the roof of his mouth. Meanwhile his hand was busy between them, positioning himself, and he slipped inside her slick wetness with a dizzying rush that made them both gasp. He pulled his mouth from her and she whimpered, but it was only so he could fasten on her other breast and devour it in the same way. God, yes.

Georgie held tightly to the bed and rode him with fierce concentration, and he held her while she set the pace, his hands hard and tight on her buttocks, his mouth worshipping her breasts. His pleasure in such moments, she knew – and when all else in her life was so uncertain it was something to cling to – was identical with hers. She had learned in the past few days, if she had not known it before, that they were extraordinarily well matched physically. She felt her body tensing itself as the sensations overwhelming her became more intense, and freed herself from his lips so that she could sit upright; he was immediately responsive, as he always was, and moved his hands to her hips once more, supporting her securely. She wanted to see his face; more, she wanted him to see her, she realised. And she had both her hands free now. She caressed her breast with her left hand, taking her nipple, wet and slick from his mouth, almost painfully engorged, between thumb and forefinger and tugging on it. Her other hand slipped between their bodies and found her nub, and began stroking it under his appreciative gaze. A few days earlier she would not have imagined herself doing this so shamelessly while he watched her. There was a great deal she would not have imagined; she was learning fast. 'Tell me what you see, and what you feel!' she commanded him.

'Oh, God!' he said. 'I hope I have the words, Georgie. I see the most beautiful woman I have ever known or imagined, and she is fucking me. Gloriously fucking me. Her perfect breasts are flushed and engorged from where I have feasted on them, her nipples are swollen and wet from my mouth, and she is pulling on one delicious little bud harder than I would ever dare. I must learn to dare, for I am beginning to realise that she loves the point where pain and pleasure meet and one can hardly be told from the other. Her delectable mouth is open and her eyes are dark with desire. Her fingers are tangled in her dark curls and she is working on herself to take her own pleasure, which Christ knows is also mine. Her thighs are gripping me with all her strength and riding me ruthlessly. She is pounding into me, or I into her, I cannot say which, both, so that the friction is almost unbearably good. I am utterly hers. I... She is very close to coming. She is magnificent. She...'

And then he could say no more, or if he still spoke she did not hear him, for his words, the feel of his body under hers and her hands on herself, his beautiful voice, his sense of her, it was all too much, and she came with a great gasp. Her climax triggered his and they fused together in desperate thrusts until they both were spent. She collapsed onto him and he held her as they panted and their hearts beat hard in their breasts. He was still inside her and neither of them moved to free him. His hand came up to cup her head and she buried her face in his neck, drinking in the masculine scent of him; her tongue came out and tasted the salt of his skin. It was good, but it was not enough. She bit him, not gently, and he chuckled. He understood, he always understood; they could not get enough of each other. She sucked on him deliberately, with mouth and teeth. It would leave a mark. She wanted to mark him as hers. He had done the same to her. The marks that were visible to the naked eye were the least of it, she thought as she closed her eyes against the ever-present nagging fear and moved up to kiss him.

34

Mrs Aubrey and her brother Captain Hart were, by contrast, having a frustrating stay in the city of York. Fraternal harmony did not reign supreme in the rather down-at-heel inn where they had taken rooms.

They had arrived just in time to attend, along with hundreds of others, the wedding of the Duke of Northriding and Lady Georgiana Pendlebury; they had stood at the rear of the crowd and Hart had witnessed the nuptials in a high state of resentment and bitter thwarted desire. Georgiana had never looked half so well, nor half so alluring, and to think that she had so nearly been his, to remember the sweet taste of those rose-petal lips and watch another man claiming her – a bloody duke! – was almost more than the Captain could bear.

He was furious that they had come too late, and felt inclined to blame his sister for it, and to animadvert upon the subject at tiresome length over the coming days.

'Nonsense,' she scolded him, contemptuous of what she saw as his flawed reasoning.

'It's not nonsense, Caro! I am sure the wench would have paid us more if we had arrived before the wedding took place. What a lost opportunity! She'd have been in the devil's own panic, scared of losing her prize at the last moment, and I dare say would have given us anything we asked for.'

'Perhaps. Or perhaps she would have set her precious brothers on us – have you thought of that?'

The Captain had not thought of that. He had offered for Georgiana's hand last spring and been summarily rejected; that had been bad enough. But later, when their clandestine relationship had come to light, he had endured a much more unpleasant interview with Lord Irlam, in which that gentleman had made it all too clear that his sister was and always would be well above Captain Hart's touch. There had been no violence upon that occasion, but there had been the threat of it – mention had been made of horsewhips – and the blazing anger and contempt in the Earl's blue eyes had left a deep impression. Adolphus Hart, despite his military profession, was not a man possessed of a great measure of physical courage, and the Earl, he knew, was an amateur boxer of no small repute. Irlam's hands had twitched involuntarily throughout that meeting, as if he barely had his murderous impulses under control, and Hart had not the least desire to develop a closer acquaintance with what was said to be a punishing right. But that prospect had retreated, and he also had a great dislike of being forced repeatedly to acknowledge his sister's superior mental acuity.

'Rubbish,' he said uneasily. 'She would never breathe a word to them. Inform her brothers she attended a damned orgy, and did heaven knows what there? I tell you she wouldn't, not for the life of her.'

'You may be right, of course,' said Mrs Aubrey with exaggerated patience. 'But you were the one who would have suffered the consequences if you were mistaken. *In extremis*, desperate to make sure the wedding went ahead and short of time, she might easily have confessed her shameful secret to them and sought their help. Of course they would have been as keen for the match to proceed as she. More so, perhaps! And they, backed into a corner, might well have decided that violence was the only answer to her plight. They might even have been so wrought up at the thought of you showing your face again that beating you to a pulp was more than they could resist, whatever the consequences. But they're gone now, the grown one and the cub together, so we don't have to concern ourselves with them. This way is better, can you not see?'

The Captain could not see. The truth of the matter was that he had become obsessed with exacting his revenge on Georgiana's sweet body; the idea of forcing her to submit herself to him before her marriage to the Duke, so that the Duke came – hah! – unknowingly after him, had taken possession of his mind and deranged such wits as he had. His sister was cooler, more patient, and explained to him that the fact of Lady Georgiana's marriage made not the least difference. 'The one thing we can be sure of is that she dares not tell her husband. She has no family here to turn to now, and she will be obliged to meet with me alone and unprotected. She will arrive in trepidation but also in anger, thinking she has only me to deal with. And then you will reveal yourself. Imagine her consternation! She thought she had seen the last of you, that you were a mere footnote to her past, a regrettable little mistake, but soon she will realise how wrong she was. You will like that, I expect.'

Hart expected that he would, too. Their last meeting had not gone to plan; he bore the evidence of that in the livid scar on his temple. Georgie had bested him then, had humiliated him, but she would not do so again. The humiliation would be hers. If she were not all sweet submission – even if she was, perhaps – he would give her a mark of her own to remember him by. He was almost past caring about the money now.

The difficulty was that three days had passed since the wedding and the Duke and his bride had not so much as set an elegantly clad foot outside the door of the mansion on Petergate. Captain Hart and Mrs Aubrey between them haunted the place to keep it under observation, and they knew that all the guests who had attended the wedding had now departed, but still the newlyweds did not emerge. The thought of what they might be doing – were surely doing – in their bridal seclusion inflamed Georgie's former suitor all the more, till at last his sister agreed that they could not rely upon a chance encounter, but must take the risk of setting something at least of their demands down on paper and sending the new Duchess a note, demanding an immediate meeting. She was forced to admit that she and her brother knew nothing of their plans; the pair might even now be intending to return to their coastal fastness, where it would be almost impossible to follow them, or to set off for one of the Duke's numerous other properties, or even to go abroad. The conspirators were severely limited in their financial resources, and could ill afford another expensive journey across the length and breadth of England or beyond. They must act now, or risk failure.

Caroline spent hours crafting her billet, and despatched it to the ducal mansion by means of a respectable messenger; her brother was there, lurking, to see it delivered. Now all they had to do was wait, with what patience they could muster: a fair amount, on Mrs Aubrey's part, and very little, on the Captain's.

35

Georgie found that the amount of correspondence she received had greatly increased, now she was a married woman and a duchess. Her family were in constant contact, of course – she had even received an atrociously scrawled but apparently heartfelt joint message of congratulation from her three younger brothers, which had made Gabriel smile when she had passed it to him. Mrs Winterton had written, and her son Leo, as had Alice Templeton and other of her friends who had seen the announcement in the paper or otherwise heard of it. Lady Georgiana Morpeth wrote in congratulation, as did her sister Lady Granville. Noble ladies with whom she was not so well acquainted had also written to her, including Lady Jersey and Lady Sefton, two of the august patronesses of Almack's and acknowledged leaders of society; it seemed she was in some sense one of them now, an alarming thought. People both known and unknown to her sent her ingenious or pitiful letters soliciting money, in great quantities. And also, she discovered that afternoon, she received letters of blackmail.

Her heart had lurched when she opened Mrs Aubrey's note,

but once the initial shock had passed she was inclined to smile a little wryly, which was surely not the effect her correspondent had anticipated. She was sitting with Gabriel over nuncheon, breakfast once again having been set aside for far more interesting ways of passing the time, and she passed the missive across the table to him, with a significant look at the footmen who stood in attendance. He scanned it impassively, and then with a brief word and a smile ordered their departure, and once they had gone turned to regard his wife with one of his more enigmatic expressions.

'Well,' he said, 'it was always a possibility, I suppose, and we should not be surprised. The news of our marriage must have been manna from heaven to her. What an unpleasant creature.'

'And I thought her a friend. It says little for my ability to judge character.'

'How could you know? You have never done her the least harm in the world, I am sure.'

'I do not think I have. But she set out to ruin me when she tricked me into that house. So much has happened since that I had almost forgot her existence. And yet she had not forgotten me. She hates me, I think – there is an anger behind her words, or am I mistaken?'

'You are not mistaken, my dear. She seeks a meeting with you, by the Abbey ruins this afternoon. Shall I go instead? I think perhaps I should.'

Georgie smiled and shook her head. 'No, Gabriel. I have said before that I must begin taking responsibility for my own mistakes, and it is true. She would never have been able to dupe me into visiting that place if I had shown better judgement and not given her so much as the time of day. I believe too that I will enjoy seeing her face change when I tell her that she cannot hope to hurt me in your eyes by telling you of my scandalous past...'

'Because the man you went apart with in that house was me,'

he finished for her, with a smile that showed he understood perfectly. 'I can appreciate how the irony of it appeals to you, and she will be well served by such a setback. But what if she recovers herself quickly – her wits appear to be sufficiently sharp – and still threatens to expose you? She may even refuse to believe you, have you thought of that? I am still of the mind that I should be there. We could confront her together; you would still have the pleasure of seeing the realisation cross her face. I own I will not be completely easy in my mind until I know *why* she bears you such malice. At present I see no reason for it, and it troubles me. The majority of people are usually so much more obvious in their motives, I find.'

She brushed his doubts aside. 'Do such creatures need a reason? What is it that you fear, Gabriel? Your concern for my safety is touching, but I cannot think it necessary in this instance.'

'I don't know what I fear,' he said, taking her hand and raising it to his lips before he released it. 'I suppose eight centuries – more – of possessive masculinity cannot be set aside in an instant just because we live in supposedly more civilised times. My Norman ancestors solved their problems at the point of a sword or lance, you must be aware. The idea of allowing their women to put themselves in danger while they stood by and did nothing would have been anathema to them.'

Georgie rose, and came to sit on his lap, twining her arms about his neck. '"Their women"?' she teased. 'Will you put me over your saddlebow and carry me off to your castle, my lord Duke, where you can lock me up in a tower and keep me safe?'

'With the greatest of pleasure, madam,' he responded with alacrity, his hands about her waist, spanning her ribcage and making her feel agreeably small and delicate in his grasp. 'I have towers aplenty, after all. You will be safe from everyone save me, and I know you do not wish to be safe from me. I fear the plate armour, not to mention the helm, will be an impediment, but I am perfectly willing to throw you down upon the refectory table, or any other table that comes to hand, and ravish you, if that is your desire.'

'I think we can dispense with the armour,' she said. 'It sounds excessively uncomfortable for both of us. But here is a sturdy table, look.'

'I do perceive it,' he said, sweeping a ruthless arm across the board to clear a space.

It was much later, and regrettably a great deal of fine crockery had fallen to the floor and broken, unregarded, when she murmured into Gabriel's ear, 'After all, what harm could she do me in a public place? She is just one woman.'

36

Mrs Aubrey had suggested – commanded – that Georgiana meet her at four in the afternoon, by a place in the Abbey ruins that she described in such an exact fashion that there could be no mistaking it. The Duke insisted on accompanying his wife there, and promised he would stay apart, but close enough that she could call on him for help if it should be needed. She accepted without demur; his concern for her was touching, and it was not, in any case, quite usual for women of high rank to walk completely unaccompanied through the streets of the city. If she was to be obliged to take her maid with her for the sake of propriety, she might as well take Gabriel rather than admit another to her secret. She would rather place her faith in her husband in such matters than any other person.

They set off from Petergate just before the hour, and so were a few minutes late arriving, having been delayed in their progress, as they always were, by the large number of people of all stations who wished to speak to them, or at least exchange nods and greetings. Once they neared their destination, Gabriel squeezed her arm and absented himself with a murmured word of encouragement before the meeting place was in sight, and Georgie squared her shoulders and made her way forward.

Mrs Aubrey was waiting, elegant as ever in a dark red pelisse with military braiding and a bonnet with an exaggerated poke. She bore a large sable muff, which was surely unnecessary in July, even a cold July, but still looked well enough. 'Duchess,' she said urbanely, omitting the curtsey that would have been correct. 'Congratulations upon your sudden and surprising elevation. I felt sure you would come.'

'I had to,' said Georgie, and saw triumph spark in the other woman's eyes. She thinks I'm frightened, she realised, and she likes that I am. She likes it excessively. I wonder if she is entirely rational? It was tempting to play along, to raise expectations and then dash them, but all at once Georgie found she could not bring herself to toy with this strange and wicked creature she had once thought a friend.

'I think you are labouring under a misapprehension,' she went on. 'You brought me here to blackmail me...'

'Such an unkind word,' said Caroline. 'But yes, if you must be crude, blackmail. I am sure your new husband would be horrified to hear what I have to tell. God knows what he would do to you if he discovered all. Divorce and public disgrace would be the least of it, I am confident. And I am sure you will pay me well to avert such a disaster. I know you thought before that you had circumvented me, and for a while you had. You believed it would ruin me as well as you if you told the world that I had tricked you into going to that house, and revealed what you saw me do there. But the stakes for you are so much higher now, are they not? I have so much more information now than I had then, and your situation too has changed. You are entirely in my power. Do you realise it yet? It is not just "your reputation" in the abstract that is at stake –

there is one man in particular, and that man your husband, who must not learn your dirty secrets. At peril of your life, perhaps, should his possessive anger be unrestrained, and certainly of all you have won by your clever marriage. I wonder if you managed to trick him into thinking that you came to him a virgin?'

Georgie said steadily, 'There was no need for tricks.' Her companion scoffed contemptuously, but she went on, 'I suppose someone else who was there in that house told you that they saw me being drawn into a private room by a man?' The letter had implied as much.

'So shocking,' Mrs Aubrey replied with a feral smile, her black eyes glittering. 'I had thought you such an innocent. Perhaps you were, till then. I do hope you enjoyed yourself, and that it was worth it.'

'Certainly it was, and I enjoyed myself enormously. You cannot possibly know the nature of the favour you did me. I owe you my thanks, in fact.'

'You will not fool me with your brave words. You will pay to keep this secret from the poor deluded fool you married, and pay, and pay again. I own you now.'

'You don't. Nobody does. I know your informer cannot have seen, or did not recognise, the man I met there. If she had, or he had, we would not be having this conversation. It was Northriding, you see.'

Mrs Aubrey gaped at her in incomprehension as she continued, 'All you did in your malice was introduce me to my husband. Your friend perhaps told you that my companion was tall, broad-shouldered, well-dressed. He was masked, of course. Did she also tell you that his hair was streaked with silver?'

'I don't believe you. You are bluffing. It is a brave attempt, but it is useless.'

'No, I'm telling you the truth.' Georgie stepped closer and said very low, her voice thrumming with conviction, 'I met him there, a complete stranger to me, but God knows an attractive one, and he went down on his knees and pleasured me with his mouth. I am weak with desire even now as I think of it. And after that he could not forget me, nor I him, and now we are married, and there is nothing you can do to touch us. Not a thing.'

The other woman gazed at her wildly, her brain whirring behind her eyes, and Georgie said fiercely, 'All you have done to me is make me a duchess. Take my thanks! But I will not pay you a penny. Nothing you say can hurt what lies between Gabriel and me. And if you think to spread the pretty tale abroad, beware. We will say that you are a liar and you tricked me there – as you did – and Gabriel was there, and saved me from your malice, as he did. My family know of it, all of it. I was the innocent deceived, Gabriel the hero, and you the villain. You will be utterly ruined and cast out from society, not I.'

The desperate woman blustered, 'Why was he even there? His reputation will be—'

'My reputation,' said a conversational voice behind her, 'is so very bad, you know, madam, that nothing you can say can make it worse. Of course I was at an orgy. Where else would I be? Nobody will have the least difficulty believing that I have attended orgies with tedious regularity. The – ah – heroic role I played there on this occasion, of course, will be something quite new, and I dare say will go a long way to rehabilitate me in the eyes of the world. It is a romantic tale, in fact, with a little spice to it, just suited to the modern taste. I expect they will make a play of it, and we shall see ourselves on the stage. And you did introduce us, after all, for which I must always be grateful. As my dear wife says, it seems we owe you our profound thanks.'

The Duke stepped forward from his place of concealment and

moved to take Georgie's hand in his, but he was not to have the opportunity to do so. With an enraged bellow, Captain Hart burst from the undergrowth where he had been hiding and charged straight at him, fists upraised in threat. His Grace was astonishingly swift in his recovery and stepped aside neatly, and the Captain whirled and came about again. They stood facing each other, both of them taking on a pugilistic stance and circling each other warily, and the Duke smiled. 'What a surprising afternoon it has turned out to be,' he said coolly. 'And who in the devil's name are you?'

'He is Captain Hart!' Georgie cried. 'You know I told you of my foolish entanglements last year...'

'I see,' replied her husband, enlightened, still smiling, perfectly relaxed. 'The importunate gentleman you struck down with a poker, I collect? What an excellent thing – I don't recall ever encountering anyone who deserved it more. I wish you might do it again, my love. But this does not explain what you are doing here now, Hart. I do not—'

The Captain launched an impetuous attack as the other man was still speaking, but it seemed he had signalled his intent to his more experienced opponent by some incautious motion of his body, for the Duke sidestepped him once again – he was the taller, heavier man but somehow much the faster – and struck him flush on the chin with a powerful and unexpected blow from his left fist that set the Captain reeling. A neat blow from his right followed it, and Hart collapsed groaning at his feet.

Mrs Aubrey had been watching all this, unheeded, and now she stepped forward. Any self-control she had previously laid claim to had deserted her when she saw her precious schemes all thwarted, her brother floored, and in Georgie's eyes she now appeared quite distracted. Her eyes were wild and her hands were trembling. 'To answer your question, Duke,' she said, pulling a small pistol from her muff and pointing it at him, or in his general direction at least, 'he is my brother, and if he cannot make you pay for what you have both done to us, I will!' She added between gritted teeth, apparently having reached the end of her patience and passed some way beyond it, 'I have observed in the past that I must always *do everything myself*! You owe us money, both of you, and you shall give it to us before you leave this place!' Glancing down at her brother with what seemed to Georgie a contemptuous look, she added, 'Or should I say, you shall give it to *me*?'

'I cannot see that shooting either of us would do you the least good,' said Gabriel, preserving his calm as the pistol waved disconcertingly about and Georgie stood frozen in disbelief. 'Unless you have an unaccountable desire to end your life at Tyburn Tree, of course, which surely cannot be the case. Put down your weapon, madam, and we can converse. You must perceive that the Captain is not seriously hurt. Nothing that cannot be mended has happened here yet.'

'You can't intend to kill anyone, Caro,' added Georgiana urgently. 'Gabriel's right. You can still walk away from this.'

'She doesn't know how to,' said the Duke coolly and, his wife could not refrain from thinking, unhelpfully. It was true – she could see that Mrs Aubrey was in a trap of her own making – but there was no need to remind her of it. They stood in a tense little triangle, quite close together, the outside world near but forgotten, Hart groaning helplessly as he lay disregarded by all of them. It was hard to see how matters were to be resolved without harm coming to one of them, since Mrs Aubrey seemed determined to cling to the only advantage she had: her pistol.

And then there was a sudden, shockingly loud sound nearby – a cry, a scream, a child, a bird, it was impossible to tell, and Georgie saw Caro's finger tighten in reflex action and knew with sickening certainty that she was going to fire, more or less by accident, not deliberately or not wholly so, and that if she did she would hit Gabriel and kill him. Without pausing to think, for there was no time for that, she flung herself in front of his body, pushing Caro down in a rush as she did so. There was a crack, and Georgie crumpled insensate at his feet. She was hit.

37

Gabriel saw the whole thing happen in slow motion. Mrs Aubrey pulled the pistol – small but sufficiently deadly in appearance – from her ridiculous muff, and spoke, though he could barely hear her words over the roaring in his ears, some farrago about Hart being her brother. He spoke, calming words, though he had little idea what he was saying. Then a sudden shocking sound – a bird's cry, some tiny cool part of his brain told him. The woman was startled, and the gun jerked up... He *knew*, he knew with horrifying certainty before Georgiana so much as moved what she was going to do. But he could not stop her. He was not fast enough. And a second later she lay stretched out on the ground, her face as pale as death, an ominous stain spreading horribly fast across the pale pink silk of her pelisse.

He fell on his knees beside her. He wanted to seize her in his arms and cradle her to him, to will life back into her as it ebbed away. He wanted to reverse time, to throw himself in front of the bullet, but he could not, he was powerless. And it would not help her, any of it, but might make things worse if there was still some fragile thread of hope. So instead he took her wrist with fumbling hands and felt desperately for a pulse.

It was there, thank Christ, she was alive, at least for now. And as the worst of his panic receded, he realised that the wound was in her left arm, not her breast or her abdomen, so it seemed she had not been hit in the heart or in the lungs, or another vital organ. Perhaps it was just her arm. Just that, though that was bad enough. But she was unconscious, insensible, and when he very gently chafed her right hand, when he touched her pale little face and called her name in pleading tones, she made no response. A wound to her arm should not do that; she should at least be moaning, showing signs of distress, not lying there terrifyingly still and silent. She had hit her head as she fell, he feared.

There were people around him now, people who would insist on asking him a great number of foolish questions, which he could not hear at all over the roaring that still filled his ears, and crowding about him. He turned on them and spoke a few words in a low, biting tone. Once more he had not the least idea of what he said, but it made them fall back and give him space.

He could not leave her here. He was afraid to move her, but he could not leave her here, broken and bleeding into the dirt. He must take her home, find help. Surely somebody competent would help him. He stood – he was dizzy for a moment, but he fought it and gained command of himself – and, with the most care he had ever shown over any single thing he had ever done in all of his thirty-one years, he picked Georgie up and cradled her to his breast. Her head lolled in a disturbing fashion, and he settled it against his shoulder with infinite tenderness. And then the Duke of Northriding set off to carry his bride home, as the frightful bloodstain spread across her garments and his.

The crowd in the Abbey grounds parted to let him pass, though he did not see any one of them, not even the many persons there with whom he was well acquainted, and a few moments later he crossed the Minster front, where he had been married with such ceremony just four days earlier, and turned into Petergate. The narrow streets of the city were thronged with people, as they often were during daylight hours, but once again His Grace was not obliged to force a passage; everyone shrank back and gave him ample room. There was something particularly striking about the slow, measured pace at which he walked, like that of a man following a funeral procession; the very obvious care he was taking not to jar his precious burden. God forbid he should stumble and cause her further hurt.

Nobody who saw the extraordinary sight was ever to forget it, and many who had not been there to see it later claimed that they had. It was a ghastly, deeply affecting tableau to behold, as so many would later aver. It was not just the blood. Such an expression of fixed, blind horror was rarely to be seen on a man's face outside of the battlefield – there were men in the streets of York that day who had seen battlefields aplenty and could attest to that – and of course it was impossible for the observers to tell, as her husband carried her so tenderly, so lovingly through the crowds, whether the poor young lady was alive or dead, and whether the Duke found himself tragically widowed so very soon after he had wed.

38

Georgie regained consciousness to find that she was back in her bedchamber and in a nightgown with not the least idea of how she got there. The curtains were drawn and a small fire crackled in the grate; apart from that, it was very quiet in the room, and somehow she felt that it must be the middle of the night, or early morning. She tried to sit, but sharp unexpected pain – in her head and in her arm – prevented her, and she fell back, gasping.

In an instant Gabriel was at her side. 'You must not try to get up,' he said, his voice level, controlled. 'Lie down, my dear, and be easy. There is nothing to fear now, I assure you.'

'What happened?' she asked weakly. 'I can scarcely piece it together, so jumbled are my recollections. Captain Hart was there suddenly, and you knocked him down...'

'It transpired that Hart is Mrs Aubrey's brother – do you remember that?'

She shook her head, then regretted it instantly as sharp pain stabbed her again. 'Try not to move,' the Duke said gently. 'I will explain everything. You have a concussion – you hit your head on a piece of masonry when you fell, for I did not reach you in time to catch you, to my eternal regret. But the doctor apprehends no lasting damage. And the wound in your arm is much slighter than I feared at first. A mere graze, really, though it bled a great deal and gave us all a dreadful fright. The bullet did not lodge in you, and so did not have to be removed: a great blessing, I am assured.'

Georgiana looked down in confusion and saw that her night-rail had been cut away and her left arm was heavily bandaged just below her shoulder. 'The bullet…?'

He smiled wryly, and raised her right hand to his lips, kissing it with enormous tenderness and saying with a lightness that appeared to cost him some considerable effort, 'You do not recall your great act of heroism? Clearly you do not. Mrs Aubrey produced a pistol from that ridiculous muff of hers, and was about to shoot me quite by accident, or so you feared, for you flung yourself in front of me and took the bullet yourself. What can I say but thank you, a thousand times thank you, though those words can never be adequate…' He broke off, impeded by some obstruction in his throat, it seemed.

'I remember now…' she said slowly. 'I thought she would surely kill you. I had to do something.'

'I thought she had killed *you*,' he replied in a low tone, looking down at her hand where it still rested in his. 'You were insensible, and there was a great deal of blood, as I think I have said. It was… I have no words to describe it.'

'That is not like you,' she said, with a pitiful attempt at humour.

'I know.'

As she looked at him, she saw that he was still wearing the grey coat he had put on before their meeting with Mrs Aubrey. It was stained all across the arms and chest – with her blood, she realised, in no small quantities. His breeches were the same. She must have let out some exclamation, for he followed the direction of her gaze and looked down, and only now appeared to recollect that he had not changed. 'Good God, I'm sorry, Georgie!' he exclaimed. 'You should not have been obliged to see that! I had quite forgot...'

'How long since it all happened?' she asked. 'Have you so much as left my side?'

'It is early morning now. You were unconscious or asleep twelve hours, I dare say, though it seemed much longer. No – I have not left you for more than a moment or two, and that under protest. I was obliged to see the authorities when they came calling last night, though I fear I was monstrously uncivil to the blameless gentlemen. Your maid was quite appalled that I would not go while she and my housekeeper cut you out of your clothes and undressed you, then put you in your nightgown. She thought it improper, and told me so, but I told her in return that she would endure my presence without complaint or I would put her from the room, by force if necessary, and do it all myself. She stopped objecting then,' he said, with a brief, wintry smile.

'I should think she did!' said Georgie, and then, 'Oh, do not make me laugh! My head hurts so!'

'I should not let you talk at all,' he said penitently. 'I was told to give you a cordial, should you wake. If you will let me do so, and promise to close your eyes for a while, I will fetch someone to sit with you for a few moments so I may go and change, and you will not see such a ghastly spectacle when next you open your eyes. I am sorry I neglected to remove these hideous garments. But I have been... distracted, and I did not want to leave you while you still seemed in danger.'

'You said the doctor reassured you there would be no lasting damage,' she expostulated weakly, as he raised her carefully in his arms and helped her to drink some liquid from a glass that had stood ready.

'He did, but... I was apprehensive.' He was excessively pale, she saw now, and there were lines by his mouth that she did not recall having seen there before. He was plainly exhausted to the limit of his endurance.

'You should go and sleep,' she said, lying back against her pillows.

'I will sleep when Blanche has arrived and can stay with you. She was to set off at first light. Your brother will be here a few hours later, I should think. I sent urgent messengers to both of them.'

'Poor Hal,' she said fretfully. 'I am for ever dragging him across the countryside to see to some trouble I have embroiled myself in.'

'I am sure he will not scold you on this occasion,' the Duke said drily. He seemed to have recovered some fragile measure of composure. 'Will you rest now, most stubborn and bravest of women?'

'I will,' she said, 'if you will tell me what happened after. I promise I will be good, if you will only tell me!'

He sighed. 'Sheer chaos reigned. It is not usual, of course, for shots to be fired in the centre of York in these supposedly civilised times. I have been given to understand that many persons fled in terror, and others, braver or simply more curious, came running to see what had happened. I recall very little of it, to be honest. But they tell me that Hart was still insensible on the ground, and you too, of course, with blood staining your pelisse in a most dramatic fashion. I was on my knees beside you, frantic...'

'I liked that pelisse,' Georgie grumbled, hoping to win a smile from him, but when it came it was a faint one.

'I am afraid it is quite ruined; even setting aside the blood, it had to be cut off you. Fortunately, when people arrived I was recognised, and so was not given in charge or suspected for more than a moment of perpetrating the massacre. The constables came, and took Hart away, once it was established that he had not also been shot but merely knocked down. I saw nothing of any of this, and cared less for it; I was carrying you home through the streets.'

'My God.'

'Yes. I believe it made an enormous impression upon all who saw it, though I was quite oblivious to it. There is, or at least there was last night, a great anxious crowd gathered outside the house to wait for news of you.'

'And Mrs Aubrey?'

'It is understood that she escaped in the confusion. Nobody had the least idea that a woman was the assailant until I was interviewed much later. She may well still be taken up, of course. Her description has been circulated widely.'

She was silent for a moment as her thoughts whirled in confusion, but after a little while some clarity emerged. 'I cannot be sorry she got away. I must hope they do not catch her.'

'You have no thirst for revenge?'

'To see a woman hang, because of me, and all for a stupid accident? I cannot wish for it.'

'I would do it with my own hands, and gladly,' he said, the blunt, assured ferocity of his words at odds with his urbane tone.

'I don't believe you really mean that, Gabriel.'

He sighed again, and she saw how bone-weary he was. 'Perhaps not, my dear. I hardly know what I am saying, I confess. Now will you rest? I will only leave you for a moment, since Blanche is not here yet, and I have told you all.'

'I will.'

He rang the bell, and when the housekeeper answered – she had plainly been hovering nearby in case of a summons – he kissed his wife's hand again and left her to change his clothing, and not before time. She closed her eyes and let sleep claim her, and hoped no dreams would come.

39

Georgiana felt a little better when next she opened her eyes, towards the afternoon, and was able to take some broth and a small glass of wine. Lady Blanche had arrived and come to sit with her as she slept, and she very kindly did not question her about what had happened or make any other demands on her when she woke; she supposed Gabriel had instructed her strictly to be as calm and soothing a companion as possible. It certainly seemed he was not currently in a mood to be crossed by anyone.

But Georgie had not previously had occasion to spend any time alone with her sister-in-law, and might well take advantage of the opportunity now that it had presented itself. To talk about something that did not in any way relate to Mrs Aubrey, Captain Hart, or the shocking events of the day before would distract her, she thought. 'Blanche...' she said, when she had eaten and the dishes had been removed.

Lady Blanche looked up quickly from her sewing. 'Can I get anything for you?' she asked.

'I am quite comfortable,' Georgie reassured her, though it was not entirely true. 'I was thinking about something Gabriel said to me – was it yesterday, or the day before? I have rather lost track of time, with everything that has happened.'

'I am sure that's perfectly understandable,' said Blanche reassuringly, snipping off a thread.

'He said that Ashby was always your father's favourite, and that he, Gabriel, was a constant disappointment to him. He seemed... I don't know, it can be hard to tell what he's thinking. But it seemed to hurt him, if that's not too strong a word. Then he deliberately changed the subject, and appeared to regret saying anything, and so I did not insist on his telling me more.'

'If my brother does not wish to address a subject, it can be very difficult indeed to have such a discussion,' replied Blanche drily. 'But I'm glad you asked. There is no great mystery, you know, and I should be happy to tell you.'

'I would be grateful. I have said to Gabriel before, we hardly know each other, and surely that must be remedied. The circumstances of our marriage...'

'Quite.' She set down her stitchery. 'Both of my brothers were always army-mad; I am sure you of all people know how boys can be when they are fourteen or fifteen. But my father would not permit Gabriel to purchase a pair of colours; it was inappropriate for his heir to put himself in danger, he said, though a younger son was different, and nothing that Gabriel could say, no matter how passionately he argued, would move him.'

'It must have been an awkward situation,' said Georgie slowly. 'But it was not an unreasonable position for your father to take, after all.'

'Of course it wasn't. But boys of that age are *not* reasonable.' Georgie laughed ruefully; she knew all too well the truth of this. 'I think only a boy could conclude that his father's willingness to put his younger brother in mortal danger meant he loved that brother *more*.'

'Oh God, they're ridiculous, aren't they?'

'Perfectly ridiculous. But all might still have been well if my father had allowed Gabriel to begin involving himself in the management of the estates, as was his right. He did not; he did not want to give up any measure of control, all the more because his health was failing by then, he was starting to let things slide and he knew it, though he did not admit it to anyone, least of all to Gabriel. Hasty words were spoken between them, words that could not later be taken back. I was not in England by then – I was married, in Ireland, and had two small children. But my mama – my stepmother, that is, but we were very close and I always called her Mama – told me of the terrible arguments, and her fruitless efforts to bring them both to see sense. She said the likeness between them had never been more obvious than when they were saying dreadful, unforgiveable things to each other.'

'I understand.'

'And then of course Gabriel reacted by becoming terribly wild, which was not surprising since my father would give him no better way of passing his time, as you can be sure he pointed out most frequently, and he was in a sense cut off from Northriding, which he loves so much, by my father's stubbornness and his own foolish pride. As anybody could have predicted, he was obliged to leave Oxford because of his behaviour there, and then worse things happened and a dreadful scandal blew up, which my father took as evidence that he had been right all along not to trust him. There was an irrevocable break between them. Papa tried to make Mama cast him off too, but of course she refused, and that caused trouble and unhappiness in their marriage, which my father, of course, blamed Gabriel for, though in truth he knew nothing of it since he was not here but abroad. Everything in the world was his fault, by this point.'

'Was Gabriel estranged from your brother as well?'

'No, thank heaven, never, or imagine how many more regrets Gabriel would have now our brother is dead. Ash was stubborn too, and refused to bow to my father's pressure. Then my father's illness worsened, he had a paralytic stroke and was incapacitated, and Gabriel returned, and at last was able to take over the running of the estates, which my father had handled very badly for several years. And Papa died, without the breach between them ever being mended.'

'That's very sad. I thought there must be something of the kind behind Gabriel's words.'

'It is a common enough tale, I dare say. Men and their ridiculous pride! And now you know, and it is right that you should. I am not sure my brother will ever speak of it, and it is ancient history after all, but you are family now. I only wish Mama had lived to meet you, for I am sure you would have dealt extremely well with her, and she would have been so happy to see Gabriel married to you. At least he always knew that *she* loved him and did not make favourites, and she never reproached him for anything more than what she saw as excusable youthful folly, such as any unlucky boy might commit. There was no nonsense from her such as blaming him for my father's illness, though I am sure he blamed himself – perhaps he does so still, I do not know, or perhaps he has reconciled himself with the past. We rarely speak of it. But I should not rattle on so when you are tired, I am sure, and need to rest. Oh – one more family thing I should tell you while I think of it, and then I will hold my tongue. Good news: I saw Isabella and her parents, and I am glad to say that she is much better. Almost her old self again, in fact. Perhaps the shock of seeing you and Gabriel helped in some way that I do not fully understand. She said it did, at any rate. She asked me to apologise to you for the scene she created, and I promised her I would do so, even though I thought it quite unnecessary. I was excessively glad to see her so well. Now rest!'

Georgie murmured her thanks, and did close her eyes for a little while, to reflect on what she had heard. It shed a different light on Gabriel, she thought – to imagine him as a passionate, wrong-headed boy much like one of her young brothers, rather than the habitually controlled, self-deprecating, almost permanently ironic man she knew now. Or barely knew, if truth were told. He had not been so very controlled that morning, when he had shown her just a little of how deeply her injury had affected him. But she could not predict how he would be next time she saw him; whether the protective shell would be back in place, defying all attempts to know him better.

40

Gabriel came back into the room soon afterwards, bathed, changed and rested, the lines carved in his face by worry and exhaustion largely smoothed away. He smiled when he heard that she had been sitting up and taking refreshment, and was even more reassured when the doctor returned and, after talking with her, taking her pulse and examining her wound, pronounced her securely on the mend. That gentleman commended her upon her heroism and her extraordinary fortitude, congratulations which she received in embarrassed silence.

As soon as she was alone with her husband, she said urgently, 'I have been on pins in case I said something wrong to the doctor! Quickly, tell me what is supposed to have happened! You did not say before, but I am quite sure you cannot have told anyone the actual truth.'

'Indeed not. The story I have put about, my dear, is that Mrs Aubrey was an acquaintance of yours who, upon hearing of your marriage, wrote you a most piteous letter begging you for aid. Because you are all compassion and trusting innocence...' Georgie pulled a face and his lips twitched, but he continued, 'Because, as I say you are known to be so extraordinarily good, if a little impulsive, you agreed to meet the lady, to see what assistance you could offer her in her time of trial. I, not being anywhere near so trusting nor so generous, accompanied you and stood close by in case you should need my help. Providentially so, for the meeting was nothing but a trap, as Mrs Aubrey was, all unknown to us, the half-sister of a rascally suitor whom your family had rejected some time past. Imagine our horror when he appeared, plainly intent on kidnapping you, whether for ransom or for some more nefarious purpose we cannot know. I knocked him down. But then his sister, deranged at being thwarted, filled with savage passion for revenge, produced a pistol, and you, heroine that you are, flung yourself upon it without a second's thought to save your newly-wed husband's life. You fell at my feet, insensible, bleeding. I clasped you in my arms, distraught. The villainess fled. And here we are.'

'It sounds exactly like something that would be set forth upon the stage.'

'It does. I am reasonably confident that it will be, and quite soon. I wouldn't be at all surprised if the company at the Theatre Royal is already in rehearsal. The house is full of flowers, by the way, brought by your many admirers. I am given to understand that next time you drive out you are in severe danger of the horses being taken from the poles and sturdy citizens taking their place, to pull you in triumph through the streets.'

'I may just stay here, in that case, and never go outside again. That sounds terrifying.'

'I don't blame you in the least. I should add that I believe the local civic worthies are having a declaration in your praise written out on a roll of parchment and illuminated, and intend to present it to you in some small ceremony. There is talk of choirs. Prints are being—'

Georgie put up her hand. 'I can't tell if you are inventing all or some of this. I hope it is all a jest. It still hurts to laugh, you know.'

He crossed to the bed and sat by her, and said with sudden seriousness, his voice cracking a little, 'My dearest—'

But she was never to know what he might have said, for at the most inconvenient moment possible a wild-eyed Hal burst into the room, still dressed in his mud-splattered many-caped driving coat, followed closely by Cassandra, white-faced and tense, both of them clearly suffering the greatest possible anxiety, and in her brother's demanding what the devil had happened to her now, the moment was lost for ever.

41

Georgie sighed and put down her book, and wandered restlessly over to look out across the silvered water with unseeing eyes. The weather was fine today, as it had not been for most of the summer, and she had taken the opportunity to sit outside, in the Duchess's Garden, and enjoy the sun, weak and hazy as it still was in this most unusual of years. The sunset later, she knew, would be a spectacular show of oranges and fiery reds. But she would probably watch it alone. Gabriel was, she presumed, busy somewhere about the estate, dogs at his heels, as he so often was these days.

They had not remained in York long after she had been wounded. Everyone was of the opinion that they would do much better in the safety of Northriding Castle just as soon as Georgie was pronounced fit to travel. She had not been left alone for a moment while they stayed in Petergate – whether she woke or slept, Gabriel, Blanche, Cassandra or Hal had always sat with her, and she had been glad of it at first, even though everybody reassured her – and themselves – that there could not be the least danger. No trace had ever been found of Mrs Aubrey, and her brother too soon departed from the city.

There had been a curious little scene soon after the shooting, which Hal had described to her but which naturally she had not witnessed for herself, that had occurred when Gabriel and her brother went to see Hart where he languished in captivity. It was unclear with what he could realistically be charged, in fact, since he had claimed complete ignorance of any pistol or any murderous designs his sister might have cherished towards the Duke or towards Georgie; he also denied with great indignation having had the least intention of kidnapping her or doing her any other sort of harm, though he had perforce admitted engaging in a foolish, drunken brawl with Gabriel, from which, of course, he had come off much the worse. And he had, he said, not the faintest clue where Caroline might have gone, although he suspected it would be abroad, if she was sensible. She had her wits to sustain her, but little money. It seemed that the authorities continued to hold Hart as much for his own protection as for any other reason, as there was a fair chance that he would be set upon and offered serious violence if he so much as showed his face in a city whose inhabitants were, almost to the last man and woman, enraged with him and his sister and desperate to lay hands on them.

Gabriel had been ushered into his fetid cell and left alone with him. Hal stood outside and watched through the bars as his new brother-in-law spoke, at length, fluently and intensely, but far too low to be audible to anyone but his intended audience of one. As he spoke, the Captain's face grew paler and paler, and he appeared to lose the power of speech. He could still nod, though, and he did, repeatedly, vigorously. Whatever Gabriel was attempting to impress upon him, it was clear that the point had been well made and well taken. 'He will not be troubling us further,' the Duke had told Hal with superb confidence as they left. 'I do not think he will wish ever to set foot in Yorkshire again once he is set free. He knows well enough what will happen to him if he does so while I am alive, or any friend of mine. I have advised him to leave the country and not to return, and warned him of the consequences if he crosses my path once more.'

Georgie was excessively glad to hear that Hart would soon be gone, and most grateful for the kind attention everyone in the city seemed determined to press on her, though she would prefer if they did not go so far as to murder anybody on her behalf, but she found as she recovered that she started at sudden loud noises, reminding her as they must of gunshots. There were many such noises to disturb her peace, despite the straw Gabriel had ordered to be laid down in the street to muffle the sound of carriage wheels and let her get some rest. The doorknocker was never still, a constant stream of visitors attempting to gain admittance to the house, and quite often noisy crowds gathered outside in an attempt to catch a glimpse of her. The Duke was obliged to issue bulletins on her well-being, as though she were the poor King in one of his crises of ill health. An entirely baseless rumour that she was going into a decline somehow gained currency, and some well-meaning imbecile set a small band of fiddles to play popular airs under her window, in order presumably to raise her spirits. This it notably failed to do. It was this last occurrence which decided Gabriel that they must return to the seclusion and tranquillity of the Castle immediately, and her doctors conceded that it might be best. As for her, she was more than happy to agree, and eager to be gone.

That had been some weeks ago. York races had for once gone forward without the Duke of Northriding in attendance, though he had a horse running. Hal and Cassandra were there in his place, and wrote that they had been cheered to the echo when the crowd had somehow divined that Lord Irlam was the Duchess's brother. Lady Blanche had had a similar experience, as had Lady Ashby, apparently much recovered and going about in society again, when they made a family party up together. It seemed ridiculous. It *was* ridiculous.

Her wound was almost healed now. Gabriel had, perhaps understandably, downplayed its gravity when he had described it to her after she first awoke, for she soon realised that it was in truth no mere scrape or graze. The bullet had caught the outer edge of her left arm and ploughed its way through it, leaving a sort of channel behind in which one could quite easily have inserted a finger, had one been minded to, though Georgie was very grateful that nobody apart from the doctor did so. It would undoubtedly leave a substantial and lasting scar, and the skin about it was still tight and uncomfortable, though she had been assured that this was quite usual. Another inch and it would have missed her entirely. But then, if its trajectory had been a few inches the other way, it would have struck her in the lung or full in the heart, and she would undoubtedly be dead. And if it had missed her completely, it might easily have struck Gabriel and killed him. She could not regret any part of it, therefore.

Gabriel, though... She knew he had been deeply affected by what happened, though he had not spoken of it since that one occasion when she first woke. She was beginning to wonder if he would ever be able to look at her and not see her falling, not see her lying insensible and bloodstained in his arms. He seemed to believe – and in thinking this she was merely guessing, seizing on clues that he let fall by accident, for he said nothing to her of his innermost thoughts and little enough on any but the most trivial of subjects – that what had happened was his fault; that somehow he had failed to protect her, failed to do his duty by her as her husband. He treated her now as though she were made of spun glass: infinitely fragile and delicate, liable to be shattered by the slightest breeze that blew. He kissed her hand, he spoke to her with enormous tenderness and consideration, if she expressed the lightest wish he would move heaven and earth to gratify it, but he did not come to her bed, and he had not made love to her since the shooting.

She had understood that he would not touch her with amorous intent while she was still in pain, while the wound remained unhealed. That was eminently reasonable, considerate, and if sometimes even now she woke in the night and cried out from nightmares of attack, and would have welcomed the comfort that his presence would have brought her, she could be patient. She had been patient.

But she was healed; she had told him so, and so had her doctors. There was the local man, who came daily, and the more distinguished practitioner who was driven out from York each week at Gabriel's insistence, and both reported to him on her progress in great detail, she knew. And still he did not come.

She was not with child. Her courses had arrived with tedious punctuality just a few days after her accident – it had not been precisely or entirely an accident, since Mrs Aubrey had after all drawn the weapon on them and might have meant to use it, but it was a good, safe, harmless word to use even to herself – and she thought it likely that he knew that too. He would have wanted to know her condition, surely, being greatly concerned with the matter and worried besides about her health, and the household staff who waited on her in York, as here at the Castle, were all his people, devoted to him since childhood, his or theirs or both. She had bled again here a month later, had just done with it.

And she was done with waiting. Her arm pained her hardly at all now, and she wanted him back in her bed, where he belonged. Tonight, she resolved. She would seduce him tonight.

She went to her chamber and dressed with great care. Gabriel had passed over the splendid Northriding jewels on their marriage, and had also bought her others as wedding gifts, which she had till now had no opportunity to wear. After some deliberation, she chose a great sapphire pendant, which nestled at the end of its silver chain just between her breasts. It had blue fire in its depths, and he had said when he presented it to her that it reminded him of her eyes. Very well. In York before her wedding she had ordered several gowns suitable for her new status as a married woman, and she paired the jewel with the most daring of them. It was silver tissue, very low cut, very simple, clinging to the curves of her breast, belly and legs in a manner that censorious persons might have described as indecent; she hoped this was true. She wanted to be indecent for him tonight. The neckline dipped down in the centre front to meet the high waist, showing a great deal of cleavage, and at the rear plunged too, in a deep vee that left her back almost completely bare. It had, she recalled, been designed to be worn over a chemise made up in contrasting fabric and edged with a piece of costly, delicate lace, which was meant to fill the gap and at the same time draw subtle attention to it, and to cover her stays, which would otherwise be exposed. But this evening Georgie was not in the mood for subtlety, and wore no stays and only the mostly flimsy of chemises. Her maid blinked when she understood her mistress's instructions, but made no comment.

The sleeves were almost transparent, and did not cover her scar completely, but she had decided that she would disdain to hide it. It was a permanent reminder of a significant thing that had happened to her, and she would not attempt to conceal it from the world. If people did not like it, let them look away. She did not think Gabriel would look away from her tonight. She did not mean that he should.

They met for dinner. They were alone, Lady Blanche and her children still being in York with a party of friends. She was the Duchess now, the mistress of this place, and, taking advantage of her new authority, had ordered that tonight's meal be served in the smallest dining room the Castle possessed; they sat in formal state at either end of the rectangular table, but it was not large, and so they were not far from each other. It was an intimate space, dark red in its decoration, with pictures chosen by some Maulev-erer ancestor with a decided penchant for semi-naked goddesses and other mythical personages, who inevitably seemed to find themselves in perilous situations in the flimsiest and most provocative of drapery. Leda and the swan were here, embracing in a flurry of feathers and naked, splayed alabaster limbs, and so was Andromeda, chained to her rock with very little to preserve her modesty and an expression upon her face of coy expectancy edging into impatience. Here I am! she seemed to be thinking, but where is he? God knows Georgie could understand exactly how she felt.

Gabriel was handsome as ever in formal evening dress, and his silver eyes glittered in the candlelight as he looked at her across the board set with shining cutlery, bright crystal glasses and snowy linen. She was intensely aware of his eyes on her, and her nipples, much like those of Leda or Andromeda, pebbled under his gaze; she thought he could probably see, hoped he could, through the flimsy layers of fabric that covered her breasts. The fine hairs on her arms stood on end, and liquid heat began to pool between her thighs. It had been far too long. But they made light, inconsequential conversation as they ate, their eyes catching, holding all the while, and then at last the discreet servants with-drew and left them alone in the quiet little room. Georgie felt that the libidinous painted heroines were urging her on, and sipped her wine, turning the glass and admiring the rich colour in the candlelight.

'You are very fine this evening, Georgiana,' her husband murmured, and his beautiful voice set her skin tingling, stoking the fire within her, as it always did. 'Are we celebrating some special occasion?'

'Yes, we are,' she replied. 'I hope you think it reason enough to celebrate. It is ten weeks tonight since we first met.'

'I know it is.'

'I thought you might have forgotten.'

'I forget nothing when it comes to you.'

This was promising. She stood, and crossed the room to him. Very deliberately she took his glass from his hand and set it down, and moved the few remaining plates and pieces of cutlery from his end of the table, leaving it clear.

'Do you have intentions towards me, my dear?' he said, with the pale ghost of a smile.

'So many intentions.'

'Good ones?'

'Very bad ones.'

'That sounds delicious.' His voice was ragged.

'I hope you will be.'

Desire flared higher still in his eyes as he apprehended her meaning. But then he seemed to check himself. With what appeared to be a great effort at control, he said almost curtly, 'You are unwell, hurt. Your wound. I cannot—'

'No, *I* cannot. I cannot endure any more that you absent yourself from my bed. My wound is better, is almost healed, and hardly pains me.'

'Hardly is not—'

'I am recovered. And I want you back. Need you back. I am not made of china, Gabriel, I am made of flesh.'

'And blood.'

'Is that the problem?' She subsided into a chair at his side and looked sadly at him; she had feared this. 'I thought it might be. Do you see me bleeding in your arms every time you look at me? Because if you do…'

He looked at her with dark hunger in his eyes and shook his head, his face pale but composed. 'No. I must admit that I did for a while, every time I lay down to sleep. It was terrible – a mere nothing to what you have suffered, of course, but still most distressing – but it is fading with time now I know you are safe. I am so very glad that you are alive, and here with me when I could so easily have lost you for ever.'

'It must have reminded you most horribly of losing your brother last year, and your cousin,' she persisted, not to be fobbed off.

'It did, of course. How could it not? But it is fading,' he repeated.

She was not sure she believed him. 'Make love to me, then,' she said.

'I don't want to hurt you. I could not bear to hurt a single hair on your head after all you have been through.'

'You won't.'

'You can't be sure of that,' he said, with sudden impatience. 'I would be very gentle, of course I would be, but even so…'

'I don't want you to be very gentle. You know I don't.'

Again the sudden flare in his eyes that showed the desire he was keeping so tightly in check. She rose from her chair and slid to her knees between his thighs, the gauzy silver fabric billowing about her as she settled back on her heels and looked up at him, her neck and shoulder bare and her breasts barely covered, the sapphire glinting blue fire between them. He reached out and touched her cheek very softly, almost wistfully, and said, 'You're so beautiful. So desirable. I know you want me too, and it's killing me.'

'Why? Make me understand, Gabriel.'

'I can't make you understand anything while you sit down there and look up at me like that,' he said roughly. 'I can barely think straight, let alone speak.' He was close to losing control, she thought, and she was fiercely glad of it. She was thoroughly sick of his self-control.

She put her hand on his thigh and stroked the black silk of his breeches very slowly and deliberately. She could feel the heat of his flesh through the thin material. 'So let me give you pleasure with my mouth and lips and tongue, and then afterwards you can explain everything when your mind is clearer. You must remember that we only did this once, the day after we were married, so you may have to remind me of just what you would like. I wish you would tell me.' Her voice was demure, in contrast with her words, and her fingers were on his buttons now, awaiting permission. Beneath her hands he was hard for her; she could feel it.

'You're deliberately trying to seduce me.' It was almost a groan.

'Of course I am. It doesn't seem to be working. I'm probably not very good at it.'

'Oh, but you are. You're very good at it. And it's so tempting, Georgie, to let you unbutton me and take me in your mouth. I know exactly how wonderful it would be. I have dreamed of this, and of so many other things, these last weeks.'

'Why won't you let me, then?'

He did not answer her directly, but shifted a little in his chair. 'Could you be content,' he asked her, 'if we always made love like that – our mouths on each other, or our hands, or all the other ways that do not lead to conception?'

She looked up at him in naked astonishment. 'I thought you wanted – no, desperately needed a child. An heir. I thought that was the whole point of marriage for you, with me – with anybody, for God's sake!'

'It was supposed to be. It is still supposed to be. Nothing has changed, and yet everything has. But now the thought of hurting you by my rough attentions, or, even worse, of you risking and perhaps losing your life to give me a child fills me with terror. And yet, if you take me in your mouth – Christ, I am so hard just thinking of it! – in a little while I know it will not be enough, and I will want to lay you down on that table, pull up your skirts and join myself with you so that I can come inside you where I belong.'

'I want that too. It is exactly where you belong.'

'Christ, I know you do. Georgie, you are so good, so brave, you are everything that is admirable, but I am a terrible person. I have always known it, but now more than ever I realise it is so. There must be something wrong with me, as my father always said.'

He grimaced; now he had begun, he was obliged to go on, little though it appeared he wished to share these dark thoughts with her. 'I said, did I not, that I wanted you so much that I was prepared to take you even if you were forced to marry me? That was true then, and that was bad enough. Unforgiveable, really, and I will understand if you feel you can never forgive me for it. But that was when I felt a mere fraction of what I feel for you now. Now, now I could almost wish that I had married some woman I did not care for, some woman I even disliked. Even though it would have meant losing you.'

She felt chilled, and could barely muster the voice to say, 'Why?'

'Because if she had died bearing me a child, I would not have cared. Not really. I would have been deeply sorry, of course, and felt responsible, I am not a complete monster, but... But if *you* do, if I cause your death by my actions, it will destroy me too. I realised that when I thought you were mortally wounded. I knew then that my own life would be over if yours was.'

Georgie saw with shock and a sudden spark of hope, so intense that it was almost painful, that there were tears on his face, running down unheeded, and she could hear the raw anguish in his voice as he went on, 'I don't want to feel like this. I never have before, God knows, and I hate it. I love you, Georgiana, with all my heart and soul I love you, and it is torture!'

42

'You love me...' she said slowly. She had never expected this from him, had barely dared even to imagine it might be possible.

'I do. I'm sorry, I never meant to tell you. Try to forget I have said it if you can. It is not your concern.'

'Not my concern...?' she repeated incredulously.

'You didn't ask me to love you. You said, if I recall, that you were determined not to fall in love with me because you were terrified that I would hurt you. That was wise of you, I think. Love is painful, I have discovered.'

She felt ridiculous now, kneeling at his feet in her provocative gown, but she could not seem to find the will or the strength to move away. Her mind was full of roiling thoughts and desperate hope. Her attempts at seduction really did seem to have gone awry in a most dramatic fashion, but perhaps it did not matter. 'I thought you would be unfaithful to me. That was what I was afraid of, I told you so; that you would leave me while you pursued other women, or, worse, come and go as you pleased, and I would be so lost to all self-respect that I would take you back into my bed and my heart, over and over again, all the while knowing that it would just be for a short time, till you became bored or restless, and then you would leave me alone again and suffering.'

'I won't do that. Not now. I might have thought that that was what my marriage would be like. Perhaps it would have been, with another woman. With Miss Debenham – my God, the thought is an obscenity, despite what I just said to you. But not with you, never with you. The idea of making love to another woman is repulsive to me. Not even that – I simply cannot think of it. It holds no interest for me. I do not believe it ever will.' He was absolute in his sincerity; the truth of what he was saying rang in his voice.

He loved her. Could he really love her? Or was he merely saying it because of the severe shock he had received, and his ever-present sense of guilt? How could she ever be sure? 'You know what else I feared. That I would become the sort of woman who takes lovers, who is so addicted to sensual pleasure that she finds it wherever she can. Who does not feel love, only lust.'

'I... The thought of you making love to another person is torture to me. Of someone else making love to you. Christ, I cannot bear to contemplate it. But... but if that is what it would take to make you happy, then I must accept it. Just as long as you do not allow anyone to hurt you, for I—'

She would not endure any more of this. She must be brave now. 'Did I describe such a life in a manner that made you think it would make me happy? Do you seriously imagine that that is what I want?'

He looked at her in confusion. Clearly he had gone so far into his own dark thoughts over the last few weeks that he had lost much of his grip on reality where she was concerned.

'Ask me what I want, Gabriel,' she said.

'What do you want, my love?' he replied, in little more than a whisper. 'God knows if it is within my power to give it to you, you can be sure I will.'

'Oh, I think it is within your power. I want your love, Gabriel, all of it and all of you. I want it because I love you too.' He looked at her in disbelief and dawning wonder and she said with a wry little smile, 'I think even when I told you I feared falling in love with you and being hurt by you it was already too late. Far too late.'

She laughed as sudden realisation hit her. 'I realise now that my family knew it – Louisa, Hal, all of them. That's why Hal told me I must marry you, that I had no choice. Not because it was true, but because he could see even then that we loved each other and should be together. I believe he thought we just needed a little push.'

Still he looked down at her in silence and she said with a curious little hiccup between tears and laughter, 'Will you say nothing to me, when I have declared my love for you? Must I beg once more?'

'Good God, Georgie, come here!' And as he spoke, he pulled her up onto his lap so that he could kiss her. He had almost always seemed at some essential level controlled to her before, even in the throes of passion, but he had no control at all now as he took her face between his hands and pressed frantic kisses to her mouth, her cheeks, her eyes. She clung to him, fiercely glad just to be in his arms again. At last he fell to kissing her properly, open mouth on open mouth, and she responded eagerly, fixing her hands in his hair and straddling his body assertively with hers.

'I have just told you terrible things,' he whispered raggedly against her mouth a little while later. 'Shocking things, emotions of which I am deeply ashamed. Something about the way I feel about you, the newness and the rawness of it, makes me reveal these things when they would be far better hidden. Again and again I will do it and curse myself even as I am speaking. And still you say you love me? You, so brave and good. Can it really be true?'

'Everyone thinks terrible things. Everyone, I am sure of it. Most people don't say them. You say them. I say them too. And do them. I am not good. Maybe that's why I love you. If I were good…' she said, and as she spoke she tugged quite hard upon his hair, where she grasped it either side of his head, and pressed her body close to his, her breasts crushed against his chest, a delicious friction. 'Are you listening to me, Gabriel? If I were good, I would not have told a parcel of lies and asked a complete stranger to put his mouth on me ten minutes after we had met. To say I love you desperately now is no excuse. I did not love you then.'

'And I did not love you. And still we both did it.' He was holding her tightly now, his hands strong and hard about her waist. How she had missed the feel of him. It was both safe and deliciously dangerous to be held like this.

'You did it at my urging. You thought I was a widow, because I told you so. I am very bad, you see. Much worse than you.'

'I seriously doubt that. And I didn't need a great deal of urging, did I?'

'Not enormous amounts,' she admitted. 'Not then. But now, all the urging in the world seems to do no good. I kneel barely clothed at your feet and offer myself to you, and you do not want me. Indeed, you say explicitly that you don't want to make love to me any more. Though you say you love me. Gabriel, I am confused.'

He took her face between his hands and looked into her eyes. 'It's not true that I don't want to make love to you. I don't think I said that or could ever say that. You must know I have never wanted anything so much in my life. I thought I wanted you before when I had not admitted to myself that I loved you, when I was only obsessed with you, but my feelings then were nothing to what they are now. Love deepens desire more than I could possibly have imagined.'

'And yet...'

He groaned. 'I have told you why! The thought of hurting you, of possibly causing your death, paralyses me. I have always been selfish – I have lived a thoroughly selfish life for thirty-one years – but things are entirely different now.'

She said, 'Not really, Gabriel. I know you are trying, and I understand your fears, God knows, but you have not thought to ask me what I feel about all this, have you? It is not your decision to make, whether I bear a child. Certainly it is not only your decision to make. Do my views count for nothing?'

'Of course they do! But I don't want you sacrificing yourself for me. You tried to do that once already and I nearly lost you.'

'It was the impulse of the moment. Perhaps it was foolish – perhaps she would never have hit you in any case, her hands were shaking so. I believe now that she didn't even really intend to kill you, only to frighten us. I did not stop to think or to calculate. But this is different, you must see. This is a conscious choice that I am free to make. It is not like throwing myself in front of a bullet.'

'Not exactly like that. But the risks...'

'My mother had six children, including a set of twins. She delivered every one of us safely. It was influenza that killed her – heartbreak, in truth, because she had lost my father, whom she loved more than life. *He* died on the hunting field – a stupid, pointless accident that need not have happened. People die every day for ridiculous reasons or none, Gabriel. We cannot keep each other safe. No one can, however strong their love is. Life is not like that.'

He pulled her closer and buried his face in her neck, whispering against her skin, 'That sounds like painful wisdom, Georgie. When did you grow so wise?'

'I am not wise. I am anything but wise; my family would laugh to hear you say so. I too have been selfish, and foolish, and spoilt.

Perhaps people like us need to fall in love to make us look outside ourselves and think of others for the first time. But that's not true, really, is it? Or at least not of you, even if it is true of me. Because you never wanted to marry, and yet you knew you must for the sake of all the people who depended on you, and you were prepared to do it. That doesn't sound very much like selfishness to me, my love.'

He laughed against her throat and ran his hands down her body possessively, her flesh catching fire anew at his touch after having been starved of it for so long. 'It is like your generosity to say so, but I do not think that you will persuade many people of your point of view. Most people would laugh to think that my agreeing to take my choice among the most beautiful debutantes society has to offer, agreeing to make love incessantly to the woman I chose until she conceived a child, then reserving the right to go back to my careless bachelor ways if I so desired, was any great sign of selflessness. I dare say most of the men in England would be very happy to be in my shoes!'

'I do not care about most of the men in England, only you.'

'I cannot tell you how glad I am of it. But I am still selfish. And now I would rather let all those people who depend on me down than lose you. You know I would. And damn the consequences.'

'I don't think that's true. Not really. I know you better than that. I think as the months and then the years passed with no heir for Northriding, you would look at the anxious faces of the people around you, people you've known all your life, and that too would begin to torment you. I know it would torment me; not even to try to have a child. I think it would be bound to cause a rift between us, a little crack that slowly opened up into something bigger. If we try and cannot, of course, that is a different matter, or so everyone keeps telling me.'

'You're sure about this, my dearest love?'

'I am not sure about anything except the fact that I love you.' She smiled and stroked his silvered head; when he heard her words, he had pressed his lips to her throat with passionate intensity, and tightened his grip on her body. 'But I am beginning to realise that I do want a child, for myself as well as for you. I felt a sharp, unexpected pang of dismay when I realised that I had not conceived, and that made me reflect. And I think too that I could come to love this place and its people, and want to be a part of it. Something about it speaks to me, you know.'

'I do know. I realised that when I first saw you walking on the beach. I can't wait to show it all to you properly, my queen.'

'And also,' she said, slipping her hand under his jacket and beginning to unbutton his waistcoat, 'I grew up in a house full of children, you must realise. It is what I am accustomed to. We may say terrible things about each other, and to each other, but we all love each other dearly, and would take on all the world and fight it if one of us needed it. I would be very happy to create a family of my own – of our own – in that image. Or at least to make the attempt.'

'Am I to understand, my love, that you would like to begin on the project this very instant?' His waistcoat was undone, and Georgie was now tugging impatiently on his shirt to free it from his breeches, so that she could slide her hands up under it and touch his skin at last.

'I think it only sensible!' she said, and as she spoke he rose to his feet, still holding her, and carried her from the room, past the liveried footmen in the hall, who stood up straighter and hastily banished grins, up the grand staircase to her bedchamber.

43

When they reached her room, he set her on her feet, though he did not release his grip on her. 'We had barely begun, had we?' he said tenderly as he looked down at her. 'Three or four precious, unforgettable days of passion, of exploration, and then I came so appallingly close to losing you. Shall we start again?'

'That sounds wonderful.'

'What do you want from me, then, my beautiful bride? I am entirely at your command. Your pleasure, as you must surely know by now, is mine.'

She told him, whispering in his ear, and drew him towards the bed. 'I think I can manage that,' he said. 'But shall I undress you first?'

'Perhaps in a little while.'

'And shall I undress myself?'

'Yes! You can do that. And I will watch you. I believe I would enjoy that.'

She slipped off her silk evening shoes, and lay back against the pillows without taking her eyes from him. He ripped off his cravat and threw it aside, then shrugged out of his coat and waistcoat. He pulled his shirt over his head and stood smiling down at her in his black satin breeches, and she drank in the sight of his muscular chest, slim waist and strong thighs. He began to unbutton himself and she bit her lip as the tantalising line of dark hair that ran down from his belly was revealed. She had kissed her way down it the day after they were married, and she would again, but not now. He sat beside her on the bed, and slipped out of his breeches and stockings. He was naked, magnificent, and hard for her. 'Good,' she said. 'Very good. Now come here.'

He came to lie beside her, and she pulled his head down so that she could kiss him. They were open-mouthed, hungry, fierce, their tongues exploring each other, and she ran her hands up his back and dug her fingers into his taut muscles. Presently he released her mouth with one long, last lingering kiss and began to work his way down her throat, pressing his lips to her skin, to the hollow where her pulse beat, and biting her gently where she was most sensitive. His warm, naked, beloved body covered hers and she spread her legs so that he could lie between them and she could wrap herself around him for the first time in what seemed like years, though it was only weeks. She was still clothed, of course, but only in two layers of delicate, gauzy material that was barely a barrier between them. Her nipples were almost painfully hard, so sensitised already that the mere touch of the lace of her chemise was arousing, yet frustrating, for she wanted more. 'This gown…' he murmured against the curve of her shoulder.

'Do you like it?'

'That's by no means strong enough a word,' he said, kissing the valley between her breasts, where the jewel still lay, and then pulling down the silver gauze with intent fingers to reveal one taut globe covered with the merest wisp of lace. He did not pull the lace aside, but fixed his hungry mouth on her with her chemise still in place, and she gasped at the heat and wetness of him and the sheer rightness of it. His clever tongue worked its way under the lace and circled her nipple, and then he used his teeth to drag aside the material, tearing it a little. His teeth just grazed the exquisitely sensitised, erect flesh with superb control, just hard enough, not too hard, not too soft, and she moaned and pushed up against him, urging herself into his mouth, arching her back, pressing her pelvis against his. His hand was on her other breast, rolling her nipple between his fingers, tantalising her through the material that still covered her there. She dug her heels into the mattress and her nails into his skin.

Presently he pulled back a little, so that he could push the gown down completely and bare her breasts. They were flushed, and she was so aroused that when he blew on one engorged nipple she whimpered and writhed under him. He laughed, a low, intimate, triumphant sound, and took her in his mouth once more and sucked on her hard, one tight bud and then the other. 'I think...' he whispered a little while later against her hot skin, and between words the tip of his tongue teased the very tip of her, and it was almost unbearably good, 'I think I could make you come like this, without laying a finger on any other part of you, without touching you in any other way.' She moaned incoherent assent. 'But you don't want that, do you? Not now?'

Before she could remind him what she wanted, before he made her beg again, he dragged her skirts ruthlessly up about her waist – another petticoat ruined – and slid into her, claimed her completely, with a breathless, slick movement that made them both cry aloud at the fierce perfection and completion of it.

She had told him, when she had whispered her desires to him a few moments since, that she did not want him to be controlled, tentative, careful of her as though she were fragile and might break under him. She was not, she would not, and she wanted all of him, all of his passion and his strength pounding into her. She locked her legs tight about his waist, gripped his buttocks tightly with both hands, and moved with him in complete unity of purpose. They came together, panting, gasping, kissing with frantic urgency, desperate to join and not be parted. Never to be parted.

When at last they lay in each other's arms in the dazed aftermath of passion, he smoothed the silvery fabric – now sadly, possibly irrevocably creased and crumpled – over her thigh and said, 'Do you know what I would like to do, Georgie?'

'I don't. I hope it's wicked and shocking,' she said lazily, her own tongue coming out to explore his nipple, as it seemed only fair recompense.

'Of course it is. Would you expect any less of me? Don't stop, by the way.'

'Mmm,' she said. 'I promise I won't. Please, tell me.'

'I would like to see you in this almost transparent gown with nothing at all underneath it.'

'I'm sure that could be arranged.'

'I'd like to see you, every precious inch of you, in this gown with nothing at all underneath it, leading me – possibly on a leash, I'd have to think about that – into that house where first I laid eyes on you.'

He saw her expression, half shocked and half intrigued, and said, smiling, 'There's no need for us actually to do it. I don't mean the dress – I must insist upon that, my love – but the public display, the house and all the rest of it. It's just a fantasy that perhaps we might both enjoy.'

Georgie did not answer him directly, though she was sure that he was right; he had given her delicious food for thought. She said instead, tangling her fingers in the whorls of soft dark hair that covered his chest and tugging on it a little, 'Everyone is always talking about your reputation – you, too. But that's one of the first things you have ever said to me that truly makes me understand how you gained it, if you have ever really done such a thing as that. And you make me realise now that you never told me why you went to that house. Perhaps you were, you are, a regular visitor? I asked you then, but you said only that I would not believe you if you told me. Is it so very terrible, your reason? We should have no secrets now, Gabriel, and if there is anything more you want from me that you are afraid to ask—'

He laughed. 'Oh, my love! The truth is quite different. I had no intention of telling you my guilty secret then; I was too busy painting myself as dangerous, mysterious, intriguing – all for your benefit. Telling you that I had gone there to look for my idiot nephew and bring him home to his anxious mama would hardly have produced the desired effect.'

She raised her head and looked at him in surprise. 'Truly?'

'Truly. You have noticed, I dare say, that he is of an amorous disposition. He attempted to flirt with you more than once, as I recall, but you gave him the cold shoulder. Yes, I was watching, of course I was watching, I was always watching… But I am straying from my point. He led a very sheltered life as a child on FitzHenry's estate in Ireland, and it is fair to say that London went straight to his head. He has no father now, and I am hardly in a position to lecture him on morality. But Blanche did call on me to restrain him from his more desperate activities when she heard of them. I spoke to him, I made sure he knew how to protect himself and others. And when she discovered from something he had let slip to his sister that he intended to pay a visit to that house, she asked me to go there and remove him, if I could find a way to do so. She was right: it is no place for the inexperienced, as I recall saying to someone else.'

'You did say that. But you did not find him?'

'No, he was not there. He told me later that he had thought

better of it, that he realised he was in dangerous territory, and becoming carried away with the idea of being a terrible sort of a fellow. God knows I understood what he meant by *that*, since it was precisely the path I followed. I was impressed that he was wiser than I was at the same age. He is really not unintelligent, when he thinks with his head and not another part of his anatomy.'

She chuckled. 'I'm sorry I did not know that sooner – why you were there, I mean.'

'Because you would have told the Aubrey woman of it? I fear she would not have believed you: my terrible reputation again, you know. Avuncular concern does not fit with how the world sees me.'

'Is any of it true, though, Gabriel, your terrible reputation?'

'Oh, yes. Much of it is. Too much. I will not have you put me on a pedestal, my love. I was expelled from Oxford for my atrocious behaviour, then caught in flagrante at eighteen with a married woman several years my senior; I fought her husband in a duel and wounded him, and was obliged to flee abroad. I lived a rackety sort of life across Europe after that, and only came back when I was forced to take on my father's responsibilities during his illness. I was a constant worry to him, and to my poor mother, and I regret that most of all, but it is far too late to mend.'

'Blanche told me of your estrangement from your father.'

'Did she? I am glad. That is a sorry tale, with faults on both sides. I was fired up with righteous anger towards him at the time, young idiot that I was, and of course when I saw what a sad mull he had made of running the estates towards the end of his life I was angrier still. But I have talked about it a great deal in recent years with Mr Summerson, and he has helped me to see things in a fairer light. We are none of us perfect, me least of all. I do regret that my father died before the breach between us could be mended, but do not be thinking of me as a tortured, mistreated soul. I am just an average sort of sinner, worse than most, not as bad as some.'

Something occurred to her that had not so much as crossed her mind before. Now that it struck her, she did not understand why she had never thought to ask what was surely a crucial question. With a sudden icy chill on her, despite all his declarations of love and fidelity, she said, 'Did you have a lover, Gabriel, when you met me? Is there some woman whom you have written to tell of your marriage, who received the news with distress and who is wondering even now if you will come back to her, and hoping that you will?'

With a fluid movement, he shifted their bodies so that they were looking each other full in the face, and said earnestly, 'There is not. There has not been anyone for a long time. And after my brother's death and all that followed it, I was... I don't know how to put it. Frozen, I suppose. Uninterested in physical contact for the first time in forever, aware that I must marry, reluctant to do so, a little revolted by the prospect... Trapped. Until I entered that house and saw you huddled in your corner, fascination warring with fear on your lovely face. Until I went down on my knees in front of you. Then I began to wake up. God knows, I'm awake now.'

His hands were on her, hers on him, and she could see that he was telling the truth. He was wide awake, every part of him, and as for her... 'I think you might undress me now after all,' she said, rolling onto her stomach so that he could reach the buttons that ran from waist to hem of her gown. The beautiful, crumpled fabric had been dragged up around her thighs, and she was, she realised, still wearing her stockings and her garters. Perhaps he would remove them, perhaps he would not. Either way had its advantages. She looked over her shoulder and smiled teasingly at him.

He smiled too, a wolfish sort of a smile, and trailed a line of butterfly kisses from the nape of her neck, across her shoulder blades and down the deep vee of her bodice. 'What a delicious picture you present,' he murmured between kisses. 'If only Boucher were alive to paint you. Being fully and most delightfully occupied, I had not until now noticed the back of this extraordinary confection. A shocking omission, I know you agree. It is just as glorious as the front, I see now, and merits just as much attention.' And he began to undo her, in every possible sense, as very slowly with lips, tongue and clever fingers he worked his way down her body.

44

LONDON, AUTUMN 1816

Mauleverer House is being opened up! was the whisper around the ton. Everyone agreed that this was excessively interesting news. It had been many years indeed since the grand mansion in Mayfair had hosted a ball or a rout party, and nobody much under the age of forty could boast of having even set foot inside. The late Duchess had been a notable hostess in her early married life, and had brought out her stepdaughter Lady Blanche in fine style some twenty years or more since, but Her Grace had lost her taste for society during her husband's long illness, and in later years spent most of her time in Yorkshire. Of course, the current Duke resided at the mansion when he was in London, but as a single man he had naturally not given any parties – or, at any rate, not the sort of parties that respectable people attended. Or admitted they attended. Young people, therefore, scarcely knew him, and it had been left to their elders to use him a species of bogeyman, a dire warning to incautious damsels of the wicked hands they might fall into if they failed to observe the proprieties at all times. (Whether such warnings had had the desired effect was entirely another matter.)

But now the other residents of Grosvenor Square could see for themselves that there was a great bustle of activity: decorators and other workmen went to and fro, furniture was removed and other furniture and furnishings delivered, and everyone agreed that the Duke and his bride must be planning to take up residence as soon as the work was done.

A handsome, wealthy gentleman with a dubious reputation, one who almost never showed his face in society but was known to have fought a duel and wounded his mistress's husband, then fled abroad to escape the consequences of the scandal he had created, was bound to be the subject of a great deal of gossip and speculation. This was particularly the case when he had so recently married a young and beautiful lady several years his junior. The current *on dit* said that His Grace *had* recently ventured into polite society for the first time in many years: several perfectly reliable people who had known him in his youth claimed to have seen his tall, unmistakeable figure at balls and parties during the season, and he had even obtained vouchers for Almack's – how? Why? – and penetrated between the august portals of that most respectable of institutions. While there he had not danced nor conversed with any young lady – no debutante had felt her virtue even slightly threatened, which was a sad disappointment to more than a few of them – and he had left quite soon after his arrival, having barely spoken to anyone at all during the duration of his stay and behaved in a manner discourteous, uncivilised, and undeniably thrilling. He had appeared, one fanciful and sharp-eyed matron had declared, to be looking for someone. His silver gaze had searched the room with electric intensity, seeking one particular person and evidently not finding them. Not finding *her* – surely, with his reputation, it must be a woman he sought, and for some amorous purpose. He had put the watching lady in mind, she declared, fanning herself vigorously, of a caged panther. Goodness, her auditors had murmured, taking up their own fans and plying them. They could all too easily picture it.

From this tantalising suggestion, this tiny nut of gossip, had sprung forth a whole forest of speculation. It was whispered that the Duke had set eyes on Lady Georgiana Pendlebury in some accidental way – in the street, perhaps, nobody was entirely sure, and it could hardly signify – and instantly conceived a violent passion for her. He had instituted enquiries and discovered her identity, then scoured the ballroom and drawing rooms of fashionable London in search of her. What, ladies asked each other, would he have done if he had found her? Asked for her hand in marriage directly – when they had never even been introduced – or carried her off a helpless captive, in thrall to his desperate obsession?

Many ladies shared an unvoiced regret that nothing quite so shocking had in fact occurred, but what had come next was in truth almost as exciting. The Duke had instituted an entirely fictitious search for a bride – for it was clear that he had with steely resolve already made his choice – and invited the cream of society to his sinister lair... that is to say, to his castle in the wilds of the North. Many ladies and their mamas had attended in innocent expectation, unaware that they were mere dupes, and, as the satanic nobleman had designed, Lady Georgiana had been among the party, entirely unaware of the danger into which she was placing herself. As soon as he had laid eyes on her once more, his passion had redoubled, and he had used all his considerable charm and experience of seduction in wooing the poor girl, to such good – that is, very bad – effect that the pair had been caught in a highly compromising situation, positively in the act, a mere day or two later by a large, horrified group of persons of rank who were attending a ball at his ducal seat. Possibly the ball had been organised with diabolical ingenuity for that sole purpose. It had all been a trap! The guilty lovers had announced their betrothal on the spot – Lady Georgiana's guardians were not consulted, and could have done nothing to prevent the match even if they wished to do so – and the Duke was triumphant, his wicked scheme having met with complete success.

But there was more! That Northriding had succeeded in mesmerising the young lady and putting her entirely in his power was made all too plain by the fact that when a deranged woman – undoubtedly, it was considered, a spurned mistress of the Duke's, one among many – had attempted to shoot him the very day after the wedding, his bride had flung herself in front of the weapon and risked her young life to save him, and been hideously wounded as a result. Her survival had been despaired of for many days, and the Duke was distraught at the thought of losing the prize he had so recently gained. Nothing half so intriguing had happened in *years*.

The activity in Grosvenor Square lessened and then ceased – the house was plainly finished – and the inhabitants of the square found all sorts of excellent reasons to pass by it and linger ingenuously near it on a daily basis, in the hopes that they would happen to be present when the residents arrived.

In fact, a pair of sisters living a few doors down from the ducal residence were one afternoon lucky enough to see an elegant black and silver travelling coach draw up outside the mansion, and immediately with great presence of mind concealed themselves, along with their accompanying maid, in the shrubbery of the square's garden to observe its occupants as they alighted. This was unladylike behaviour, but their mama later conceded that in their shoes she would have been sorely tempted to do the same. And the results of their subterfuge were all that could have been hoped for.

The carriage steps were let down by the waiting footmen, and a gentleman got down, then turned to assist someone inside the carriage. He was undoubtedly very tall, well-dressed and handsome, but he did not – at that precise moment – show any obvious signs of wickedness. The younger lady, an impressionable damsel of only sixteen summers, had half-expected him to be of a reddish complexion, sporting horns and a tail, and this was rather disappointingly not the case. A lady emerged from the coach and put her hand in his; she was of medium height and elegant figure, very stylishly dressed in a travelling pelisse of blue trimmed with silver braid, and she looked about her with bright interest as she alighted.

Georgie – for it was she – murmured, 'Is it usual for there to be people watching us from concealment in the bushes, Gabriel? It seems most odd. And I feel – perhaps I am mistaken, but I do not think so – that there are many eyes on us, observing our arrival from the windows that overlook the square.'

'I'm sure you're right,' her husband said, with the wicked glint in his eye that she had come to recognise. 'I showed you Blanche's letter; I dare say she did not exaggerate the extent of the gossip that our marriage has created. Shall we give them something to talk about, my love?'

As he spoke, he took her in his arms and commenced kissing her ruthlessly, and when her lips responded eagerly to his and her arms came up about his neck, he picked her up and carried her up the steps and into the house, leaving the astonished footmen to scramble after them with a sad loss of dignity.

'Well!' said the elder of the young ladies who had been witness to this thrilling spectacle with great satisfaction. 'Just wait till we tell Mama! She will be mad as fire that she missed such a shocking sight!'

45

The news spread like wildfire: the Silver Duke and his bride had arrived in Town. Anyone who was even remotely acquainted with Lady Georgiana – with the new Duchess, as one must learn to call her – and many persons who were not, called and left cards in Grosvenor Square. She was a bride, of the highest rank outside royalty, and as such was clearly owed every civil attention. Bride-visits were paid, and ladies who had been fortunate enough to find her at home were interrogated by those who had not. How did she look? She looked ridiculously happy, it was generally agreed. Mesmerised? Not in any obvious fashion. Did she have the appearance of a young lady who had been caught in the most intimate of acts by half the nobility of the North of England? One lady who had called on the Duchess and found her devoted husband at her side at the time of her visit said thoughtfully that she did in fact present very much that appearance, and furthermore did not seem to regret it in the least.

The truth of this assertion soon became apparent when the couple held a ball to celebrate their marriage – surely the most coveted invitation of the autumn. It was understood that the Duke and Duchess would commence the dancing together, and that the first dance would be a waltz.

Northriding was immaculate in evening black, with a waistcoat of white and silver, but he was a mere foil for the magnificence of his wife. Her gown was simple white satin, but any adornments of embroidery or beading would have been superfluous, since she wore for the first time the Mauleverer diamonds, a spectacular necklace that extended from her throat to her decolletage and flashed fire with every tiny movement of her body. She also sported a curious rosette on her breast, an unusual, richly jewelled order fashioned from enamelled gold and set on coloured silk. It had been presented to her, to her enormous embarrassment, that very day, when she and her husband had been summoned to Carlton House at the behest of the Regent.

Like so many epically selfish persons, the Regent was a pathetic sentimentalist, and the news of the Duchess's heroic self-sacrifice had affected him very deeply. (No lady had so far felt prompted to risk death for his sake, although there was of course still time and he had not yet given up hope.) Finding that there existed no official means that he considered appropriate to reward a noble lady for heroism, he had invented one, commissioned Messrs Rundell and Bridge to realise his design at enormous cost, and presented it to Georgie in a simple but touching ceremony. One of his rare flashes of good taste had fortunately prompted the generous prince to delegate the task of affixing the decoration to the lady's bodice to the Duke rather than undertaking it himself. Since His Royal Highness had graciously intimated his intention to attend the Northridings' party (despite not being invited), Georgie had thought it prudent to wear the garish thing this evening. The thought of what her irreverent younger brothers would say when they heard of it was something she resolutely pushed from her mind. This was easy enough, in all truth, when she found herself in Gabriel's arms and saw him smiling down at her.

Though there was nothing obviously incorrect in the way the ducal pair held each other and moved through the steps of the waltz, still there was something about their intent focus on each other, the way their eyes, blue and silver, locked and held, the instinctive physical and mental harmony in which they glided across the floor, that created a powerful impression on many of those watching. Those old-fashioned persons who still thought the new-fangled foreign steps indecent – and particularly the extended embrace which was the novel feature of the dance – were observed to turn to their companions and say, 'Do you see what I mean now? Most improper!', although if they were challenged as to what precisely was improper about it, they found themselves unable to say.

Lady Carston, another bride, was resolute in her decision not to take to the floor, and since she was several inches taller than all but four or five of the gentlemen present, including her own husband, her refusal was perhaps understandable. That she would have liked nothing better than to waltz with the person of her heart – but that her choice of partner was not permissible in the prevailing social circumstances – was not something she was able to share with most of her fellow guests. And so she stood and watched with Louisa as the Duke and Duchess owned the dance-floor, and they shared a little secret smile. They owed Northriding and Georgie a substantial favour, they were well aware, for the furore around their marriage and the startling events that followed it had quite eclipsed any interest that malicious persons might otherwise have shown in the recent and very quietly celebrated union of Lord Carston and the authoress Miss Spry.

'Perhaps when you are ready to let it be known that you are in an interesting condition, love, we can arrange for someone else to attempt to put a period to Northriding's life,' said Louisa, in a dry tone meant only for Jane's ears.

'That would be most convenient,' agreed her companion, with a perfectly straight face, 'as long as your niece performs no more heroics. I am convinced that Northriding's hair will go completely white if she gives him another such fright.'

The dance came to an end, and the Duchess swept the Duke a magnificent curtsey. He bent low over her gloved hand and kissed it in a manner that was either heart-stoppingly romantic or disgracefully indecorous, depending on one's point of view.

Much later, Gabriel lay with his head cradled on his wife's breast, and she stroked his black and silver hair. Outside, the autumn dawn was breaking in smoky red and gold over the rooftops of London. They had not slept. 'My love,' she said, 'I have been thinking...'

'That sounds promising.'

'Yes, I think you will agree that it is. I was remembering that you threatened – or perhaps promised – when we were so memorably together in that house to lay me down and spank me.'

'I did. And you asked me then if I thought you might enjoy it.'

'And if *you* might, Gabriel, don't forget.'

'I am of the opinion that we both might.'

'And I am of the opinion that you may be right.'

He took her hand and pressed his lips to it, and said, 'I wonder, while we are on the subject of our first meeting, do you still have that red suit, Georgie? I will never forget my first sight of you, and how you intrigued me and drew me from my purpose, and changed my life for ever. You might wear that once more, and this time I could undress you very slowly and completely, as I so longed to do last time you wore it.'

'No, I do not have it, or you would have seen me in it long

before now, I swear. But I know exactly where it is kept. I will ask Cassandra for it, and I am sure she will let me have it.'

'And understand exactly why you want it, I dare say? You Pendleburys really are extraordinary people, my love.'

'We are. And what's even better, we marry extraordinary people too.'

'I cannot disagree with that!' the Duke said, kissing one rosy nipple.

Georgie smiled and stretched languorously. 'Jane – Lady Carston – told me this evening that she is in an interesting condition already. She is so very happy.'

'I am glad for her. There's a woman who knows exactly what she wants, and how to get it. Speaking of which, do you suppose they...?'

She tugged hard on a lock of his dark hair. 'Oh, no! Where Jane, my aunt and Lord Carston are concerned, I do not suppose anything at all, I refrain entirely from supposing, and I suggest you do so too! But Gabriel...'

Her tone had altered, becoming suddenly serious, and he raised his head from her breast and looked at her. A curious little smile hovered about her lips, and found an instant echo on his face. 'Do you have something of a most important nature to tell me, love of my life?' he said gravely. He had known – of course he had known – but he had been waiting for her to tell him in her own time. It was her secret, after all.

'Only that I think I should obtain that suit from Cassandra quite soon, for I am afraid if we delay, those very tight breeches that you liked so much will no longer fit me.'

He moved up so that he could look straight in her eyes; they swam with sudden tears, and he was aware that his did too. 'My love, my love, my love...' he murmured, touching her face very tenderly.

There was so much to say, and so much that need not be said, or not now. A little while later, when she lay with her head on his shoulder, his arms tight and safe about her, he whispered, 'I don't think I want to spank you, love, now I know your news. Well, I do want to, if indeed you want it too, but I should be afraid...'

'Perhaps you could do so very gently. Just a tap or two, just enough to make me tingle...'

'That's possible, of course. I would like nothing more than to make you tingle. Or perhaps we could find other things to do.'

'I'm sure we could...'

EPILOGUE

SEPTEMBER 1817

Could anything be more glorious than an Indian summer in Yorkshire, when the sun was shining and the sky a superb blue? Such days were rare, and to be appreciated and enjoyed all the more for that reason. The Duchess of Northriding sat in her garden in the sunshine with her friend Lady Carston and talked idly, or did not talk, as they shared a rare moment of peace.

It was a family party at the Castle that autumn. All the Pendlebury siblings were present, and the Duke was swiftly coming to understand why it was that persons of a sensitive disposition had been known to start and grow pale and wild-eyed when the names of the three younger boys were mentioned. He, however, was not of a particularly sensitive disposition, and had this afternoon taken all five of his brothers-in-law, Cassandra, Bastian's particular friend Matthew Welby, and his own nephew and niece down the stair to the beach to play a noisy game of cricket. Ten persons, and two very excited dogs. If he had formulated the plan in the hope that the three boys would be exhausted by the activity and less likely to get up to mischief afterwards, mused his wife, he would soon discover that he was sadly mistaken. But no doubt the practice would be good for him: Fred, Jonathan and Hugh were an education in themselves for a man newly embarked on fatherhood.

The thwack of leather on willow and yells of triumph or of protest could faintly be heard in the garden high above the beach, along with volleys of barking from Tam and Nico, but all this presented a pleasant sort of a backdrop when mingled with the soothing sound of the waves and the plaintive cries of sea birds. It was certainly not enough to disturb the sleeping babies, nor Lady Louisa, who was dozing unashamedly in a comfortable chair.

'Were you up much in the night, Jane?' said Georgie lazily, closing her eyes and basking in the sun. She was tired, but also contented. Life was good.

'The better question would be, did I get any sleep at all?'

'She looks so tranquil now, it is almost impossible to imagine.'

'Monster that she is,' said Miss Eliza Louisa Georgiana Carston's fond mother, looking down on her daughter with an expression of doting idiocy quite at variance with her words. 'I'm surprised you weren't disturbed by her. As you can see, Louisa was.'

'Eliza would have had to yell very loudly indeed to make herself heard in our chambers,' replied the Duchess drily. 'And now they sleep, and we should too, and yet here we are, awake and talking.'

'And you don't regret a moment of it.'

'I don't, and nor do you, I can see. Would you contemplate having another, Jane?'

Jane Carston chuckled. 'Poor Louisa! She has always made it eminently clear how much she dislikes the bustle your brothers create, and what must I do but bring a horrid noisy baby into our lovely, tranquil home. Should I inflict another on her?'

'Well, that wasn't what I asked.'

'Yes, of course, the answer is yes. We have discussed it.'

'Lord Carston joins us in a week or so, does he not?'

'And it was very good of you to invite him,' said Jane, with a perfectly composed countenance that was undermined somewhat by a wicked twinkle.

Georgie met her eyes and began to laugh. 'Is he not your husband, and an old friend of my family besides? Of course I invite him. Oh dear! I am sure anybody looking at us now would imagine that we present a picture of perfect respectability.'

'I may not be terribly respectable, Duchess, but I am sure nobody can say that about *you*. A duchess, married to a man she adores and who adores her, a mother, decorated by the Regent for her bravery...?'

'You'd be surprised, I dare say,' said Georgie, with a secret little smile.

'I dare say I wouldn't be surprised at all. And do *you* contemplate having another child?'

'Of course, in a little while,' said the Duchess lazily. 'There is no terrible urgency to the matter, after all.' And just as she spoke her twin sons, Ash and George – or, to give them their proper titles, His Grace the Marquis of Tollesby and Lord George Mauleverer – awoke together and began to wail for food and for attention, and Miss Eliza was disturbed by the commotion, and all peace was banished for a time.

ACKNOWLEDGEMENTS

I wrote my first novel in my kitchen in lockdown. I'd never have developed the confidence to do it without the encouragement of all the complete strangers who commented so positively on my Heyer fanfic on AO3. But the real inspiration came from my good friends in the Georgette Heyer Readalong on Twitter. I'm particularly grateful to Bea Dutton, who spent many hours of her precious time setting up and running the readalongs. I can't possibly name everyone – there are too many of us – but thank you all, amazing Dowagers, for your continuing support with this novel and far beyond it. We have brainstormed insane plot suggestions involving rakish dukes, and I have cried with laughter. Clare Wilson, we're all waiting to read YOUR novel!

Like many people in the writing, publishing and reading communities, I've loved Twitter. It's called X as I write this, but who knows if it'll even exist by the time this book is published? Whatever it's called, it's been this introvert's ideal place to socialise. So I'd like to thank all my Twitter friends for the years of chat and mutual support, especially the very talented Katy Moran and the wonderfully kind and endlessly gracious legend among women that is Katie Fforde. Thanks too to all the other lovely authors who took the time to read my work when they have so many other demands on their time, and gave me reviews that made my day, month and year. And anyone writing romance owes a huge debt to the RNA for their tireless work in ensuring romantic fiction finally gets the respect and recognition it deserves.

I've been obsessed with Georgette Heyer's novels since I first read them when I was eleven. They have their faults, but they've provided solace and escape for millions of people in tough times, so thank you, Georgette, even though you would have absolutely hated this book.

Thanks also to my family for putting up with me while I wrote one novel and then another in quick succession. And then another three. Thanks for understanding when I just have to write another 127 words before lunch so I can stop on a nice round number.

My lovely work colleagues Amanda Preston, Louise Lamont, Hannah Schofield and Amy Strong have also been extremely supportive: thanks, Team LBA!

I am very lucky to have a superb agent in Diana Beaumont of Marjacq. She has believed in my writing from the first time she read it, and will always be my champion. Her editorial suggestions are brilliant, and she's just an all-round star. Thanks too to everyone else at Marjacq, including Catherine Pellegrino and Guy Herbert. I know better than most people how important the whole team at an agency is.

Many thanks to everyone at Boldwood, including Cecily Blench for the fantastic copyediting, Gary Jukes for the proofread, Rachel Lawston for the gorgeous cover, and to Amanda, Nia, Niamh and Claire of Team Boldwood as a whole for your amazing professionalism and unflagging enthusiasm. And of course grateful thanks to my wonderful editor Rachel Faulkner-Willcocks, whose superb edits have made this a much better book. One of the many special things about Boldwood is the wonderful spirit of mutual support that the authors share, so I'd like to thank you all, particularly the amazingly talented Jane Dunn, for your generosity and friendship.

Finally, if you're reading this because you've bought the book, or a previous one: THANK YOU!

ABOUT THE AUTHOR

Emma Orchard is the author of several well-reviewed regency romance novels. In her other life she is a literary agent, helping others realise their dreams of being published.

Sign up to Emma Orchard's mailing list for news, competitions and updates on future books.

Follow Emma on social media here:

x.com/EmmaOrchardB

instagram.com/emmaorchardbooks

pinterest.com/EmmaOrchardRegency

Printed in Great Britain
by Amazon